Ramona,
Thank you! Y...
years means ...
... whatever it is,
give it your BEST!
Enjoy!
Brenda
_2011_

THE BEST
I HAVE TO OFFER

Brenda A. White

Choices

Within

Houston

Copyright Choices Within Publications © 2010 All rights reserved. No part of this book shall be reproduced, stored in a retrieval system, or transmitted by any means without permission from the publisher, Choices Within Publications.

The following story is fictional and does not depict any actual persons, places or events. The use of certain names and places is to give this novel a since of reality.

ISBN 13: 978-0-9819-3440-2
ISBN 10: 0981934404
Library of Congress Control Number: 2010900807

Printed in the United States of America
Choices Within Publications

DEDICATION

To my Mom and Dad
R.I.P.

ACKNOWLEDGEMENTS

I'm so happy I could just sing…Thank you Lord for all you've done for me! Thank you for giving me the passion to write and for the tenacity to complete this book! It is certainly a dream come true. You are truly an awesome and incredible God, and you deserve incredible praise! I PRAISE YOU!

ReShonda Tate-Billingsley, my editor and hero! Thank you for all of the red marks! Thank you for helping me to write a much tighter story.☺ I learned so much from you. The next one won't take three years!

Thank you to my sisters, Juanita Robinson (I'm putting the books in your hands, finally!), Shirley Hicks, Tina Burton, and Cynthia Holmes, (and my niece Cassandra Postway) for being there for me through every single moment in my life. You always make me feel like I can do anything. You read my writing whenever I asked, even if you had to blush your way through it. Speaking of blushing, thank you to my niece, Barbara Williams, and my sister-in-law, Shirley Postway for reading several excerpts and then just giggled.☺ Thank you to my brothers, you always bragged enough to spark a continuous challenge for me to do even better at whatever I set out to accomplish.

Thank you to Angela Osborne and Tarisa Busby for the excitement and interest you showed around the developing characters back in 2007; reading every single page that I wrote, every short story, listening to every idea, critiquing and helping me to get better at my new craft. I'm striving for continuous improvement! Shelia Benson, Charlotte Pitts, Alia Bushell, Sharon "Smooth" Bankett, Rechelle McArthur, Sandra Hatley, Sherry Gibbs, Monica Holiday, LaVern Shaw, Nora Autry, Kim Davis, Shelia Kemp, and Ebony Hobbs, I thank you so much for your perspective and for reading my one-liners or anything that I put in front of you to read. I know I had you all excited about the next part for three years! Here it is! Alia, thank you for the stories and I'll stop there. ☺

Thank you to Tyrone Bennett, Kevin Williams, Michael McFrazier, Troy Landry, Steve Terry, Dave Thomas, Ronald Punch, Daryl Willis, and Corey Hinton for giving me your opinion when I asked for it or didn't ask ☺ and helping me to understand things from male's perspective. Thank you so much! Tyrone thanks for allowing me to invade your privacy and showing me Bed-Stuy. In the beginning, you allowed me to ask anything that I wanted. I quickly realized that instead of asking you if there were any questions off limits, you should have asked me if there were any comments off limits. Now what now? Whew! Bruce Cayton, thank you for asking at random, 'Where's my book?' with some bass in your voice, believe or not, your tone was encouragement for me to keep going! Thank you to Darlene Hernandez at MAC for doing my makeup and to Isom Washington for taking one-hundred photos for me to choose just one. Thank you Isom!

To all of my friends and family including nieces, nephews, sisters-in-law, brothers-in-law, cousins, aunts, Class of '87, my sisters of Delta Sigma Theta Sorority, Inc., and my Facebook friends ☺ thank you for your support, prayers, words of encouragement, and the sparkle in your eye when I told you that I was writing a book. Thank you so much!

One more thing before I go, you all can continue to talk around me, not every story will end up in a book, I promise, I think. ☺ We've only just begun!

PROLOGUE

Dark Secrets

S he broke one of her truisms, *some things you need to go to your grave with*. She sat in the low back contemporary-styled Italian leather chair, cigar in hand, right leg crossed—never inhaling—blowing circles into the air, her four-inch black patent-leather stiletto rhythmically swinging from her foot.

"They both were laid out when I left. She was sprawled out on the chaise-lounge and he went down after the gun went off." She paused. "Hit his head on the wall." She looked down, then back up. "He should have known, I am not to be messed with. I told him that, several times. I told him that I learned how to shoot—I'm licensed to carry—self-defense. You name it, and he still tried me. Damn fool. You know, I've been told that I'm just like my grandmother. I must say, people will learn, one day."

She sat up straight, tapped the cigar in the ashtray, crushed it, picked up her wine glass, took a slow sip, and allowed the taste to linger on her palette for a moment. She swallowed and leaned back again, took a deep breath, exhaled through her nose. Her breast rose and fell. She stared at the ceiling. All of the feelings and memories of that dismal evening crowding her mind like the fans at Cowboys Stadium to see the Dallas Cowboys play. She fidgeted in her chair as her heart sped up. Though she tried to pretend she was confident and cocky, she was scared.

"His wife came in acting all crazy, had a knife in her hand waving it like a fool. He started acting like a damn wimp. He suddenly charged at her, took the knife and took her down, then had the nerve to try the same thing on me and I stopped him, dead in his damn tracks. That simple, but just too much drama that I didn't expect. I felt like I was moving in slow motion. You know, I never heard anything about them again, absolutely nothing about the story. I guess because they covered it locally and I left immediately, and went back to Dallas; though I thought about it every minute or every day for months. Nevertheless, I'm past that now. That was years ago when I first moved to Dallas. I dabbled with that for a short time against my better judgment; suffered minor consequences and scars, and moved on. Dealing with him was hazardous for my health."

She stood up, looked down, smoothed out the wrinkles in her black pencil skirt, and started her casual and slow stroll toward the door. She stopped and turned around. "You know what? I'm never smoking again."

She gave her signature wink and walked out, leaving so many unanswered questions.

PART ONE

IGNORANCE
IS
BLISS?

CHAPTER 1

MIA

I was standing in my office window on the thirtieth floor, looking over downtown Houston. The sun was forcing its way between two buildings, onto the expressway and directly into my face. What a beautiful sight.

Thank you Jesus, I thought. I sure was going to miss this view. I sat back down in my chair amid all of the boxes in my office, leaned my head back, and meditated for a few moments. This had been my morning ritual and now it was being interrupted by my cell phone ringing. I sat up straight, inhaled, and exhaled, before picking up my Blackberry. I smiled when I saw the picture displayed on the screen. "Talk to me, talk to me!" I sang into the phone.

"What's going on, girly?" It was Dena Thomas, one of my very best friends.

"Good Mernin', Good Mernin'," we both said in unison, mocking Dena's great-grandmother.

"Hey, I want you to meet me at the park for lunch, on the swings. I feel like being a little girl today and I need to talk to you," Dena requested.

"Okay, I'm down for that." I sat up straight and continued to put more of my personal items into the boxes. "Today is my last day here. So I'm out of here early. I'm done with recruiting, policies, and procedures. I have recruited my last college student, from this position anyway. I have a few things to wrap up and then I can meet…"

"Yeah, that's right," she interrupted. "Today is your last day over there."

"Yes indeed." I thumbed through a few papers before tossing them in the trash. "I'm ready to do what you taught me and try this entrepreneur thing. Learning and Development here I come! It is about time I utilize my hard-earned education from Associate's Degree to Ph.D. It's a little unnerving but I'm ready."

"Yes, girl you are. You lined it up because you knew the layoffs were coming. You said they were discussing it three years ago, right after they promoted you to run the place."

"I know." I sat back down in the chair. The guy from the mailroom knocked on the door and pointed at the boxes. "Hold on for a second, Dena." I rolled my chair closer and pointed at the labels to guide him to the boxes that were going to storage because they were outsourcing my entire team, including me. "Okay, go ahead."

Dena continued. "Girl, they just gave you that gentle push that you needed to get started on your dream, with a ninety day notice and a nice severance."

"Thank the Lord and I am not complaining about that." I stood to look out the window.

"You've spent two years planning and focusing on the right things, breaking that entrepreneur dream down to little manageable pieces. What's that board you created?"

"A vision-board," I added as I paced back and forth.

"Yes, the good ol' vision-board, you sacrificed and saved, you will be okay. I assure you, Mia," she encouraged.

I needed to hear that again because a hint of fear had landed on me this morning like a heavy weight. My company, ACC had given me a heads-up in early January that lay-offs in the recruiting division were imminent. I had eight recruiters on my team covering forty cities across the U.S.

"Whew! Thanks, Dena." I fanned myself with a folder as I scanned the office to make sure I wasn't about to leave behind anything important. "You always know what to say and when to say it. You are the angel on my shoulder encouraging me keep moving my feet and I thank you."

"Yeper. That's what I'm here for. You can do it, girl. I got your back! But, one thing you will miss is the nice bonus in the spring. Umph."

"And I know it. So keep my bedroom ready over there just in case. But anyway, enough about me, what do you need to talk about?"

"Didn't I say meet me at the park?" She huffed, jokingly.

"I know but I wanted to get my mind ready for the conversation. And pray and meditate and all of that good stuff."

She paused for a moment and then said, "I just want to go to the park and swing and chill."

She was not telling the truth and although I didn't know what was going on, I had planned to hang up the phone and continue my morning ritual, which now included a longer prayer for her. I knew my friend very well and when she wanted to go to the park, on the swings, and become a little girl all over again, something was bothering her. Sitting on the swings allowed us to go back, if only for a moment, and relieve some stress. I prayed she didn't have an impending confession because she had done something to that deadbeat boyfriend of hers. Because Lord knows, they have had enough drama for everybody.

I conceded with no pressure. "Okay, I'm down for that. I have some things that I must do today so I need to skedaddle and get to them. I'll probably be ready by eleven-ish."

"Okay, well, we can eat and then go to the park or have a picnic. I'll pick up some food. Hopefully we won't get hit in the head with a golf ball. I can see it now, in the headlines— DENA THOMAS, HOUSTON'S FINEST EVENT-PLANNER EXTRAORDINAIRE, KNOCKED OUT AT THE PARK WHILE EATING A BOLOGNA SANDWICH." I moved my hands dramatically as if she could see me.

"Yeah, and right beside that, DR. MIA NIXON, HOUSTON'S MOST ELIGIBLE BACHELORETTE WAS EATING SARDINES." She laughed.

"Now that's disgusting! Yuck!" I pretended as if she grossed me out. Truthfully, I had never tasted sardines and had no plans to ever do so.

"You are so silly. I'll be out there by eleven. Your clubs in the car? Maybe we can either hit a few buckets at the range or play nine holes."

"We'll see." There was no commitment from me. It was hot! Swinging on a swing under a tree in the shade was one thing but swinging a golf club in the Houston humidity and heat was a different story.

"Okay, holla bay-beh!" she yelled into the phone and hung up before I responded.

Gosh, I love that girl and all her drama, crazy and all. I prayed, finished packing more boxes, loaded my car, ran a couple of errands, and was at the park by 11:15 ready to hear what she wanted to talk about.

It was eighty-nine degrees. The park was beautiful as always at the beginning of spring. A golf course sat next to it, the grass looked like thick green carpet, sand boxes with fallen and half-constructed sand castles adorned the area, which was evident that happiness had visited the spot. The flowerbeds and trees were placed strategically throughout the park, an allergy nightmare.

Dena enjoyed sitting in the swings, staring at nothing. It was a great stress relief to go back to childhood, enjoy the outdoors, listen to the birds, and just be thankful.

I had seen Dena handle tragedies from a young age. I believe that was the reason for many of her demons, despite her success professionally.

My mind went back to the summer of 1985 when Dena and I met in elementary school. Dena was walking on the sidewalk in Queens with one of her friends, Tory, a car drove onto the sidewalk and hit him, then just kept going. Tory died on the sidewalk. Dena's mother found out that Tory had been hit on purpose so she sent Dena to Arkansas to live with her grandmother as the "investigation" took place. We were at recess when I invited Dena to join my friends and me on the swings. At the time, she appeared very shy. All of the swings were full, so I volunteered my swing to her, and pushed her until she got her momentum going. From that day on, she joined in our daily competition of who can swing the highest. She really enjoyed it. Sometimes the two of us would go to the swings and just sit, we did not talk until she was ready to talk. She was going through her grieving phase of losing her friend and being taken away from the environment where she was most comfortable. We would always go to the swings when we needed to talk and that has been our tradition ever since.

I pulled into a parking space beside Dena's Lexus and spotted her already sitting on the swings in her golf attire. I hopped out of the car and walked toward her. I noticed a woman standing at a distance with a camera that had one of those long lenses on it, like the professional photographers use.

"Hey Dena." I reached for a hug. "How are you doing Missy? Did you notice if that lady was snapping pictures of you or was she just taking pictures of the park?" I motioned my hand in the air and walked over to the blanket that Dena had spread on the ground, dropped my bag, and returned to plop down in the swing next to Dena.

"What woman? I wasn't paying attention."

"My gosh, Dena, please pay attention. That woman over there." I moved my head toward the woman, trying not to be obvious as I thrust my legs forward to get a slight momentum of my swing.

Dena lowered her sunglasses to get a better view of the woman. "She's too far away, I can't see her."

"You're not under surveillance for any reason are you?" I joked.

"I'd better not be. But there's no telling who Monty's dumb self has hired. Oh no, wait. He's broke and hiring anybody to do anything would require money, huh?" She scoffed.

"Well, that camera is aimed in this direction for some reason and it's making me nervous. Why would Monty hire somebody?"

"Because he's trifling, broke, about to be homeless, and accused me of cheating this morning," she blurted out.

"Umph. Glory." I mumbled.

I decided to wait to see if she would elaborate before I made any comments. I knew all about Monty and his tricks but for him to be on the homeless track, he had really pissed her off.

She remained quiet and kept her eyes on the woman with the camera. She stood up and stretched as I struggled to stop my swing because I knew she was getting ready to do something that she had no business doing.

"Who is this woman? She is really bold standing here just snapping away. I know she's not taking pictures of the scenery," she muttered.

"Dena, uh, maybe she's uh…" I stood beside her.

Dena ignored me and started a brisk walk that turned into a sprint, in the direction of the woman. The woman saw Dena coming toward her, lowered her camera and rushed back to her convertible Volkswagen and drove away.

"Damn it!" Dena declared when I caught up to her. She rushed back to the picnic area, dropped to her knees and rummaged through her things until she found a pen. "I'm not gonna chase her ass but I can write those license plates down."

My eyes followed the direction of the Volkswagen until it was out of sight.

CHAPTER 2

∽

GARY

"Mr. Matthews, do you have any children?" a little boy asked.

"Do you have a daughter?" a little girl yelled out before I could answer the first question, as the whole class giggled at their questions.

"I bet he has a son!" another little boy yelled.

"Hold on, guys." I placed the palms of my hands together, leaned forward and smiled "And girls. No, I do not have any children."

I couldn't remember how this conversation went from understanding money to my personal life.

"Well, do you want some?" another kid yelled.

I looked at the teacher in a 'please help me' expression. She appeared to be enjoying the barrage of questions by the class.

"Okay, now class, that's enough," Mrs. Griffin conveyed.

"Thank you." I mouthed, as I nodded, and smiled.

The bell rang and the kids scrambled to line up at the door.

I was actually impressed because they were so quiet. One little boy kept looking at me. I gave him the peace sign and he gave it back. The students left and Mrs. Griffin and I went through the normal 'thank you so much for coming' speech, I stopped by the principal's office to sign out and I left the building.

I volunteered for Operation Hope, a program that teaches children how to become financially savvy. It was a six-week commitment and I had just enjoyed week number three. My parents shared financial knowledge with me at the appropriate time and I took pleasure in giving it back.

I took my jacket off as I always do when I drive. I put my cell phone within reach, as I got in my truck because I needed to call Sean before I got to the office. We used to talk at least twice per week but I was so busy, I hadn't talked to him in over two weeks. Sean is my very tall, dark, muscular buddy, born and raised in Houston, Texas. I met him on one of his visits to New York through my cousin, Sam over ten years ago. When the three of us walk into a room, most people mistake us for members of a professional sports team or bouncers. Sean and Sam look a lot alike and are both larger than me and I considered myself a pretty sturdy dude.

"Mr. Matthews," I heard a female voice call out before I closed the door. It was Mrs. Griffin running toward me, waving a piece of paper.

"Mr. Matthews, you forgot something," she panted as she tried to catch her breath.

"Oh, I'm sorry, I would've come back in. You didn't have to run. What is it?" I stepped out of the truck.

She appeared to be at least ten years younger than me, nice hair, was a little on the heavy side, and not bad looking but I could tell that she wasn't up on her cardio regimen. Her chest was noticeably moving up and down.

"I wanted you to…I wanted you to… have this." She slouched on the door of the truck.

"Are you okay?" I gently touched her elbow to try to steady her. "You sure?"

"Yes. I'm fine. I just didn't want you to leave here another day without me giving you this."

"What is it?" I asked again.

I opened the folded piece of paper. A flyer for a little league football camp that had already happened but there was also a name, phone number, and email address written in the corner. My eyes scanned the flyer.

I was puzzled. "What is this for? Who is Melinda G?"

"It's me." She wiped her forehead with the back of her hand. "I just used this paper to make it seem like something legit, just in case someone saw it."

"Oh. Melinda Griffin." I looked at the wedding ring on her left hand.

Her eyes followed mine. "Oh. That. I just wear it for school." She wiggled it in the air. "I'm separated for over a year now. I decided to get back into the dating scene and thought I'd just put myself out there and see what happens."

"Oh, I see, with your ring on, huh?"

"He won't be needing that." A familiar female voice resounded as the paper was removed from my hand, ripped into several smaller pieces, and tossed into the air.

"Oh hi, Nina. I'm sorry, Ms. Briggs, is this your man?" Mrs. Griffin asked sarcastically.

Ohh damn, I thought.

"He was and you know that." Nina bolstered.

"Yes. I did and the keyword here is *was*." Mrs. Griffin stepped toward Nina who didn't flinch.

Nina Briggs was my ex-girlfriend whom I had not spoken to in several months and hadn't seen in a year. When we dated, she was short-fused and bad-tempered and blamed it on the hours she worked on two jobs and the people she worked with. Nina allowed the work she did as a nurse to control her mood. She was very unhappy. Her second job as the backup school nurse brought her to the school and I could see that nasty mood hadn't changed.

"Ladies, come on now, there is no need for this." I glanced around the parking lot to make sure no one was watching and stepped between them. "Nina, what are you doing here?"

"I work here. Remember?" She folded her arms and shifted her weight to one leg.

"No. I don't remember. So, why are you out here?"

"I drove up and saw Mrs. Griffin slouched all on your truck so I decided to come over here and save you from yourself, so you won't mess around with a married woman."

I gasped. "What? Save me from myself?"

"I'm not married, Ms. Briggs." Mrs. Griffin chimed in and stepped around me. I'm sure her plan was to give me her number and saunter back into the classroom as if nothing happened but Nina stopped all of that. "I've been separated for months and you know that."

"Nina, you stay right there." I turned toward Mrs. Griffin and gently grabbed her shoulders. "Mrs. Griffin, I'm flattered but I, I uh, I will be in touch, okay? Please go back inside, we don't need this. I promise, I'll be in touch."

She looked disappointed but she turned on her heels and

headed back toward the building. "I'll be in touch," she said loudly. She and Nina glared at each other as she walked away.

"No. You won't," Nina called back.

I turned back toward Nina. "Nina, stop! Save me from myself? Are you serious?"

"Save me from myself," she chortled derisively. "That lady is married Gary, and you, being the bona fide player that you are, I needed to save you, from, yourself." She leaned forward.

I folded my arms and narrowed my eyes at her. *I could argue with her or I can concede. I want to argue because she just disrespected me and I want to make my point but if I argue that will cause a scene so I must concede and deal with her later or not at all.* "You know what? Thank you, Nina. Thank you so much for saving me because you know I don't do married women."

"I know." She swirled around and started her walk into the building.

I got back into my truck and wondered what just happened. I sat there for a moment and watched Nina. I rested my head on the headrest. *She is nuts. What in the world is going on with her. Nahhhh, I can never go back there. Ever.* I shook my head and cranked the truck.

Within fifteen minutes, I was back on the 610 West Loop. I decided to wait before calling Sean and called my assistant, Lynne instead. I wanted to see how many people were in the office before buying breakfast, being very conscientious not to waste money especially since I had just finished teaching good habits to the children.

"Good morning, Lynne, how many…"

She interrupted. "Yes, Good morning, Gary. Nina called in here this morning. Three times."

I threw up my hands in frustration and paused because I didn't know what to say. I wondered if she told Nina that I was at the school.

"She just asked where you were and what time you will be back," she continued.

"Did you tell her?"

"No, I didn't," she snapped as if I dare ask her such a question. Lynne always said she wanted me to find a good woman but every time there is a mention of me with a woman, her attitude gets really nasty.

"Good. How many people in there today?"

"Just me and T.J."

"Okay, I'll be there in less than thirty minutes."

"Okay, see you when you get here." She perked up, satisfied that I showed no concern for Nina.

I ended the call and scratched my head. I was even more puzzled about what Nina could want with me all of sudden. I thought we were free and clear of any lingering issues. I had not heard from her meanness and I didn't want to, but I needed to figure out what she wanted and get a mutual understanding as soon as possible.

I pulled into this little bakery, a couple of blocks from the office, ordered a couple of breakfast sandwiches and pastries, and headed toward the office.

"All righty now, got that part over with. Next thing on the agenda for today. Let's see, maneuvered traffic, talked to the kids, had a dose of drama, picked up breakfast—all before mid-morning." I chuckled because I was talking to myself.

This was going to be a long day in the office. I had three meetings back-to-back including lunch. I had been working long hours because of my business partner, T.J.'s illness. The doctor diagnosed him with prostate cancer and for the last six months, it's been Lynne and me.

T.J., Thomas Jamal Jefferson, is a tall, slim cyclist and runner in his mid-forties that, prior to his diagnosis was on a very healthy diet from my point of view. I met him several years ago when I moved to Houston from Seattle shortly after I finished law school and passed the bar. I had been in insurance for about seven years on the claims side. He had been in insurance for some time and wanted to start his own business, as did I. We connected, had several meetings, became business partners first, then friends. We've been at this for about five years, successfully.

My cell phone rang. I answered and before I could say 'Hello' my friend, Sean yelled, "Hey dude, what's good?"

I pulled the phone away from my ear before he burst my eardrum. "It's all good. I just finished teaching nine-year-olds how to save money and balance a checkbook," I responded. I decided not to mention what happened with Nina and Mrs. Griffin.

"What? That's what's up. I didn't know what a checkbook was when I was their age."

"Yeah, you telling me. I think the kids can teach the parents, too. Some of them missed the boat on that one." I added.

"Yeah man we gotta teach these kids. Yo, what you got up for today?" He changed the subject mid-sentence.

"I have meetings all the way through lunch. Why? What's up?" I slammed on brakes to keep from driving through the red light with the camera and all of the food fell to the floor.

"I wanted to grab lunch and then play a few holes or just hit some balls. I need to relieve some stress."

"Man, you need to do more than play some holes to relieve

some stress. Call one of those women you got and get you some. You'll be all right," I joked as I reached to get the bag of food off the floor.

He chuckled. "Nah man, not right now. I got that lined up for later."

"I am not surprised. What time are you trying to go?"

"Around eleven. You know it'll be hot as hell after that."

"Naw, it's hot as hell now. Eleven o'clock? That's less than an hour away. Let me see what I can rearrange in the office first. You might have to play in the heat today, buddy." To tell the truth, I needed to relieve some stress, too.

"Man, I thought that was the beauty of working for yourself?" he said. "You can do whatever you want."

"It is, but bills gotta be paid too, dawg. T.J. is back, too."

"Yeah, that's what's up. Good for him. Well, let me know. But you will go to the sports bar tonight, right?" He stated, more as a commandment than a question.

"Let me check my schedule, man. I have things to do today and I need to get to this book club discussion party tonight." I pulled into the parking garage.

"Book club? Reading? You must be trying to meet a woman or something?" He quizzed. "Because I know your ass ain't into no book club. That-is-so-gay," he expressed exaggerating every word.

"Okay, you know damn well I'm not gay, and reading is not gay. I can't believe you're saying that, 'Mr. Teacher of the Year'. Besides, we're not reading girly books," I explained. I stood outside my truck trying to determine how I was going to get my briefcase, my coffee, and the food while holding the phone.

"Oh, that's nice." His voice dripped with sarcasm. "You're still after something else if you're already planning to go."

I chuckled because he was definitely telling the truth. "Yeah, you're right. You remember Dena's friend, Mia, I was telling you about?"

Dena Thomas is a very dear friend from Brooklyn. Our cousins used to be married, so we've always said we were cousins. I have known her for several years. She moved to Houston before I did and started her own business after working in the hotel industry for years. She helped me, I helped her and we were cool.

"Yeah, yeah, I remember."

I pushed the bag of food into my briefcase, with coffee in hand and the phone cradled in my shoulder. "Well, she's been talking about her again. Dena has been trying to play matchmaker for a while now, even while I was with Nina." I lowered my voice as I walked toward the building.

"Yeah, I remember ol' junky ass Nina. I couldn't believe you dated her as nasty as that house was. And you know you like your joint tight."

"Man, I keep telling you that her house was not always like that. She was depressed."

"Depressed my ass, G., I was at her house twice with you and both times that house was junky as hell. She stayed depressed then. Matter of fact, I know I heard 'Sanford and Son's' theme song playing in the background when I walked in the house."

I laughed out loud as he continued. "At first I thought she was watching it on TV, but no, that shit was playing in my head, loudly."

"Man you are nuts." I continued laughing. He has told that story for months to anybody that would listen. "May I finish my story now?"

"Yeah, go ahead." He started making the music sounds of the

theme song with his mouth.

"Good Morning, Mr. Brown." I greeted the security guard as I walked through the lobby of the building toward my office. "Man, you know you're crazy right? Anyway, for some reason, Dena didn't like Nina either." I lowered my voice again.

"What about that chick from Queens, or was it LA?"

"Both, but nah, I just dated them for a minute after Nina, nothing serious. Plus, neither of them wanted to be serious and neither did I. We knew that in the beginning. Dating is about numbers man. You date several and see if one tickles you to settle down. If they do, then you settle down."

"So you think you're ready to settle down, huh?"

"Yeah, man. Don't you think it's time?" I asked as I walked into the office and Lynne met me at the door. "Hold on for a second, man. Lynne I'm sorry that I had to smash these but I couldn't carry all of my stuff. No hands." She took my briefcase from me, pulled the bag out, and looked at it as if I handed her a bag of dirt. "The food is still good. I promise." I winked at her and walked into my office. She followed carrying my briefcase.

"Thanks, Lynne."

She shook her head in a motherly way and walked back to her desk. She always told T.J. and me that we needed to slow down and smell the roses.

"All right, sorry about that man." I sat down at my desk and made sure I lowered my voice once again because I definitely didn't want Lynne to hear anything that I was saying. I respected her like a mother but I did not like my personal life crossing into business.

"Not a problem, but what if Dena's girl is ug-gly? And you're talking about getting serious." He exaggerated his words again.

"But what if she's not? As a matter of fact, I know she's not. I don't remember her looking like a wolf. Besides, beauty is in the eye of the beholder."

"Okay, eye of the beholder. If she is the one, you want to be able to take her out without a leash." He laughed at himself.

I laughed, too, which gave him a little bit of satisfaction.

He continued. "But seriously, man, I'm ready to settle down, too, but with Holly acting the way she is, I just don't know, and this other lady that I'm dealing with is crazy. She told me this morning that she had a miscarriage a few months ago. I'm not even sure if it was mine or her husband's. She's seeing a psychologist about it. But man! I never thought sex could be this good nor have me acting like this."

Sean was a good guy, schoolteacher, who taught tenth grade Biology. But he was playing in dangerous territory, sleeping with a married woman, one of the student's stepmother. He started the escapades after getting upset with his fiancée, Holly about their wedding plans.

"This woman must be fair-skinned with long wavy hair, since it's apparent your judgment is off." I handed him some of the sarcasm he'd been giving me.

"Whatever, man. But the more she gives it to me the more I want it. You know this woman licked my ass? At first I tried to stop her but, man! Man! That shit felt too damn good. I'm almost ashamed to say. You know I'm greedy when it comes to sex, the more the merrier. But, dawg, I've been messing around with this woman since August? September? Yeah, September, and man I tell you, she is, whew!" He paused for a few seconds as if he was visualizing the acts.

"Man, come on now, snap out of this. What about Holly?" I

pleaded with him because for some weird reason I thought that if his relationship worked then I had a fighting chance at one.

"Well, you know that's who I really want to marry, eventually. I guess, I'm pissed off and trying to punish her ass, though. But this shit I'm dealing with now is just unbelievable."

"Man, but she's married. How good can it be, sneaking around? We're too old for that."

"I know," he said somberly.

"Why don't you teach Holly how to do what this lady is doing? Then you'll have the best of all worlds."

"Man, have you lost your mind? Did you hear yourself? Hell, nah, I'm not teaching Holly shit! What am I gon' say to her, 'Yo, Holly the next time we have sex I want you to lick my ass?' Holly will cuss me out! She's already not planning the damn wedding from over two years of engagement."

Sean wanted to settle down with Holly, his girlfriend of four years. But he's feels a little resentment toward her after their engagement party over two years ago on a rooftop condominium near downtown Dallas. She was serenaded by a group of dudes singing acappella. All of the close family and friends were there, as he presented her with a three-carat princess cut platinum ring. He had so many flowers, you would've thought they were getting married that day. My man went all out. Since that night, Holly has made no efforts or preparation for the wedding. So now he has allowed someone else to get his attention, since no wedding plans were underway. But he was still in love with Holly and didn't want to leave. He said he was just having fun while it lasted. Holly was the aggressor when they first met. She approached him. He spent some quality time with her, felt it was time to settle down, start a family, and be the man that God wanted him to be. Now he was bitter because he thought she felt the same way but she obviously changed her mind and didn't tell him.

I laughed. "Man, why are you cursing so much? Have you been drinking this early? Anyway, that's not how you approach that type of conversation. You can either discuss it first or you do her first, satisfy her and then maybe she'll want to satisfy you."

"Right, right. Well, all right, man. I'll see you later or what? I guess I'll go meet up with this woman since you're so iffy."

I could tell he was in a foul mood now, probably thinking about Holly and her lack of desire to plan their wedding.

"I'll call you later. I can tell you now, I doubt if I can get out of here early enough to play but maybe we can catch a brew at happy hour or something."

"Auight. Later."

I pressed the End button and picked up my office phone to dial Dena's number to see if they were still having the party tonight and if her friend was going to be there. Lynne walked in so I decided to send a text message instead.

"Hold on just a second, Lynne." I completed the text and placed my phone in the drawer.

"I just wanted to give you your messages." She handed me a legal sheet of paper where she had drawn a grid and had written the words *Name, Date, Time, Nature of Call,* across the top.

The notes filled over half of the paper. On the list I saw Nina and Mrs. Griffin's name several times and a few of our clients. I tried my best not to react while Lynne was standing there. I eyed the blinking voicemail light on my office phone.

"I'll be out here if you need me."

"Thanks Lynne." I sat back in my chair, closed my eyes and prayed, *Lord please, let me have a good day.*

I decided not to call Nina but I wanted to see why Mrs. Griffin had called so many times. As soon as I placed my hand on the phone to return her call, I heard my cell phone vibrate in the drawer.

It was Dena's response. *Yes and yes. She'll be at the door with Ms. Emma.*

Ms. Emma was the owner of The Networking Spot, where the book club party would be held.

I picked up the office phone again to call Mrs. Griffin.

CHAPTER 3

MIA

Dena and I sat on the blanket eating turkey sandwiches, potato chips, dill pickles, and chocolate chip cookies with pecans, not in the cookie. We hadn't said much since Dena ran after that woman with the camera. Given that we were at the park because she wanted to talk, I was trying to keep my conversation to a minimum until she was ready. The melodic sounds of Jill Scott on her iPod stereo filled the air.

"Jill Scott's lyrics make me feel so sexy. I mean, if you internalize them and sing them in your head or pretend you're singing to your man. Sexy. Yeah." She broke the silence.

"Yeah, just like Musiq Soulchild makes you feel like you're in love when you're not even dating. Whew!" I laughed and gave her a high-five, remembering that it had been way too long since I had quality sex or even a meaningful hug.

I gazed across the park at couples in professional attire taking a break and enjoying each other for lunch.

Her cell phone rang. She answered, "Hey… Yeah, he'll be

there, at least he said he was… Sure… Okay, I can do that. Bye."

"Who was that? You were very short," I asked.

"Lonnie. You remember her? She's very desperate for a black man, wants everybody to know it and taking the tips for single woman way too far. She wanted to know if my cousin will be there tonight because she wants me to introduce her. I really don't want to because I don't think they're a good match. She saw him one time, at the gym and has been asking about him every day since then. He needs to be with somebody else. Lonnie has run off every guy that I have introduced her to and then everybody looks at me as if I'm the crazy one. Ugh." Dena sighed. "Crazy people. Besides, I don't think her butt can be faithful anyway." She looked at her phone and smiled as she sent a couple of text messages.

"Well, crazy people don't usually let you know they're crazy. It just comes out at the wrong time, and then you know." I laughed at my own little joke. "Who knows he might like a cheater to play with. Most of them cheat anyway. So let him be the judge of whether he wants to date her or not. You know, put it out there up front."

"I am. I got a plan. Believe that and it's not for her." She gazed across the park absentmindedly and nodded.

"People shouldn't blame you for their poor decisions. And when did you become cupid, Miss Missy? You don't have time for that." I smirked at her.

"I've always been cupid and I'm gonna find you a man, too, just you watch, Sissy." She smiled a mischievous smile as she moved her eyebrows up and down.

"I'm not holding my breath." I stood up and smoothed out my pants.

"Know this. If you did hold your breath, you wouldn't die.

That's how close it is." She tossed her cell phone into the picnic basket, got up, and snapped her finger into the air as she did her runway strut toward the swings.

I noticed the handle of her gun in the basket where her phone landed. "Dena, uhh." I glanced around the park and hurried behind her but quickly decided not to say anything about the gun. "Well, you make sure, if you EVER run across a man for Mia Nixon, please just make sure that he has all of his teeth, and that they're clean, make sure he's clean. He'd better be saved. He needs to be affectionate, respectful and his ass better not be broke. I have to spell it out for you because that last clown you introduced me to was a mess!"

She laughed. "Don't you worry, dear heart. I got it covered this time."

"Whatever, Dena."

"And another thing, you need to come out of that shell and stop waiting on a guy to approach you. You should become more aggressive, go after what you want."

"The Bible says that man that findeth a…"

Dena stopped abruptly and turned to face me. "I don't care what the Bible says, you need to be more aggressive." She snapped her finger in the air and started her runway strut again.

"Whatever, Dena."

We usually went through our competitive game of who can swing the highest first, and end with seeing who can jump out the furthest distance. I always won because it seemed Dena's mind was usually elsewhere.

"Well, Mia, we can't do our competition today since you came out here like you were going to an interview."

"I'm gonna let you have that one today since you're the reason

I'm out here in these clothes, as hot as it is."

She brought her swing to an abrupt halt and started talking. "Monty is going to make me hurt him. He's always asking for money and his temper is off the charts now-a-days. I can't believe I let him move in with me. He stormed into the house yesterday just as one of my clients was leaving. He was all huffed up, looking like he thought he was going to catch me doing something. But when my client shot him a strange look, he calmed down and pretended he had just experienced road rage."

"Oh, wow. Do you think your client bought it?"

"Yes, she did. Because she started talking about one of her experiences. Monty eventually left the room until my client's boyfriend showed up to bring the deposit for his brother's birthday party and then he started lurking around my office again. Now does he think I'm stupid enough to mess with one of my clients?"

"He hasn't tried to put his hand on you has he?"

She jerked her head toward me. "He's still living, ain't he? Girl, I'd have to bring Brooklyn out on that ass."

"Just checking." I held up both hands. "So, uh, is that why you have your gun with you?"

"No. Not really. I just bring it with me all the time since I'm licensed to carry it. You never know when drama will jump off. Remember that woman a few minutes ago? You need to be carrying yours."

"Dena, that's not how people live, just carrying a gun around just in case something jumps off. Whatever happened to talking. You used to, before we took the gun class." I said regretting that I talked her into taking the gun and the self-defense classes.

"People in Texas do. Brooklyn, too."

"Dena, you are, we are, professional women and we... you

know what, never mind, tell me about Monty." I decided not to go into a lecture.

Dena was dating a guy named Monty from D.C. He was supposedly great in bed, professional, bad to the bone, spiritual and just had it all together. For some reason though, after the IT industry experienced layoffs, he hadn't found a good paying job and was always asking her for money. He had one sob story after another… he's working on a venture that he needs to save up for or he needs to have his credit clear and he only needs to be in a holding pattern for six months because his nephew reneged on a car he cosigned for and he has to help his mother because his father is nowhere to be found and then his brother got caught up, went to jail and he's waiting on a check and on and on. He said his layoff was a blessing in disguise because that allowed him to do some things that he's been wanting to do for a long time. But what the hell is that? I hadn't seen him do anything "for a long time." Finally, the ultimate foolishness, he asked her if he could move into her house and she let him. What the…? But what does it matter? He was always at her house and he has a key. I guess his few little pieces of furniture would make it official.

I was single and contrary to popular belief, would certainly rather stay single than deal with some of the drama that Dena dealt with.

"Monty is not that crazy. Trust me. Girl, please. I don't know what I would do if he tried to hit me. Oh my, God." She paused as if she was contemplating what she would do. "Girl. Umph."

"Has he moved all of his stuff in yet?"

"All of what stuff? He didn't have much more than clothes. He had pawned most of his other stuff."

Listening to this conversation was very difficult for me because

I knew she could do so much better. They had good history but he did a one-eighty change after he lost his job. I was trying not to commit too much to memory because her feelings would all change quickly anyway. I always try to make sure I was careful in my comments, so I was not labeled as a single bitter female, which was what Monty frequently said because Dena sometimes told him too much about what we discussed. But when he had done something wrong, he was good at distracting her or better yet pissing her off by bringing up her "bitter" friends.

"Let me get my phone." She walked over to get her phone. As soon as she picked it up, it rang again. "Dena Thomas... no, today is not good. What about tomorrow afternoon? Okay... Thank you... See you then."

"Business is booming, huh?" I smiled.

"Yes and praise God for that. Mia, can I ask you something?"

"Well of course you can."

"Do you think that God will punish me if I keep living in sin? I mean, like, allowing Monty to move in." She started stretching as if she was getting ready to go for a run.

I stammered my words for a moment as it seemed that every scripture that I have ever known left my memory at the same time. "Dena, I uh, I uh, know that God hates sin and I don't think he just starts allowing punishment to fall upon you." I stood up and walked over to the blanket.

"Allowing punishment to fall upon me?"

"Yes. Let me explain it like this. I believe that when you purposely live in sin, and I said purposely because everybody sins whether it's intentional or unintentional. So if you purposely sin, I believe you block blessings that would come your way if you were doing things God's way. Does that make sense?"

She stood there with her arms folded and pondered my comments. "Yes, it makes sense. I get it."

"Dena you know what I want for you?" I walked over and stood directly in front of her.

"What?"

"I want you to be happy. I want you to have joy no matter what because you deserve it. Think about it." I rubbed her arm.

"Thank you, Sissy." She reached for a hug. "Okay, let's get out of here. Are we going to the range?"

"Oh, God, is that Monty right there?" I said.

"Where?"

"Right there. Pulling in beside your car, Dena."

She started gathering her things as if she didn't see him.

"He didn't even say goodbye when he left the house this morning and now here he comes tracking me down at the park." She tsked. "I think the clown is bipolar, for real."

"How did he know you were here. You think he'll act foolish?"

"Girl, nah. Monty is not one for public display. Catch the other end of this blanket please."

We folded the blanket so many times; you would've thought we were soldiers folding the flag.

"Good day, ladies!" Monty smiled and walked over to Dena, hugged her and kissed her on the cheek. Her body was tense.

"What's wrong with you, Dena?" He rubbed the back of her neck and pulled her close.

"Monty, did you hire someone to follow me?" She handed him the picnic basket and the blanket. Her mood had changed slightly. She appeared more tolerable than she sounded a few minutes prior.

"What? Hire someone? Dena, please?" He looked at me.

"Well, there was a woman out here earlier snapping pictures and when I tried to approach her she ran." She folded her arms and waited for him to answer.

"Dena. Come on now. You know I wouldn't do anything like that?"

"Do I?"

"You should." He threw his arm around her shoulder as we walked toward the car. He whispered in her ear, her naturally curly, light brown hair blowing in the wind.

I walked slightly behind them to make sure he didn't make a wrong move. I did not have a gun but I was ready to fight if I had to but Lord knows I prayed that we didn't have to.

CHAPTER 4

❧

GARY

Mrs. Griffin asked me to meet her for lunch; she said she had a business proposition for me. I had decided not to play golf with Sean so I figured I would take at least an hour to see what she had to say. Besides, she peaked my interest when I returned her call. I knew I was making a mistake when I agreed to it. But my inquisitive side told me to do it anyway. I would like to think it was because I liked making money or maybe because Nina didn't want me to. Nina made that known in the four voicemail messages that she left before I got to the office.

"Mr. Matthews, thank you so much for meeting me here." She looked around the restaurant as if she was hiding from someone. The hostess had sat her in the back corner in a secluded area. So all of the extra ducking and hiding that she was doing was really unnecessary.

I sat down. "Not a problem. But why are you acting so

secretive?" I frowned. I was puzzled. "Look, maybe this wasn't a good idea." I stood to leave.

She reached for my arm. "No, no, Mr. Matthews, please wait. I do have something to tell you, well a favor to ask you."

"I tell you what, let's trade seats so that I can face the entrance."

"Okay, no problem." She hopped from her seat and quickly moved to the other side of the booth. "How's that?"

"Better." I gave her a quizzical look because she was behaving peculiarly.

The waiter set two glasses of water and a basket of bread on the table and took our drink orders.

"Okay, let me just cut to the chase here. You're in insurance and I need your help. What type of insurance do you do?"

"Property and casualty."

"Okay. Do you adjust or appraise or what?"

"Both."

"Okay, I need uh, you to appraise my house for more than it's worth so that I can sell it. And I need you to take a look at some water damage at my house and uh—you know, uh my husband, well soon-to-be ex-husband is trying to get over on me and I don't appreciate it."

"What? Melinda are you asking me to lie so you can get paid?"

"Yes. Well, no. I uh—" She put her hand on her chest and took at a deep breath.

I absolutely wanted no parts of her scheme and I was very disappointed that she thought she could ask me to lie and jeopardize my business to benefit her. "You know what? I'm going to forget you asked me this question. This day didn't happen. I'm out." I stood up, reached in my pocket and dropped a twenty-dollar bill on the table and left. *Gosh, why did I agree to meet this clown? Now I can't go back to finish my obligation at the school.* I was talking to myself as I walked out the door.

As soon as I arrived at my truck, I saw Nina standing there with her hand on her hip.

"I told you not meet her for lunch."

"Drop it, Nina." I gently pushed her out of my way. I hated to admit it but she was right.

"No you're not going to just ignore me!" She slapped the window.

I cranked the truck and began pulling away. She kept yelling expletives and then threw a bottle that skipped across the hood. I slammed on the brakes but quickly decided to keep driving.

CHAPTER 5

MIA

Thanks for hanging out with me today, girl. I'm sorry that Monty put a slight damper on it." Dena and I hugged as we prepared to part in order to rest and get ready for the book club discussion party.

"He didn't dampen anything for me. Your mood was the one that went from hot to cold and back to hot then cold, until he drove away. I was beginning to think you were bipolar."

She laughed. "Cut it out, Mia."

Dena had cheered up tremendously while we were at the driving range. Of course it was after she met a tall fair-skinned man with blue eyes, named Dwight. He kept flirting with her until they eventually exchanged phone numbers. She invited him to the book club party and he appeared to be excited about the invitation. Dena knew that Monty would not be there, which would have been a total disaster if Monty knew that she flirted with another guy. Monty had come to the park to inform her that he was on his way to Austin for a job interview and was staying overnight.

I asked, "Did you get it all out today? Is there anything else you need to talk about?"

"Nah, I'm good. Thank you."

"You sure? I can stop by for a few minutes. I need to finish the book though," I said hesitantly because I knew what was coming next.

She swatted my arm. "I know you didn't, Mia. Now why haven't you finished the book?"

"I'll finish it, Dena. I'm almost done. I'm stressing because I don't know what I'm wearing. I've been mentally going through my closet since we got here. Anyway, last call, you need me? I'm here."

"I'm good, I just wanted to vent about Monty. I don't know what I'm going to do about him. I bet he had something to do with the camerawoman and he's probably not gone to Austin either. But I'm done talking about him for today. We need to get ready for tonight. We have less than four hours to rest and get ready to look fabulous!" She pretended to be excited.

"Okay Miss Missy?" I joined in her excitement.

She acted as if everything with her was fine. She rubbed my arm. "Sissy, I'm sure. You know sometimes people need to stop talking about it and just do it."

I smiled and looked at her with concern but said nothing.

"Okay, Sissy. See you tonight. Come fierce!" She winked.

"Okay." I smiled as I walked toward my car.

I was glad to see her show an interest in someone other than Monty. She appeared to be in a better mood. I, on the other hand, had tried to show interests in a new guy a few times before and it just didn't work, so I continued to wait on God to do what He does. One guy I dated had a yellow tooth smack-dab in the front of his mouth and he was shorter than I was. Another guy chewed with his mouth open and smacked so loudly that I wanted to smack him. Still another one apparently wore big bloomers-looking underwear, that were all bunched up in the back of his jeans. I remember thinking, *What is all that fabric bunched up in the back of his pants?*

I stopped in my tracks when I noticed the woman with the camera in the Volkswagen drive by slowly. I looked back to see if Dena was watching. She wasn't. She was distracted by her cell phone.

I rode home in total silence, thinking about the gun, the lady with the camera, and just all of Dena's issues. I meditated for a few minutes, finished reading, took a nap, got dressed, and headed out the door for an evening of fun.

En route to the location, Dena called. "Mia, are you on your way?" She sounded frustrated.

"Dena, yes, I told you I'd get there thirty minutes early." I looked at the clock and pressed the gas pedal a little harder.

"Well, I was just checking."

"You need to calm down. I'm on my way now." I looked in my rear view mirror to see flashing lights on top of a black Dodge Charger. "What the… Dena, I gotta go, this cop is pulling me over. Shoot! I don't have time for this." I pulled over to the side of the road.

"No ma'am, put me on speaker please so I can hear everything and make sure you're okay."

I noticed the cop get out. "Great, a female cop! I do not have time for this crap today."

"It'll be okay Sissy."

"Dena, just make sure you don't say anything, please?"

"I'm not, Mia."

After all of the driver's license and registration routine, the cop asked, "Do you know why I stopped you?"

Hell no, I don't know why you stopped me! I thought and then said, "No, I don't." I placed my hands on the steering wheel in the ten and two position.

"You were going eighty miles per hour in a sixty-five." She leaned down to look in my face.

I might have been. I just didn't know but it was quite possible. "Oh."

"Where are you headed in such a hurry?" She handed my driver's license and registration back.

"I have a book club meeting that I'm hosting. I didn't realize I was speeding. I'm sorry."

"Well, slow down." She tapped my arm and walked away.

I paused as I watched her walk away. "Dena, she's walking back to her car. Can you believe this?"

"Now, I know her tail didn't just stop you to say that. You weren't speedin' then! Did you get her badge number?" Dena bellowed.

"Yes, I got it." I jotted it down on a TJMaxx receipt.

"That's weird."

"I know."

"What did she look like?" Dena said pensively.

"That lady from the park." I pulled back onto the highway and headed toward my destination.

"You're kidding?"

"No. I'm not."

Dena hosted the first Thursday, monthly book club discussion party. She said I should help since I had the combination of qualities that she needed in this venture—outgoing personality, loves meeting new people, attractive and most of all, I enjoyed reading.

Dena and I met when we were ten years old. She was a "new student" at my school back in Arkansas. She stayed for about a year and then went back to New York. She came back to visit her grandmother every summer after that. We wrote each all the time. We were both cheerleaders, went to the same HBCU, pledged the same sorority, at the same time, but were total opposite in all other areas so we always learned a lot from each other.

When I co-hosted an event with Dena, my duties consisted of mingling with most of the guests to make sure they were having a great time. When I was at the door, the rule was "Greet each guest individually with a handshake, a hug or a simple nod with eye-contact." I usually wore one of my slinky black and classy numbers but spring was approaching and the weather was nice, so I wanted to lighten it up. I chose to wear a different color: latte, two-piece with four-inch heels. The skirt had a waistband that folded down, which allowed just a hint of my belly-button ring to show. I didn't have any tattoos, just the ring. A belly ring said one thing and tats said something very different.

I was standing at the door when he walked into the party. He greeted Ms. Emma with a hug. They exchanged pleasantries and then he moved toward me, giving me total eye contact, smiling and greeting me with a firm but gentle handshake. Both of us used the 'shake with one hand as you cover the back of the other's hand', which was considered comforting, more inviting.

"How are you tonight?" he said as he gave me a once-over without being disrespectful, unlike several other guys that came by. He was definitely eye candy, with his pearly white teeth. He had a very low haircut, and thin, perfectly-edged sideburns that connected to his beard, and a neatly trimmed mustache, which was not connected to his beard.

"I'm doing well." I smiled back. He released my hand slowly, as he stared attentively as if he was trying to memorize every detail of my eyes. He moved past me and began to scan the room as if he was in search of someone that he knew. His cologne pleasantly danced in my nostrils.

The owner of The Networking Spot stood next to me at the door. She was an older, elegant vibrant woman named Emma Reed.

"Girl, I think he liked what he saw." Ms. Emma teased.

"He's probably married," I said. "I think I've seen him before. I'll bet he's married or at least taken." As always, I thought every good looking guy was already taken.

"No, dear he's not," she sang.

"How do you know?" I said with a hint of excitement in my voice.

"Trust me. I have a friend, Vaughn, and that's his friend-slash-mentee-slash-nephew. Something or another. His name is Gary Matthews. I've heard Vaughn talk about him and I've seen him a few times myself at Talk Sweet."

"Huh, friend, mentee, nephew? What's Talk Sweet? Saw him with whom?" He is way too cute. I need to figure out a way to meet this one.

"Yeah, I'm dating this… well kinda seeing, well…you know what I'm saying? They call him V., short for Vaughn." She scratched her head and blushed.

I looked at her with a perplexed look. "Yeah, I get it." My lips curled into a smile. "You go, girl. You've got more action going on than I do."

I didn't know much about Ms. Emma's personal life but I knew she was a strong, sophisticated, and successful lady that I aspired to be like. She retired from American Airlines after thirty-five years, went to church regularly, got fulfillment from giving her time to non-profit organizations that helped women and children, and she had her own business that is booming because of the concept and the ambience of this place.

"You'd better get some." She chuckled as she turned to hug another guest. "I got V. and he's a younger version of him, just taller."

"Now who is V.?"

"Mr. V., Vaughn Matthew James, my male friend. I use the names interchangeably. He calls himself a teacher and counselor now. He is well respected by many people in the community. He is a good man. He loves to share his wisdom, time, and money with the people he loves. He owns Talk Sweet. You ever heard of it?"

"No, ma'am, I have not."

"It's on Westheimer, near Kirby. It's a really nice restaurant and lounge. It has a bar area in the front, restaurant in the back. It has an ambiance set for singles and couples. You should check it out sometimes." She shuffled flyers on the podium.

"I should. It sounds nice."

"It really is and I'm not just saying that because I'm dating him. You know I have my own stuff." She gestured her hand in the air and chuckled.

"I need to check it out. What's the age of the crowd?"

"Maybe Gary can take you there," she said playfully, covering her mouth, and widening her eyes as if she'd said something that she shouldn't have.

"Ms. Em-ma, stop it. You are too much."

"I know, but it's all ages there, it depends on the night. For your age, mid to late twenties, Friday night is the best night for you."

"Uh, Ms. Emma I'm older than mid to late twenties, and thank you for the compliment but I'm grown." I smiled.

"You're still a lil' young thing to me." She winked. "Many singles in the Houston area make this their Happy Hour hang out Monday through Friday. I'm sure the two young bartenders that are not stingy with the alcohol have a lot to do with that and V. is not worried about them taking his business under. He's open seven days a week from eleven to eight. Dinner has a waiting line, especially if you don't make reservations. The lunch rush is even busier, but it's in and out, great food, great service, at a great price. Business is good for him."

"That's good. I'll have to check it out."

"Excuse me for a moment, Mia. I need to go check on the D.J."

Ms. Emma excused herself from the door to ensure the D.J. was ready to play some old school jams, loud enough for dancing but low enough for enjoyable conversation. Unlike the nights when there are live bands playing here, you could barely hear anything.

She made her way through the dimly lit room, lined with enormous high-back lounging chairs and ottomans. The networking tables with mirrored tops and blue hurricane vases with votive candles to match the wall sconces lined the outside perimeter of the rectangular dance floor. The bar was a few feet away in the center of the room with more tables on the other side.

I continued to greet people as I kept an eye on the crowd looking for that fine "young tender," Gary Matthews. I was sure he was younger than I was. If he were covering the room hitting on every woman in his path then I'd know just a little bit about his character, what type of girl he liked, maybe he was a player. I'm usually not able to put it into words the type of guy that I want but I can give you a long list of qualities that I do not want but now I can just give you a name. Gary Matthews.

Although Ms. Emma and Dena listed a desired dress-code when they sent an Evite about the party, they had no control over whom the Evite was forwarded to and if they actually read past the date and time, so sometimes she cut some people some slack and let them in anyway—especially if they read the book. The target audience for the party was small, about fifty people, equally men and women mainly because the book was *The Measure of a Man* by Sydney Poitier, but the crowd was always larger. This kept the group smaller, allowed for good conversation about the book, good icebreakers for some, and not just idle chit-chat in which the conversation always ended with it anyway. The Networking Spot, an obvious place to network.

Ms. Emma came back to relieve me at the door. She started stacking papers that didn't need to be stacked. She had an expression that told me she had something to say. "Oh, Mia," she sang. "I think someone is interested in you."

I was suddenly embarrassed and excited all at the same time but trying not to show it too much. "Oh, please. Who?"

"Mr. V. Jr." She smirked.

I knew she was talking about Gary. "How do you know?" I said in anticipation. I couldn't believe my reaction. I knew nothing about him.

"Because, I told him that you were interested."

"Ms. Emma, no you didn't!" I exclaimed.

"Well, not really, but I did point over here toward you."

"Ms. Emma!" I whined.

She winked. "Sometimes Mia, you need to go after what you want. Be aggressive or at least assertive, honey. You single young women need to get over that old school move of waiting on a man to approach you. There is absolutely nothing wrong with stepping to a man and saying, 'You seem like someone that would be interesting to have coffee with or having a five-minute conversation.' If he says 'no thanks,' then move on. It's not as if you asked for his hand in marriage. It's just coffee and maybe a conversation. Men deal with rejection all the time and they're not dead, but why are we so afraid to make that move?"

"Ummhmm." I folded my arms as I pondered her words of wisdom.

I wasn't sure if I was ready for an aggressive move yet so I decided to be assertive and subtly let him know that I was interested. I sauntered across the dance floor to the smooth sounds of Cassidy Stewart, piano player extraordinaire, as I danced with some of the guests that had decided to groove to the up-beat tunes. The party was only to last until ten and then the doors opened to regular customers. I made sure that I walked past Gary just to get another look. I stood close enough to do a flirt wink at him as I talked with some of the guests, acting as if I was interested in what they were saying. Mission accomplished. I was nervous but I did it.

I could usually flirt with the best of them, but when it came to action, I usually sat back and waited on the guy to make the first move, and if he didn't, then nothing happened.

I looked at my watch as I made my way back over to the door. It was nine forty and I was sure there were no more book clubbers coming. I stood there thinking about Gary Matthews, just wanting to find out his story. There was a soft touch on my elbow. It was Dena with Gary in tow.

"Mia, I want you to meet my cousin, Gary. He's single, girrrl. Just what you've been waiting for." She leaned in and sang in my ear in a giddy school girl tone. "I told you that I was going to find you a man, girrrl."

"Dena, stop that, you're acting like I'm a desperate hooch," I said through gritted teeth as I smiled.

"Well, if the shoe fits… no I'm just kidding." She smiled and started talking quickly as she used many hand gestures. "Gary, Mia, Mia, Gary. Both of you are single, saved, professional, looking for a mate, love people. I can't be-lieve this! Finally! I've been working on this hook-up for months! And Lonnie was about to ruin it for me. Gary! You'll like her because she is not just dying to get married. If you happen to be the guy then she will consider but she won't bug you every time you turn around. She is not one of those! Both of you are extremely down-to-earth. Gary, you were always dating someone or busy and Mia you've, well anyw—"

Gary interrupted her. "Hi, Mia. It's a pleasure to meet you formally. Forgive Dena. I don't know if she told you that she was dropped on her head about a month ago and she just blurts out foolishness from time to time," he said as he playfully pushed Dena to the side.

I smiled and then replied, "It's a pleasure to meet you, too, Gary."

"Have fun, girl." Dena slapped Gary's arm and walked away.

"Behave, Cousin. You too, Sissy," she said as her voice trailed off into the distance that she put between us.

"So, how long do you have to stand here?"

"A few more minutes, unless Ms. Emma or Dena relieves me. I'm a woman of my word, so I gotta stand here until ten."

I was extremely nervous all over again. The leg shaking, heart palpitating kind of nervous. I patted my hands against my skirt.

He turned his wrist to look at his watch, a Rolex. "Well, let me see if I can make your last fifteen minutes enjoyable." He stepped closer then turned to lean his back against the wall.

"How do you plan to do that?" I said as I folded my arms with a flirtatious flare.

"Conversation only." He smiled a mischievous smile as he held up both hands.

The conversation started with the usual questions, but he was only verifying what Dena had already told him—when I moved to Houston, career aspirations, marital status, dependents, personality, hobbies, etc. He told me all of the same things after I asked because Dena hadn't told me anything.

"So, you come here often?" I asked as I studied his face trying to remember if I had ever seen him before. I was certain that I had at least seen him in passing.

"Well, occasionally."

"I don't recall seeing you here. I would've remembered you." I scratched my head.

"Is that right? I asked Dena about you a few months ago, same place, same time." He flashed another smile. "You weren't at the door when I got here and you left early that night. So, I didn't have an opportunity to meet you but I was determined to meet you tonight."

"Wow, Dena didn't tell me any of this."

"Really? Well, we've discussed you several times." He rubbed his hand over his mustache.

"Wow." I was slightly flattered but wondered why Dena didn't tell me.

He said, "Listen. I like your style. I want to get to know you. No games, no drama, just conversation for now, see where it goes."

I was short on words. "I'd like that." I prayed I was right. Dena wouldn't put me out there with a buster. Not again, anyway.

"Starbucks?" He pointed toward the door.

"Sure."

"Well, I think we were supposed to talk about the book," he joked, making the cutest face with raised eyebrows.

"Oh yeah, did you like it?" I asked.

"Very much. Did you?"

"Yes, I did." I nodded.

We chuckled at the fact that we tried to stick to the rules of the night after being lost in conversation for at least ten minutes without mentioning the book.

Franky Beverly's "We Are One" started to play. Ms. Emma and the bouncers took their places getting ready for the second part of the night. Ms. Emma winked and nodded that I was done with my duties.

Gary grabbed my hand and led me to the dance floor. He was wearing True Religion jeans with a white button-down shirt that showed his muscular and broad shoulders. He was so sexy.

"I guess you're assuming that I can dance and won't embarrass you," I yelled over the music.

"I know you can dance and I know that you won't embarrass me."

We danced as if we had been doing it for years, as if we were the only two people on the floor. We did a combination of Chicago Style Stepping and Salsa. During my free-style moment, I held my arms in the air and moved my hips in an alluring manner as he moved his feet back and forth. We gazed into each other's eyes with seduction. We ended the dance as he took my hand and turned my back to him and embraced me.

He whispered, "Thank you."

We swayed as one as the song ended.

"Gary, wait here a second. I need to tell Dena that I'm leaving."

"Sure." He watched as I walked away.

I walked swiftly toward Dena. My legs felt wobbly, my heart was beating faster with every step. *What is wrong with me? I am not usually like this over a man. I am so excited! I have to get some type of control here before I make a flat fool of myself.*

"Dena, I'm getting ready to go to Starbuck's. Do you have anything that you need to tell me? Why didn't you tell me about him but you told him everything about me?"

She smiled. "Because I know you, Mia. You would've brushed it off and made all kinds of excuses because you're not ready to seriously date yet." Her tone turned serious. "You've taken enough time to mourn and grieve your loss, Mia."

I reflected on her words for a moment. It had been two years since Byron, the guy that I was dating had passed away and I was sometimes conflicted when I met a new guy. I had gone on a few dates in the past year, but nothing too serious. I got what I wanted and kept it moving just as it had been done to me more than a few times. I wanted to believe that I kept it moving because I wasn't interested and not because I was still grieving. The dating scene had changed slightly and I wasn't sure I was ready for it.

I turned to look at Gary standing at the door messing with his Blackberry. The sight of him made me tingle all over. "Well, do you have something to tell me before I go with him? I'm ready for this. I think."

Her smile returned as she started to ramble. "Nah, not really. Well, he's kind of my cousin, pretty laid back, was in a relationship until about a year ago. I've always known him to be dating someone. I guess you could say cousins by marriage. Our first cousins were married to each other, so we just claim each other as cousins. I call his mother my aunt. I met him a long time ago, twenty years maybe. He's really cool and a good guy, no heavy baggage. He's good people, no children that I know of, no drama, he was the guy that I told you that asked about you, like I sa—"

I interrupted, straight-faced. "You ever slept with him? I'm just asking." I had to know because I was so not in the business of sleeping with someone my best friend had been with. If she slept with, kissed him, or was even interested, he was so off limits to me. If I followed her track of men, then I was essentially sleeping with her. Eww!

"Hell no! I just said he was my cousin! I said! Damn!" Her eyes widened and her neck rolled. "He asked about you before. I never told you because I wasn't sure if he was over that bitter-ass girl he used to date annnnnd, I know that would've given you an excuse not to meet him so I wanted him to approach you on his own when he was ready. You'd better get your ass over there and not lose him to one of these hoochies up in here! Especially Lonnie.

She thought that was who I was introducing her to."

"I know girl, it just seems too good to be true. I mean, one minute I'm single with a crazy past, no real prospects, just guys to pass the time but very interested in meeting someone for something permanent; scared to even go for coffee with guys that I met online, and now, I'm headed for a potentially meaningful relationship, friendship or something just out of the blue. And he's fine as—oh my gosh!" I shook my head and looked back at him again. "He said 'no games no drama, see where it goes'. You think he's interested like that?"

"Girl, yes! I set it up for him to be 'interested like that'. You've been good and you've waited long enough for this day to come. It's time to move on, Mia. Byron would want you to move on and get serious for a change. I set it up for you, honey. I've been working on this for almost a year now." Her tone was empathetic. She placed both of her hands on my arms and rubbed up and down. "Go get your man, girl. Y'all looked fabulous on that dance floor. You need this, Mia."

We hugged, tears welled in my eyes. I dabbed my eyes and I turned on my heel to go get 'my man'.

"Lover, maintenance man, cobweb cleaner, bus driver, plumber, or whatever name you want to call him." She playfully yelled over the music as I walked away and fanned at her. I couldn't believe she'd worked this without me knowing.

I arrived at Starbucks within ten minutes. I powdered my nose before getting out of the car. There were quite a few people there, mostly bikers just hanging out. Gary stood and waited for me at the door. I really like the way he looked at me.

I ordered a green tea. He stood slightly beside me with his hand on my lower back, and he ordered a regular coffee.

"I need major caffeine," he joked.

My knees were weak from his touch. I was so excited and struggling not to show it. I hated when a woman got so giddy around a man that she lost herself to a point of looking goofy. I refused to do that.

He moved his hand to his pocket and pulled out a silver money clip. Unwrapped a ten-dollar bill and handed it to the cashier. She was very friendly so he dropped the extra dollars into the tip jar. I was impressed with him already.

Luckily, we found a table in the corner. He assisted me with my chair and then sat down. "So, Dena didn't tell you that she was concocting an introduction?" he asked.

"No, she did not. I do, however, remember her saying that she would introduce me to someone and if I held my breath I wouldn't die."

"Oh really?" He raised his eyebrows.

"Yes, really."

"Dena is cool. She's good people. I trust her." He paused and smiled as if he was trying to determine what he would say next. "So, Miss Mia, let's get acquainted. Dena told me you are a girlie girl and you like to golf, you like football, basketball, and you ride a bike."

"Wow. She said all that, huh? Well, all true. I like variety. I try to play golf, I love watching football, I enjoy watching basketball but I will try to play also, and yep, I ride." I held out a finger after naming each one. "And, if I can do all of that without breaking my nails, I'm happy."

"Really? That's the girlie part, huh?"

"Yep."

"Who's your favorite football team?" He smiled and narrowed

his eyes.

"America's team baby, the Dallas Cowboys," I said with excitement.

"Ohhhhhh, come on! You meant to say the Giants, right?"

I leaned forward. "D-Dal-las Cow-boys, say it with me, D-Dallas. Marion and 'nem."

We laughed.

"We'll just watch the game in different locations," he joked.

"Works for me." I twisted my lips.

He held up his hands.

We sat, talked, laughed, and shared for over an hour. We discussed everything from sports to community service to anal sex. He listened intently as I talked, occasionally scribbling on a napkin. We discussed so much, asking questions for clarity and the conversation flowed. Whatever came up, respectfully came out. Some of it, I must admit was kind of out there for a first visit but we threw caution to the wind and just went for it. If we didn't want to elaborate, we didn't. Dena carefully planned the introduction, so part of our freedom of speech came from both of us trusting her.

Gary pushed the napkin that he had been scribbling on toward me. It read, 'I like you, do you like me? Yes No'. He reached across the table and drew check boxes beside the words.

I started laughing. "How cute!"

Neither one of us revealed anything major in our lives that would raise the other's eyebrow. No felonies, no major jail time, fantasies, motivations, and likes were in the same direction. I reached for his pen, covered the napkin with one hand as I checked the 'Yes' box, and pushed the napkin back to him. He looked at it and laughed.

"You're funny, you know that, right? Excuse me, please," I said playfully as I stood up to go to the restroom to say a little 'Thank you, Jesus' prayer.

I could tell that he was watching me so I held my head high, shoulders back and kept a sway in my hips.

I stood in the handicap stall for a few minutes, inhaling and exhaling into my hands. I thought about Byron for a moment. I dismissed the thought. I needed to calm myself. I chanted, "Thank you, Jesus" several times in what I thought was very low voice but apparently, it was loud enough for the woman in the next stall who was in major need of a pedicure to ask if I was okay. I didn't respond. I flushed the toilet, walked out, washed my hands, and strolled back toward Gary.

On my way back to the table our eyes locked on each other, as I walked, he watched every step with his hands in a steeple on the table, talk about desire in his eyes. *Whew! That's what a woman wants, to be desired among other things.*

We sat with our eyes dancing, studying for a few moments.

He reached for my hands. "You did wash your hands, didn't you?" He laughed at his own joke.

"No," I said without smiling. "Why would I?" I smiled. I couldn't keep up the façade.

"You're quite the jokester aren't you?"

"You are, too."

I relaxed my shoulders and extended my hands across the table. "You okay?"

I nodded. "I'm cool."

"Sure?" he said easily.

"I'm good, I'm good." I nodded and smiled.

He paused for a moment, looked down at his hands, and then

back up at me and into my eyes. It appeared that we had what each other needed at the moment, quality conversation, attention, and time.

"Look, I know that I took the rudimentary route with the napkin but on a serious note, I know we've only officially met a few hours ago. We've sat here and exchanged some very detailed information about ourselves. You've said that nothing I said turned you off and I'm totally impressed with the information that you've shared with me." He paused. "I don't usually move on anything so quickly but I definitely know what I want now. And since you know my cousin and she considers you her girl, best friend, like a sister, and we've discussed you several times, I guess I can count that." He smiled. "I'm sorry, I'm rambling."

I interrupted. "So, do you just want a friend with benefits or just someone else in the pool for dating to see who you get to choose from?"

He held up both hands. "No, no, no. I'm done with just dating. I want to be serious, you know, just two individuals coming together, complementing each other. I'd like to take this a step further. Start with dating, of course, then to whatever it leads to." He looked at me and didn't appear surprised by my question. "So, what do you want?"

I gave him a semi-smile. "I don't know, dating and see where it goes, I guess."

He nodded. "Eventually I want a serious monogamous relationship, not marriage, so don't panic, and run out on me." He held up his hands again and chuckled. "No sex." He paused. "Yet." He smiled and held my hands again, rubbing the back of my hands with his thumbs. If only he knew. I was two more thumb rubs away from melting right into this seat and sliding to the floor. "I mean, dinner this weekend, a movie, museum, a game or all of the above, you know, get to know each other, behavior, reactions, like I've said before, we can see where it goes." He was definitely charming and sexy. Dimples showing, he raised his eyebrows, narrowed his eyes, and studied me. "Look, I'm ready to move from one point to another in my life, elevation. I want someone that can complement me doing that, not someone that's going to be so draining that it would have me standing still or going backward. I've been there, done that."

I looked at him with a quizzical look as if I was trying to determine if he was telling the truth or a lie. I decided he was telling the truth.

"I'd like that. I can do that. I'm looking for the same thing." I returned the smile, studying, trying to read a little more. "So, you're turning in your playa card?" I joked as I sat back and playfully folded my arms.

He smiled and continued. "You're tough. Geesh." He paused. "No card to turn in. Gave that up a long time ago. Not worth it. Trust me, putting the expectations out there up front keeps you out of trouble." He paused again. "I'm serious."

"So why don't you put the expectations out there up front, Gary!" A mature looking woman in nurse's scrubs exclaimed as she glared at him.

He returned the glare and lowered his head as if he was trying control his impending anger. "Nina, what do you want now? Please. Can't you see I'm busy?"

"Who is this?" She put one hand on her hip and fingered her burgundy highlighted afro.

My irritation was threatening to build but I decided to remain calm until I witnessed how he would handle the situation.

"Nina, please?" he said, attempting to show patience.

"Hi, I'm Nina and you ar—" She thrust her hand toward me.

"Leaving!" He interrupted her as he stood to usher her away from the table. "Mia, excuse me please. I am so sorry. This is nothing. I assure you." His eyes were pleading.

Nina jabbed him in the chest with her finger. "I hate you, Gary." She said through gritted teeth.

He extended his arm to push her away. "Nina, I promise you don't want to do that. What is wrong with you?"

I didn't know if I should stand just in case I needed to defend myself or remain seated and not add fuel to the simmering fire. She was about four inches shorter than I was and about the same size. I was calculating my moves if she attempted to get out of hand with me. I could think of only two words at that moment—self-defense.

After another minute of Gary trying to keep her at arms-length without causing a bigger scene than she already was, she huffed and stomped out. He looked confused as he watched her leave.

He returned to our table and sat down slowly. With his eyes lowered, he opened his mouth but nothing came out. He rubbed his hand over his face and looked at me. "I'm sorry, Mia. I am so sorry. I don't know what else to say. I'm sorry and I'm embarrassed."

I nodded my head because I didn't know what to say either. He seemed sincere.

"Let's get out of here." He stood up and extended his hand to assist me from my seat. "Hey look, I know you didn't ask but I feel like I owe you at least a simple explanation."

"I'm okay. You don't o—"

"No, I want you to know, because I don't want this to be the last time I see you." He pushed the door open.

"It won't be, Gary." My lips curved slightly upward. "As long as this is not a frequent occurrence."

"Trust me, it's not. That was my ex-girlfriend, Nina. We dated for several months and then we broke up but that was about a year ago." He pushed his fists into his pockets as he looked around the parking lot. "I'm doing a community service at this elementary school and she is a nurse or something there and she showed up today as I was leaving and caused a scene with one of the teachers."

"Ohhh." I rambled for my car keys.

"I don't know." He shook his head. "I need to stop this before she goes way too far because I am not one for public theatrics." We walked toward my car. I could tell he was pissed off about what had just happened.

"You okay?" I asked.

"Yeah, I'm good." He paused. "Look, uhh Mia, I had a great time. Thank you so much for sharing your evening with me. Great conversation. I am so sorry for what just happened. I assure you it won't happen again. I will make sure of it. I would love to see you again soon. Like tomorrow." He smiled.

I smiled. "Sure Gary."

He pulled me close and hugged me. "Thank you."

CHAPTER 6

⁓

GARY

I knew it was a mistake but I had to go to Nina's house to see what was going on in her mind that she had to cause a scene three times in one day. I had never experienced the behavior with Nina but I had with another stalker and I knew the situation could get worse. I was determined to stop it before it got worse and I didn't care that it was after midnight. I looked at my phone and I had missed several calls from Mrs. Griffin and one from Dena. I called her back. "Hey Dena, she's everything you said she'd be. You did good. I owe you big time."

"That's great, Gary. I told you." She beamed.

"Okay well, I'll hit you back, I need to take care of something here quickly."

I pulled up to Nina's place, hopped out and walked briskly toward the door. I pounded the door several times with my fist and called her name. "Nina!"

The door opened but Nina was not standing on the other side.

"What's up, man?" Her short and burly twin brother, Leonard, asked with an attitude. He folded his arms across his chest.

Leonard and I had always been cool. We hung out a few times in the past. I hadn't seen him in several months either. From his stance, I figured he had a problem with me pounding the door the way I did.

"Nothing man. Where's Nina?" I looked down at him.

"Hold up, man, you lookin' like there's a problem."

"Where's Nina?" I didn't respond to his accusation. I pushed past him.

"Hold up, man! Don't make me have to—"

"Don't make you have to what?" I was indignant. I turned around to face him.

"Y'all stop it." Nina said nonchalantly as she tied a scarf on her head. "Leonard, I got this."

Leonard's chest was moving up and down, with fists clinched as he walked into the living room and sat down.

"Oh, you got this? Well, Nina, since you got this, why don't you tell me why the hell you've starting popping up all over the place when I haven't seen you in a year?" I stepped closer to her.

She flopped down in a chair and started to cry. "I'm sorry Gary, I just, I just—saw you today and I, I—wanted to be, I thought I wanted to be with, I thought about our baby."

"What? Wait a minute. What baby?"

"I was pregnant when we broke up and I was so upset with you that I had an abortion because I didn't want to raise the baby by myself."

"Wait, Nina. What? You were pregnant and you what? You just decided to have an abortion without letting me know anything?" I didn't believe her. Something about her demeanor made me think she was lying and unless she had changed her position, she didn't believe in abortions.

She wiped her tears, placed her hands over her face, and then rubbed them over her hair. "I didn't know what to do. I just—I was mad and I just did it."

"So, at thirty-six years old, you decided to have an abortion? Why?" I stood and walked toward the door.

"Gary, I'm sorry. I just thought you didn't want me anymore and didn't want anything to do with me, so I just did it," she said through loud sobs as she buried her face in her hands.

"You thought?" I said sarcastically.

Leonard appeared in the doorway, he glared at me as I stood with my arms folded. "What's wrong with you, Nina?"

"Nothing, Leonard. I'm fine."

"Well, why you crying then?"

"Leonard, I told you I was fine. Get out of here!"

"Leonard, hold on, did your twin tell you she had an abortion?"

I said that because I knew Leonard had always protected Nina, always had her back but he never supported her when she created drama. He loved kids, he had seven of them. I knew he was against abortions, too because we discussed it many times. He coached his son's Little League teams and everything.

He frowned. "Abortion? Yeah right."

"Thanks, man. I'll holla." I walked out.

"Gary, wait, please wait. I just want you back, I'm sorry!" She called out as she followed me.

"Nina, get back in this house causing all of this drama," Leonard commanded.

In the past, I assumed Nina was not stable but now, she proved it.

CHAPTER 7

❦

MIA

Gary and I departed ways and I was headed home to think about all that had happened in the past three hours. I started to feel somewhat guilty for having a good time. I had slipped back into a moment of mourning Byron. I knew I was single. I knew he was gone but I couldn't understand why I suddenly felt like I was cheating. As I reached the toll road ten minutes later, speeding and holding true to my personalized license plate "*ZUUMIN*," my cell phone rang. I answered. "Hey, girl! Are you done having mad passionate sex with my cousin?" Dena's voice boomed through the phone.

"I wish I was, but I don't know Dena." I tried to say without sniffing through the tears. It didn't work. She noticed.

"Are you crying? What happened?" she said in shock. "Stop the damn car right where you are, I'm on my way." She knew me too well.

"I'm fine Dena. He was so adorable," I said as I began to cry.

"He really is, but I—"

"Where are you Mia? Have you passed my exit?" She continued to interrogate.

"No."

"Sweetie, please stop by my house. What's wrong, why are you crying then, if he was so adorable?"

"I don't know! I just…"

"Oh honey…" she sang in a sympathetic voice. "Please can you come by, Mia? I just don't want you to go home alone and be miserable."

I just held the phone and didn't comment because I was very comfortable going home alone. I was used to it. The guys that I had been playing the juggling act with never stayed over. I didn't allow it. She, on the other hand, had always been in a relationship, good or bad and she enjoyed having people around her.

"Mia, Gary just called and said that he had a really wonderful time and thanks for introducing him. Oh honey," she continued to sing.

I rang the doorbell and Dena opened it immediately with widespread arms.

"Okay, tell me what's wrong."

"Nothing. I just feel like… like I'm… like…" She knew exactly why the tears were there but I was shocking myself at the emotions that I was emitting. I had dated a few guys and had never done this or felt like this about any of them even after a few dates. It was definitely something different about this one.

She ushered me to the sofa. She rubbed my face. "Trust me, Mia. Byron would want you to move on, girl. I know you allow yourself to stay in the grieving stages sometimes but trust me honey he would want you to move on. If things happened the other way around, trust me, he would be dating by now." She said emphatically.

She was always careful about what she said about him, most of the time asking questions and never really commenting on my responses, just an attempt to get me to verbalize my feelings.

"Think about this. Do you feel like you've allowed yourself to grieve or do you feel like you've busied yourself to avoid your grief? And when you think about him, do you think about the day he died or do you think about the good memories with him? Think about Mia. You did your part. It's time, Mia. Just think about it," she said as she walked into the kitchen grabbed a bottled-water, sat it on the coffee table in front of me, then walked down the hall toward the guest bedrooms.

I sat there in silence—thinking about what she had just said. Still crying, I slid down, curled into a fetal position, and drifted off to a light sleep. Cold.

She tapped my leg, startled me.

"Mia, your room is ready. You can lie down in there."

I got up, stumbling, rubbing my eyes as I walked to my room that I decorated to my liking in red and brown, comfortable, cozy, romantic, from the window treatments to the lamps to the duvet cover to the rug on the floor. All of the feelings from Gary just moments earlier had subsided because the guilty feelings from my past attempted to take over. Dena was right. I needed to move on.

I changed clothes quickly and assumed the same fetal position in the bed, asleep within five minutes. Hoping I would dream about Gary, the gentleness of his touch, and the charm that exuded from his pores and caused my body to implode from the way he looked at me.

I know Dena would have so much to say about some of the topics that we discussed. She'd probably be appalled but I wasn't and neither was he. All was fair in the conversation. I felt it was better to be taken aback in the beginning than to endure heartache and debt later when you find out that you're dating, or even worse, married to a monster. My position had always been, find out the answers to what you want to know up front and pray that your potential mate is telling the truth. That way your feelings are not tied up in it when he asks you to cosign for his momma a car and she never pays the car note, acting as if the car was a gift from you and to top it off she stops speaking to you because her daughter doesn't like you. I digress, but that actually happened to my cousin. From the lunatics that Gary has dealt with, I should be the apple of his eye in no time. I trusted "Nina" was not going to be a problem. He didn't appear to be the type that would entertain drama anyway.

CHAPTER 8

GARY

I pulled through the gate, waved at security, down the street and into the garage, went in, and didn't make it past my media room. Undressed, sat down and started channel surfing, local news, ESPN, Fox Sports Net. The phone rang, I pressed the talk button.

"Talk to me."

"Hey, Gary, its Dena. What are you doing?"

"Didn't I just talk to you?" I joked. "I'm sitting in my recliner, flipping channels, chillin'. Why? Oh and thinking about your girl." It sounded corny but I said it. I had to think about her to get my mind off Nina's crazy ass. I couldn't believe she pulled that stunt. It hadn't started well, but I thank God for Leonard.

"Yeah, well good, that's what I'm calling about." She sighed.

I sat straight up in my chair. "Why? What's wrong? What happened to her?"

"Nothing man, she's here," she whispered.

"Well, what's going on? And why are you whispering?" I

furrowed my brows, concerned.

"Because she's here, duh, damn, listen! Remember I told you that she has gone through some losses in her life and sometimes she has these moments where she'd cry, cry a lot. She thinks you're very adorable and wants to…"

"Dena, first of all watch your feisty assed tone and then get to the point. Please." I was getting anxious because Dena exaggerated sometimes.

"I'm sorry, man. I just want you to help her, love her, cherish her, which is why I plotted, prayed and planned the introduction, and I…"

"Dena, that's what I want and plan to do. I need to get to know her first, though." I was getting slightly irritated wondering where all of this was coming from. It was way too much pressure for me in one night.

"Can you come over here to talk to her, please? I just think that it would be best if you knew the details sooner than later so you'll know what you're dealing with."

I squeezed my temples and rubbed my hand across my face. What have I gotten myself into now? If there is drama, Gary seems to walk his ass directly into it. Just like old times in Brooklyn. I didn't want to deal with more drama. It can't be that bad, though. We talked about so much. What the heck could be causing her to cry? And why do I need to get over there, like right now? I hope Nina's show hadn't gotten to her.

"What do you mean, sooner than later and what am I dealing with Dena?"

"Gary, just get your ass over here, okay? Please?" she said as if we were plotting a conspiracy.

I sighed deeply. For some reason, I trusted Dena. I wanted to go because I'd love to see Mia again but I didn't want to appear too pushy by invading her privacy and I sure as hell didn't want any drama. I have had enough of that in one day.

"I'm on my way. No drama, Dena," I said firmly.

I put my clothes back on, brushed my teeth, strapped on my boots, and was on my bike within ten minutes, on the toll in fifteen minutes and at Dena's within thirty minutes of hanging up the phone. It usually took a little bit longer to get to her house but this time there was a sense of urgency.

It took Dena a few minutes to get to the door after I rang the doorbell. When she opened the door, we both just stood there. I broke the silence as I stepped inside and reached to hug her. "What's up?" I placed my helmet on the bench in the foyer and removed my boots. Dena's house had a very contemporary flare, everything was very sleek, clean, black, red, white, squares, circles, rectangles similar to the look of a downtown loft from a design magazine.

"Hey, thank you for coming. Come on, she's in here." She started walking, her bare feet quickly slapping the marble floor through the foyer, across the living room and down a short hallway toward one of the guest bedrooms.

"Hey wait, does she know that I'm here?"

She never stopped her stride, just turned her head to the left, and said, "No."

"What?" I whispered with animation.

"She'll be okay with it," she whispered back the same way.

She knocked on the door of the bedroom. There was no answer so she turned the knob and peeped in. I stood on the outside in silence.

"Mia, are you sleeping? Somebody's here to see you." Dena sat on the side of the bed.

I inhaled deeply, exhaled slowly through partially closed lips, and expanded jaws. I could see Mia's feet, perfectly manicured toes, and firm legs. I heard the bed move.

"What?" She said in a confused tone as if she was awakening from a deep sleep.

"Gary's here to see you?" Before Mia could respond, Dena continued to explain. "Sissy, I called him because I knew that he could help you and I wanted him to understand the situation and just see you sooner than later, you said he was adorable and you wanted a rela—"

"Dena? Help me? Why did you do...oh my gosh, Dena?"

"He's cool, he's cool. He won't judge you?"

"What?" She sounded just as confused as I felt.

What is there to judge this early in the game? I thought. *Damn, I should leave, I don't feel like this tonight, I don't want any drama. Damn, damn, damn, Dena!*

I paced the floor back and forth. I closed my eyes, rubbed my head from the base of my neck to my face, and slowly removed my hands as I exhaled. Preparing myself. Dena kept rambling on and on. *She means well and I know she would not have introduced me to a drama queen on purpose, so I know this is not as bad as it seems. This is minor. I know it.*

I stepped forward and gently knocked on the door. "You mind if I come in?"

Dena immediately stood up and walked toward the door, she walked behind me and gave me a gentle push toward the bed. She pulled the door to close just enough, being careful not to close it all the way. She was nosey and didn't want to cut off the sound of her "monitors" called ears. Closing the door all the way would cause that.

I sat down on the side of the bed next to Mia's feet but decided to change to the chair sitting across from the bed to get a better angle of her face. I couldn't help but wonder why this chair was sitting here in such tight quarters. Mia sat up and leaned her back against the black leather headboard, wiping her eyes that were swollen and red. The dim light from the brown and red lamp on the oak nightstand illuminated the room in a romantic ambiance. I had to remain focused because it was apparent that I was not there to be romantic, though I wish I was, and I couldn't help but wonder what was going on. *Could she be pregnant? What did she not tell me? I know she's not married.* I was nervous but hopeful. She seemed uncomfortable by the attention. She held her head down, staring at her hands, wiping away tears. We sat in awkward silence for at least five minutes. I wanted to touch her, hold her, caress her, and let her know that whatever was going on, I would be right there to help her through it, at least that's the confidence that Dena had in me and the confidence that I usually had in myself. My mind was racing trying to figure out any situation that could possibly have me running for the hills. I had left a different person an hour and a half ago. I didn't expect to see this side until months later but the sooner the better. Though I'm sure if it was up to her, I would not have seen it.

"If you'd like to run out and act as if you've never met me, I'd understand," she sniffed.

"No, no, I'm not going to run, I just want to understand what's going on. Dena asked me to get here right away."

"Dena is so crazy. She should not have called you." She continued to look at her hands.

"Babe, what's wrong? Why the tears?"

"I'm fine, really. I promise. I just have times when I get sad, I'll cry, and I get over it, that's all, and I know that I'm not the only one to deal with stuff, so I just have my moments, get over it and keep it moving. I promise that's all. Dena made it sound far worse that it is. I'm sorry she made you come over here." She folded her arms.

"I'm cool, but what are you crying about?" I ensured my tone was empathetic. I really felt it was the least I could do especially after Nina's stunt. I still wanted to get to know her.

She was silent for a moment.

"Gary, you know what? I really like you, a lot, although I just met you. I think you're a good guy, and I want to have a friendship, a relationship with you," she said in a monotone voice and vulnerable disposition.

I was certainly relieved but I felt a 'but' coming.

She continued. "I cry sometimes over the losses that I've endured over the past few years. Like I said, I cry, I get over it. The episodes are very infrequent now. I'm not a crybaby by a long shot."

Feelings of mourning started rushing back to me. I had to control myself. I touched her leg and scooted closer to her but made sure that she understood I was comforting, not taking advantage of her vulnerability.

"Do you want to talk about it?"

"It depends, if I don't, will you be mad that you drove all the way over here," she joked, tried to smile.

"Nah, it was worth the trip, plus it's not that far and I'm seeing you again." I smiled, knowing I sounded corny.

"I'm gonna kill Dena." Her voice had a morsel of additional

energy.

"She's concerned, although over-exaggerated sometimes, but concerned. She cares about you."

"I know," she conceded, clearing her throat. "Do you want the long version or the short version of the story?" She tried to muster a smile again.

"Which version do you want me to hear? I'm all yours."

"You're all mine for real?" she joked.

She got serious again and began to explain with rapid fire. "I've been through the grieving process more than I care to think about. I won't hit you with every single case, just the most recent one. A couple of years ago, the guy that I was dating was hit by a car that was driving too fast in the parking lot. He was trying to keep two kids from getting hit, a little boy and a little girl, five and four." She paused for a few seconds, wiped away tears and started again. "It was a hit and run. The little boy suffered minor bruises but the little girl died. He pushed both of them out of the way but the driver swerved, lost control, and hit them." She paused again, wiping away tears with the back of her hands. She continued. "I spent a week at the hospital with him, watching him, watching the monitors, listening to the nurses and doctors imply that there was no hope, still praying to God that he would recover, and the nurses wanting him to be that miracle 'wake-up' just as much as I did. I traveled back and forth from Dallas to Charlotte every weekend." She fidgeted with the thread on the comforter. She sat thinking for a few moments. "I was on my way to see him the night he passed away. I guess God had another plan, expected me to say goodbye forever. How do you do that?" she asked, not expecting an answer. She continued. "You know that happened with my mom and dad, too? They passed away when I was on my way, en route, they didn't hold on to wait for me."

Tears started to stream again. I moved closer, held her hand.

"They finally found the lady that hit him. They gave her ten years. Can you believe that? Only ten years?" She paused for a moment. "The mother of the two children had a nervous breakdown after the accident, but coincidently she remembered enough for the police to make an arrest. So messy."

She sighed.

"You know the weird thing about all of this?" She didn't wait for me to answer. "We had recently stopped dating because we realized we were on two different paths. Lies, deceit, it was all coming out in the open. Obviously, we still cared about each other though because we were friends. I haven't really desired to date seriously since then until recently. Grieving, anger at him, all set in. I know you think I'm stupid, right? I guess that can go on the list of silly things that you do for love." She shook her head as if she was awakening from a bad dream. "I haven't been on a quality date in months, not meaningful ones anyway. Guys can really be a lot of work." She smiled and stretched her legs out.

I smiled and laughed quietly.

"And now I meet you. I do apologize for rambling so much but I was feeling somewhat guilty for having a good time tonight and I have the potential of moving on to a wonderful friendship, relationship and I know I deserve it. All of the things that you were saying tonight had me thinking about a lot. Afraid I would mess it up and I know that my parents wouldn't get to meet you and—" She sighed deeply. "What I had planned to do was cry the tears of sadness and then joy, in the comfort of my own home but who knew that Dena had something else up her sleeves tonight. She knows me very well, that's why she begged me to come over here to stay so that I'm not 'home alone.'" She mimicked Dena moved her hands in quotation gestures as she spoke. "I'm gonna get her. I hadn't planned on sharing this story until we were well into the friendship, not four hours in." She looked up at me, an intense stare.

I said, "I understand."

We sat in silence for a moment longer. I tried to find the words to say. I couldn't. Therefore, I allowed her to talk for as long as she needed. In my grievance counseling sessions several years ago, we had to learn to listen to the person that was grieving, offer a hand, a hug but just basically be there, mostly in silence.

She began again. "I remember a few years ago, there was a lady, a prophetess, at my sister's church. She used to hug me tightly every time she saw me. She'd pull back, look at me with a perplexed look, and say, "Be careful." At first, I didn't think anything of it since I was traveling back home and that was the usual send off message of well-wishers. After several times of hearing the same message, "Be careful," I somewhat started to worry. I guess that's what she was trying to tell me, perhaps she saw danger, an accident, around me." She paused for a moment as if she suddenly thought of something and then continued talking. "You know? It was a weird thing, because after he was hurt, she never said that again. But she did, however, tell my sister that she did not have a good feeling about his recovery." She frowned. "My sister didn't tell me that until later, obviously, he didn't make it."

I sat silently wondering what I should do, what should I say because I can certainly relate. I had been on that side of pain and in some cases, I still was.

She fidgeted with her hands. "I just … I just … I just don't get it. Ya know?" She looked up from her hands, another tear fell. She wiped it away, took a deep breath, and wiped her face with both hands, "You said that you understand, how so? Tell me some of your hurts."

"You know what?" I had to clear my throat. "I'd rather stay focused on you right now. The day will come when I'll tell you everything you want to know about my hurts, and trust me I have plenty." I smiled and used my thumb to wipe away her tears. I rubbed her jaw with the back of my index finger as I studied her face. Even with swollen and red eyes, she was so beautiful. She had the cutest dimple to the left side of her mouth, almost on her cheek that showed occasionally when she spoke but always when she smiled. If my friends from back on the block saw me right now, they would say that I'm a wimp, a duck, and soft, but thank God, I gave all of that up years ago. I can express my feelings and no longer am I trying to come off as being "hard," as if men don't cry and don't show affection.

"So, I guess it was nice meeting you," she mumbled.

"Huh?" I looked perplexed, "No, you're not getting rid of me that easily." I placed my hand on her leg, rubbed up and down as if I was trying to warm her. "Seriously, Mia, I do understand."

She nodded.

To break the awkward ten minutes of silence in the room, I reached for the radio on the nightstand, turned it on and Franky Beverly was singing "We Are One." We looked at each other and giggled.

I wanted to kiss those juicy full lips but I had to contain myself. I reached into my pocket and pulled out the napkin that I had written on earlier and handed it to her.

"Oh my," she cooed.

She flashed her pearly white teeth, opened her arms, and

reached for a hug. I moved closer and took her in my arms. We held on tightly with occasional rocking, for a while. I am really feeling her, everything that Dena told me is definitely true. She is very open, honest, affectionate, but vulnerable right now. She rested her head on my shoulder and hugged with a tight passion. The last song that I remembered was Eric Benét's "Pretty Baby." I was beginning to feel the pain of the uncomfortable position.

I loosened the grip just a little and she let go and said, "I'm sorry, I'm about to break your back."

She let go and leaned back on the bed. She stared into my eyes, her eyes were glistening. She took my face in her hands, reached to rub my eyebrows with both of her thumbs, she pulled me toward her, closed her eyes, and kissed me softly on my lips, no tongue, just lips. I was excited! However, I had to maintain control.

She asked, "Will you close the door and lock it? Dena is a sleepwalker and I don't want her standing over me if I fall asleep."

We laughed.

I stood and walked toward the door, pushed it closed, wondering about Dena and her sleepwalking.

"Dena we're closing the door now," I yelled.

My cell phone rang within five seconds.

"What?"

"I said I closed the door."

"Why you gotta announce it?"

"Because I knew you were listening to make sure that I didn't do anything to your girl."

"How is she?"

"She's good. Everything is good." I looked at Mia as if to make sure.

Her expression showed she was.

86

"I wasn't worried about you doing anything to my girl. Are y'all staying the night?"

"What? No, I hadn't planned on it."

"Why not? You're both consenting adults. And it's the wee-hours of the morning."

"You're nuts, Dena."

"Mia knows there are towels, toothbrushes and everything in the bathroom in there, so it's your call and besides, you don't need to be driving that bike all fast back home tonight anyway."

I chuckled. She had this all planned, her way.

"I live only thirty minutes away and you're just 'Johnny on the spot' aren't you?"

"Yes, I am, I have to take over since y'all moving so slow, and there are babies to be had within the next year or so and y'all need to practice, I told you that. I'm in charge here, remember that."

My jaw dropped and a baffled look covered my face. "Well have at it, Dena."

"Oh, there are some condoms in the drawer in the bathroom, too, and don't make the headboard hit the wall too hard." She laughed and hung up before I could respond.

Mia said, "She is out of control," as she laughed at the look on my face and I know she heard everything that Dena was saying.

My cell phone rang again.

"I forgot to say, take care of her. Trust me, Gary, she's the one, and for the record I was not listening to y'all."

Straight out of New York, she had certainly picked up that Southern term "y'all" and used it frequently.

"Bye, Dena and thank you. Oh and by the way, I ride my bike not drive it!"

"Whatever you do, you do it too damn fast."

I ended the call and put the phone back into my pocket. I looked at Mia and smiled. She had moved down from the headboard to the pillow. She patted the bed next to her.

"Will you lie down right here?"

I climbed onto the bed next to her. She had changed her clothes. She had on orange short shorts with a blue and white stripe around the band and a double orange and white tank top, no bra. She was tempting me. Intentionally or not, I had no idea, I just flowed with it. She took my hand and pulled it over her.

She said, "I'm not ready to make babies yet as Dena is suggesting, I just want you to hold me."

I did just that. I pulled her close, rested my hand on her abs, and allowed the scent of her body to invade my nostrils in a magnificent way.

CHAPTER 9

MIA

Dena and I sat in the kitchen eating Honey Nut Cheerios as she quizzed me about the detail that Gary and I got into in our first conversation. I absolutely hated it when she "put me on the couch" though. She claimed she was trying to make sure that I was sure.

I retorted with, "Are you sure? You introduced me. I felt comfortable because you claimed you set it up. It took you over a year. Remember?" I mocked her. "I'm trusting you, so I went for the gusto. Now, is he a good catch or not? Is he faking?" I said when I got irritated. "He seems cool. It's amazing how it's acceptable to have sex on the first date but not acceptable to look directly into a person's eyes and ask questions to make sure you're connecting to the right person, have the same goals and aspirations, are going in the same direction and besides, he asked me just as many probing questions as I asked him. Perhaps you should start asking more questions when you meet these men you run across."

That last statement slowed her just a bit. "Mia I'm not judging your conversation, my dear, I'm just asking questions," she calmly said. "So, what did you two talk about?

My mood had simmered some. "Everything from anal sex to zodiac signs."

"What? Are you serious?" She raised her eyebrows.

"Almost. Everything from A to Z. He is so adorable. He asked about my passion, my fantasies, marriage—"

"What? He brought up the marriage question?"

"Yep. He just asked how badly did I want it, what kind of wedding did I want, and if I wanted children?"

"Wow."

"I asked him simple stuff like, What did he enjoy most? What sport did he play or like? What was his greatest fear? What was his relationship like with his mother? His father? Does he have any addictions? Has he ever been considered a workaholic? How and why did his last relationship end?"

"Gosh, you talk about me interrogating, look at you." She picked up her bowl to drink the remaining milk.

"Well, he was piling on the questions, too and it was cool. We talked about everything. I'm telling you, background checks, dreams, motivations, housekeeping, HIV status, community service, politics, and he's saved. I am way cool with him." I went to pour my milk in the sink and washed the bowl.

"So, you sure you don't think all of this questioning was a bit much on the first date?"

"No. I don't. And besides it was not an interview. It was a conversation between two intelligent adults."

Despite her grilling after Gary left to shower and change clothes, the weekend with him was wonderful, marvelous. Neither one of us worked on Friday. We slept at Dena's house Thursday night, totally unplanned. He was a gentleman. I still felt a little uneasy about showing my emotional side so soon but I guess that could be okay. I am so much stronger than that. At least that's what I try to display. On our first night together, both of us remained fully clothed. I wanted him so badly and I knew he wanted me. I could tell. Be he controlled himself and so did I.

We went running Friday morning, golfed in the afternoon, only nine holes, it was too humid! A movie on Friday night, it was a fast food day for the meals and I was okay with that.

We went to the gym Saturday morning, ran several errands together including satisfying my craving for the Breakfast Klub, standing in line for at least thirty minutes to get the Breakfast Special with turkey, scrambled eggs, potatoes and a side of grits. I knew I had to run extra miles after my three-day eating habits. We chilled for a few hours in the afternoon and then went to Groove's Saturday night. On Sunday, we went to church, dinner and a walk in the park, and enjoyed the sunset.

We slept alone each night with the phone plastered to our ears. I couldn't take the chance of messing up my reputation so early in the game. But hell, what did it matter with two consenting adults. Allowing grown folks activity was okay if we wanted to.

The Monday after our first weekend together, I dressed as a floral delivery employee, trying to be incognito, and made a delivery to his office: one yellow rose, a basket of gourmet cookies and a handwritten note that read *Gary, Thanks for the best weekend ever!! Your New Friend.* My outfit was black sneakers, black pants, a red golf shirt, and a black hat and to top it off, I had a clipboard. I think I passed.

I rang the buzzer. An older woman looked sternly over her

glasses toward the door with a frosted name, *Jefferson, Matthews & James Insurance Consulting.*

"Good afternoon, how may I assist you?"

"Hi, I have a delivery for Gary Matthews." I looked at the name on the door again to make sure I was in the right office.

She didn't say anything, I heard the buzzer so I turned the knob and walked in. She smiled at first but it turned to a frown when she noticed the rose and the basket of cookies. I guess she thought I was delivering some books or something.

"Hi, I have a delivery for Gary Matthews." I tried to ignore the frown and appear friendly.

"Hello," she said dryly and rested her chin in her hand, as her eyes were darting around the basket.

I placed the basket on the desk and carefully placed the rose on top of the basket. She pulled the card out and read it as soon as I sat the basket down. My eyes widened. I wanted to say, "Um excuse me, is your name Gary?" I decided to be nice to the little old woman although she was a tad bit rude. She must know that I am not against karate chopping rude people but of course, she did not know that this gift was from me. I gave her a pass since she didn't technically know she was being rude.

She narrowed her eyes at me as if she knew that I didn't work at a floral delivery shop but then she said, "Thank you, I will make sure he gets this." She gestured toward the basket and rose.

She stood up and walked toward a closed office door.

I moved out of the office at the same brisk pace that I walked in. I was back in my car and down the street in no time. My phone rang, I answered on the first feel of vibration on my thigh and beeping in my ear singing "hello."

"You are too much. Thank you." I could tell he was blushing.

"What are you talking about?"

"Thank you for the cookies and the rose."

He had mentioned during one of our many conversations that he loved chocolate chip and oatmeal raisin cookies, although he looked as if he had never had a cookie in his life.

"Oh, you are so welcome. I had a great time, and I wanted to say thank you."

"Well I did, too. Can I thank you with dinner again tonight if you're not busy?"

"I'm sorry I can't. I have a class at church tonight." I came up with that right on the spot. For whatever reason, I was all of sudden trying not to get too close too soon. It wasn't working. I though, *Duh, you spent every waking moment of your weekend with him and then sauntered into his office and dropped off a rose.*

"What time do you get out? I want to see you again."

"I'm not eating that late, I–."

"Will you drink that late? Help me out here. I want to see you."

"Okay, okay, okay." I bit my bottom lip. "My class should be over by eight o'clock, I can see you after that on Westheimer and Post Oak, there's another Starbuck's, can you meet me there?"

"Of course, of course. I'll be there."

"Cool."

"Tell me one more thing, who'd you get to deliver the rose and…"

"I did."

I could tell he let out a quiet laugh of satisfaction. "You are too much, and I like it."

"Why did you ask?"

"Because I thought I saw your car at the traffic light on my way back from my lunch appointment. Personalized plates will give it away every time."

"Oh, did you now? I'm glad I have no secrets."

"Yeah, me too. See you tonight."

His voice just sends me over the edge. Velvet. Smooth. A late night-radio-personality voice.

I was tempted to make a comment about his assistant but thought better of it.

CHAPTER 10

GARY

Mia and I went to her house after talking and drinking coffee and tea for nearly two hours. I could tell she wanted me. Her body language was talking loudly. I could see it in her eyes, her nipples were showing it also. I was willing to bet her panties were wet, too. She flirted in such a sexy way. Since I did not bring condoms, there will be nothing jumping off tonight. I know she didn't have any because she told me she didn't want to embarrass or insult the guy, so she always thought she'd allow him to buy the condoms first, never getting too heated to go without one. Being embarrassed was undeniably not my concern, insulted maybe, but never embarrassed. And I'm not bragging.

I tried to focus on something else. I refused to act as I did when I was in my hoodlum stage. If I saw a woman that I was very attracted to, I hit it that night and on occasion, my dumb ass did it without a condom. Thank God, those days are gone and I, luckily, suffered no consequences.

Her house was immaculate. She definitely had an interior designer's talent. Her house could beat any model home that I've seen in this price range.

I said, "I like your style."

"Thank you."

We sat down on the sofa and started watching her new DVD of "Martin," the first full season. Both of us are big fans. We laughed as if we had never seen the show. After the first episode, she jumped up and went over to her iPod speaker system, pushed her iPod into position, rolled her thumb over the controls.

"Let's see if you re-member this, bruh!"

She muted the TV and pressed 'play.' The familiar drum roll beats from the late eighties started pumping from the speakers. I started bobbing my head. She started bouncing around like she was on stage singing with the five-boy group, New Edition… "I don't love her, I tried to tell myself, but you can see it in my eyes …" I stood up and got in sync with her, singing and dancing. We danced around and reminisced for at least twenty minutes. This girl is so cool. She knows how to have fun. I like that.

"Okay, okay, I'm tired now." She plopped down on the sofa, leaned her head back, breathing as if she just finished running a race. I sat down beside her, allowed her to rest for a few minutes. She stretched out, resting her head on the throw pillow and I pulled her feet into my lap. I rubbed her feet, very soft and pretty. She channel surfed through a few nightly talk shows, reality shows, and then turned back to the DVD, pretending she was not affected by the foot rub.

After the last episode, less than forty-five minutes later, she got up, straddled me on the sofa, and started kissing me. I succumbed to the pressure and started groping her breast, her back, her butt.

Heavy breathing ensued. This was a pleasurable surprise.

She whispered in my ear, "I want you so badly."

We continued kissing, passionately. All kisses in the past have been tender, gentle, hot, but short.

Damn! I can't believe I don't have any damn condoms. I want her so badly but I don't want her, not like this. We will wait. We have to.

We continued to kiss. I sucked her tongue, her bottom lip. I wanted to taste her, more. Her nipples were protruding through her white blouse.

Eventually I confessed, "Baby, I want you so badly but I don't have any condoms."

My manhood ached in anticipation for her. Although we knew our HIV status, both negative, it is still automatic to use a condom.

We walked upstairs to her bedroom, removed our clothes, kept our undergarments on. Beautiful. Made love without penetration. It was late, we were both tired, and so we went to sleep and I was hard as a rock.

CHAPTER 11

MIA

Knowing my best friend's likes, dislikes and moods, I took a chance, stopped to get coffee, tea, and muffins for Dena and me. It's a beautiful morning and I have so much to do today, but not before stopping by Dena's office. I pop into her office to surprise her from time to time with her favorite Caramel Macchiato and banana nut muffin. I was in a fantastic mood and was determined to put her in one also, if she wasn't already.

"Hey Nyla, I'm Mia Nixon. Is Dena busy?" I said in a cheerful voice as I extended my hand to her very firm handshake. I have a firm handshake, too. I feel it's important but my fingers were still stuck together after a few seconds. Damn. If I didn't know any better, I'd think she was trying to hurt me.

"Nice to meet you finally, Ms. Mia. Yes, she's back there, hold on a sec. I'll tell her you're here." She picked up her phone.

Nyla was Dena's fourth personal assistant in two years. Every time Dena gets a new assistant, I get a new person to mentor, eventually. The work is not that difficult as they answer the phone and must be able to keep client information confidential and occasionally manage a project, working side by side with Dena. She was hoping to have Nyla for a few years, they seem to click. So far, Nyla was truly the one. She just needed to lighten up that handshake a bit. Dena told me that Gary's assistant, Lynne, gave her the referral. I felt Dena needed to keep an eye on her for that reason alone.

"Hey, Dena. Someone is here to see you," she stammered as she tried to understand my mouthing and hand gestures not to tell her my name. "Okay." She hung up the phone. "She said come on in."

"Oh, Nyla, what kind of coffee do you like? I should start bringing you some, too."

"Oh, that's okay. I'm fine. I get mine on the way in," she said shyly.

"Well do you like muffins? Banana nut?"

"Yes."

I handed her my banana nut muffin as I walked toward Dena's office. I was in a giving mood and since I knew Dena really liked her and thought she was a keeper, she was cool with me, for now.

"Coffee, tea or me?" I joked as I struck a pose like a server balancing the drink tray on my hand.

"Coffee!" she yelled and rolled her eyes.

"Good answer and I don't want your skank butt either; you don't have the tools that I need anyway!" I said as I worked my neck from side to side.

"Hey, girl. What's up?" I extended my arms and embraced.

"What's up, hot girl?" She looked me up and down as if I had on a pair of short shorts with my butt cheeks hanging out.

Instead, I had on a pair of black cuffed wide legged slacks, peep-toe pumps and a white cotton blouse with silver links and a hint of breast showing.

"I'm not hot, just a little warm. Always looking sexy, never know who I'll see," I joked.

"Well, you'd better not be looking for anybody else, you are already hooked up." She paused and rolled her eyes, "Thank you dear for my coffee and muffin. You're something special to me!"

"No problem, this is what I do but you gotta share that muffin since I gave mine to Nyla."

"Damn, Mia!" She made a face. "Just kidding." She let out a goofy chuckle and proceeded to cut the muffin in half.

"I was just getting ready to acafool up in hur," I said playfully.

"You gave Nyla your muffin? How nice is that? She's a sweet girl."

"That's good."

"She was in here this morning talking about her dad and how her mother didn't want her to see him. That is so sad, it reminded me of my younger years. She said the more her mother talked bad about her dad, the more she missed him and the more she dreamed about him. She said she found him on her own and he's coming to see her."

"Wow," I uttered as I tried to understand because I couldn't relate. My parents were together until death.

She changed the subject. "So you and Gary are still hitting it off well, huh? I knew you would. I am so happy for you two."

"Me too. He's a really good guy. We're having dinner and … dinner tonight, at my place," I cooed and adjusted myself in the chair.

"Dinner and what, sex?" She smirked.

"I'm not here to talk about me. You're on the couch today, Miss Missy! So how youuuu doin? What's going on with Monty?" I sat my muffin and tea on the table, crossed my legs and folded my arms.

She sighed, "Girl, I don't know how long this one is going to last. He just… I don't know. You know that fool asked me to go to a Swingers Club with him. Knowing his lil' raggedy heart can't take it. He asked what I thought about an open relationship."

"What? You have got to be kidding." I sat up and put my elbows on her desk, waiting to listen to this story, totally ignoring the heart comment. Because the truth was, I didn't care about his heart.

"Yeah, tell me about it. He is something different, I tell ya. I'm open to a lot of things but this one is a bit far for me. It's right up there on the same level as recording sex as being too much for me."

"Dang, you think he's bored with the current sex life? I guess so if he's wanting to add some spice with other people."

"He's crazy, too. I just don't know about him anymore. He's just all over the place, from one thing to the next." She shook her head.

"Well, you usually bend over backward to accommodate his ass, what happened, you're at the end of your rope?"

She stared at me as she bounced her pencil up on the eraser. I waited and wondered if the end of her rope was because of another guy, Dwight.

"Mia, you know there was a note on my garage door the other day?" She changed the subject.

"Really?" I said with concern. "What did it say?" My mind went back to the note on my car.

It said, 'I'm back and I'm watching you'."

"Oh, my goodness. You know, I feel like an idiot for being so careless, but I found a note on my car after I left Starbucks the first night that Gary and I met. It may have been on there before I left Ms. Emma's place."

"Mia, why didn't you say something? Where is it?"

"I threw it in the passenger seat, I couldn't understand the writing, plus my eyes were full of tears that night and I forgot all about it."

Nyla rushed into Dena's office. "Dena you have a call on line one. There's an emergency at your house."

"What?" Dena picked up the phone before Nyla could answer. "Dena Thomas." She paused. "O-okay! I'm on my way!"

"What's going on?" I asked in a panic as I read the look on her face.

"Let's go, Mia. Nyla, please cancel all of my appointments for this morning and then lock this door. I'll call you."

"Sure thing." Nyla rushed back to her desk.

As I rushed past Nyla's desk, following Dena, I know I saw that muffin that I had given her, in the trash. I did a double take, looked at Nyla as she glared at me. *What's her problem all of a sudden?* I thought. *Trust, I will find out later. Right now, we need to figure who has the emergency jumping off at Dena's house and who this "note bandit" is.*

CHAPTER 12

⁂

GARY

Another class at the school with the children, completed. I made up a lie to cancel my commitment at the school where Nina and Mrs. Griffin worked. They moved me to another school. It was farther away but I didn't mind. I had only three more weeks and I was lucky to be able to switch with someone.

I was in meetings all day discussing acquisition strategies, partnerships and communicating a few spot-bonuses. Most of my team worked outside the office, adjusting claims or appraising homes for one of many insurance carriers where we have contracts. We had five employees, including our assistant, Lynne. All of the other people are contract workers. Thus, the reason for the small office space on the first floor of a bank building near Beltway-8 West. The building consisted of two offices, one receptionist/ administrative assistant area, two bull-pen cubicles for sharing among appraisers and adjusters when they are in the office.

In between one of my meetings, Lynne walked in and abruptly

asked, "New woman in your life or new problem?" She leaned against the door frame and fingered her short salt and pepper hair.

I chuckled without making eye contact. "What are you talking about Lynne?"

"You're distracted. What's her name? I mean it's not one of my daughters so who is it?" She spouted about five more questions.

"You got me, I won't lie to you. That's why I'm moving through each meeting quickly so I can get out of here."

Her tone slightly irritated me.

"I can reschedule some for tomorrow if you'd like," she said in a tone that was dryer than her usual perky one.

"Nah, I won't be here tomorrow. I need to take care of some things. Plus, I want everyone to know about their money today."

She smirked.

"I have two remaining and I'm done, right."

"Yes." She didn't change her facial expression. "I saw the treats that she brought you yesterday."

"Lynne, I know that. You put them on my desk and I'm not telling you anything so stop smirking and get my next appointment in here, both in thirty minutes, tops." I mustered a smile.

The statement was her cue to keep me on track with my time and let her know I didn't want to get into a conversation about my personal life. She read the card prior to bringing me the basket because I saw her makeup fingerprints all over it.

I could trust Lynne with almost anything, just not my personal life. She tried hard to stay in the know about any woman that I was dating, but I usually didn't reveal too much. She figured out that I worked long hours if I wasn't dating and normal hours if I was dating. She is the best administrative assistant that has ever worked with me in my career. She also recommended Dena's assistant, Nyla. She had two daughters that she gave up trying to fix me up with over a year ago. Both of them had children out of wedlock with a lot of baby daddy drama. I remember she brought them in to meet me, acted as if I requested it. I stood there in awkward silence. The oldest daughter, December, baked some cookies for me. I politely declined and lied that I was preparing for a body building competition and had to be very particular about my consumption. That was a terrible lie because I had to remember to eat right for weeks after that.

I had to finally tell Lynne that I was not interested in her daughters. She apologized for overstepping her boundaries and offered to resign from her position if that would make me interested in one of her daughters, particularly the oldest one, December. She was very persistent. I told her that she didn't have to resign and then assured her I was still not interested in her daughters, December nor June. Even at my age, I was not interested in a woman with children, especially small ones. Been there, done that, didn't like it, plus neither of them were my type. My experience in that baby-mama area was not good. Intelligence and independence are high on my list of qualifications and her daughters hadn't shown either one. Since I told her there was no need to resign, I prayed that I didn't regret it later. Lynne also has twin sons, the ideal family, two sons, two daughters or should I say four daughters sometimes, since her sons weren't sure what they wanted to do. One day they were married with children and then they were divorced and dating men, and then switched back to women. Whatever one does the other does also. It was crazy. Lynne was extremely stressed out during their season of uncertainty. Her husband died of a massive heart attack. He was a minister. I can only imagine what killed him. Lynne had no shame about it. She said she still loved all of her children the same but for different reasons no matter how crazy they seemed.

I called Mia before leaving the office to ask her if we were still on for dinner. She was always so busy so I wasn't sure if she'd keep last night's promise. She totally took control of the situation for tonight and bluntly said, "Of course I'm ready for tonight and I refuse to go through another night of heavy teenage petting. Well, on second thought maybe we need to act like teenagers because they aren't petting anymore. I need you to stop at Condoms R Us, Wally World, or wherever! Just handle your business."

I was shocked but pleasantly surprised by her sudden outburst. Astonished, I said, "I got it covered. What are we eating?"

"Don't worry yourself with that, you just get here," she flirted, "Trust me, you'll definitely enjoy it."

"I can't wait." I smiled.

"Hey, on a different note, I was at Dena's office this morning and we had to rush to her house for an emergency. The security company told her the zone that caused the alarm, which meant the back door, could've been opened."

"No forced entry, huh? How did Dena react?" I quizzed.

"She appeared very nervous at first but she calmed down after the police checked everything out and all seemed clear."

Mia tried to appear confident but I heard worry in her tone.

"Oh." I did not say too much. Time will tell what that was all about.

Both of us were silent for a moment.

"Okay well honey, I will see you tonight! Be there or be an L seven." She perked up.

She had everything set at her house for the ultimate physical connection in our relationship. She was adamant about no sex anywhere but at her place. She wanted to feel more comfortable and ensure there were no hidden video cameras anywhere, so sex had to be in her living quarters until she reached that comfort level. She didn't tell me why she felt that way and I didn't ask.

She came to the door wearing a silk tangerine sundress, clinging in all of the right places. I stood in a trance for a few seconds longer than I anticipated. That color was gorgeous against her caramel-colored skin.

She waved her hand in my face and sang, "Hello! Are you coming in?"

"Yes, yes. How are you?" I reached for a hug. "You look nice."

"Well, thank you! Mission accomplished." She winked. We both said that phrase when we intentionally set out to impress the other.

I handed her the flowers and the bottle of wine that I stopped to get on the way to her house.

"Thank you, Gary." She reached for another hug. "Let me put these in some water. "Come on." She started to walk away. And the way her body moved in that dress had my mind in another place.

Dinner was light and great and so were the three rounds of lovemaking. I was truly amazed. First impressions are lasting impressions so I had to make it good. I wanted to make sure she was satisfied.

Soothing instrumental music flowed softly through the speakers. I started with a sensual massage to relax her but I knew that it would be sexually stimulating at the same time. Lights low, oil on the night stand, pouring oil into my hand, I glided over her skin using firm but gentle pressure, making sure that I covered every inch of her body. I intentionally avoided her hot spots that we had discussed in previous conversations, wanting her to ache with anticipation for my touch. After torturing her, making love without penetration for at least twenty minutes, she started begging me to enter her.

"I want you inside me," she whispered as she tried to pull me toward her.

"Hold on, not yet," I whispered as I started to kiss every area that I had previously stroked with my hands, including her hot spots. I sucked her breast and she came. Then my lips found that pulsating spot. I sucked and licked and stiffened my tongue and pushed it deep inside.

"Please, just … jus … I … wan … oh … my… Gah … Gary! Mat-thews!" Heavy breathing and moaning, her back arched, toes curled, and handfuls of the sheets. She trembled. I smiled inside with pride and satisfaction.

I protected us without missing a beat, I came up and entered her slowly, remembering that she told me that she enjoyed long, slow, gentle strokes when she's relaxed. I got pleasure from watching her. I held on until we both exploded at the same time. We were loud. Round one, over, and I enjoyed every minute of it.

Round two. Round three. Her body was so telling. She's very flexible, perfect height and she talked to me. She called my name several times, she trembled repeatedly. I felt her heartbeat and her pulsations against my body, all of which entices the hell out of me. I made sure that she was satisfied from every position and she insisted that I was also.

CHAPTER 13

MIA

Sitting in the chaise-lounge in the courtyard of the Doubletree Gateway Center, not far from the Sky Harbor Airport, people watching was very peaceful. I was trying to read one of my James Patterson's novels, "The Quickie." A friend told me that this book had drama jumping off from beginning to end and I intend to find out.

I took an early flight this morning to speak for thirty minutes in the ballroom at lunch and I'll be back on the plane by two-thirty. The weather was pleasant, birds singing on such a beautiful morning. I stretched out and took in the peaceful sounds of the water fountain, my iPod repeating the play list 'Gospel House Play,' all of my inspirational gospel music on background volume. I certainly had a lot going on at the moment but it was still so peaceful to me. I had a great evening with Gary last night and had rushed to catch a flight so I was trying to regroup. I had a few more trips coming up and I was certainly grateful that my marketing and networking efforts were paying off.

I picked up my phone to call Dena. We really needed to talk about these notes popping up everywhere.

"Hey girl, how are you this morning? Any more notes? You know we really are being a little careless by not trying to figure this out."

"I know. But no I haven't gotten any more. You?"

"None. The one on my car was the first one that I saw."

"You think it's Sylvester?" she asked.

"I don't know, but could be, especially since the notes are coming to me, too. Gosh, I so regret that entire ordeal."

"I know. I'm sorry I got you involved."

"No. You didn't. I was concerned and nosey all at the same time, which was why I followed you that day." I tried to comfort her.

"If it is Sylvester leaving notes everywhere, he's probably trying to scare us. You just happened to be my friend and you know a quick Google search can find anybody. All you need is a name and it will place you on their doorstep with pictures and all."

"Girl, I know it," I emphatically agreed.

"So where do we go from here? Did you tell Gary?"

"No, I haven't. I think we should, though. He'd probably go nuts."

I thought about Gary and many of the conversations that we had about him protecting me, giving me his best, being there for me. I wondered if he'd go running for the hills when he found out the real deal about Dena and Mia.

"He'll be okay, as long as you give him the details. You know he knows a lot of people and he can probably," she paused as if she was suddenly distracted, "he will probably. Probably, uh, protect you."

It sounded like she was distracted, but I let it slide.

"When are you back?" she asked.

"My flight leaves at two-thirty."

"Okay, stop by on your way home," she muttered. "I mean, uh, I'll see you tonight. Gary still cooking dinner, right?"

"Yes. He is."

"Okay, talk to you later."

That was a weird conversation. We didn't joke at all. I shook it off and continued to listen to my inspiration to get my mind settled for my speech to teenage girls about "The Hype" that they didn't need to believe in. A lady that I used to work with asked me to come out to speak to a group of girls in a not-for-profit organization that she founded. She gave me the title and told me to fit into some of their recent themes with my personal twist. I was more than excited to accept the offer, very flattered that she remembered me and thought enough of me to ask me to share my story.

Those young girls probably knew more than I did in some areas. I was just perplexed by some of the stories that she told me. I remembered her saying, "I need to prepare you before you come here so you'll be ready if things goes left when you have your question and answer session. We got on this subject recently and they seem to want to discuss it frequently—a blowjob is just like kissing now. They prefer it that way, they're still considered a virgin actually because there is no penetration. Nowadays, parents need to talk to their children about sex, drugs, and alcohol way before the age that I learned about any of it. My mother had one statement about it all, "If you do it, I'll kill you." And believe me that was enough for me. One thing is for sure, if the parents don't tell it, someone else will and that someone is probably another misguided child with erroneous information. And Mia, that's why I want a successful woman like you to talk to them, but make it fun and relate to them." I remember just holding the phone with my mouth agape in surprise and praying that the theme she gave me would go over well with them.

I usually started my presentation off with a quote, a poem, or a song and depending on the audience, a dance. For this one, I started with music, dancing down the isle with the girls to India's "There's Hope" and then I stopped the music to the claps and laughter from the girls and began, "Live the life that you seek …"

I finished my presentation, had lunch with the girls, chatted with some of the teachers, and was rushed to the airport by two. I was instantly irritated by the extremely long check-in lines. I took a few deep breaths because I had just finished being positive and had a great time. I was not about to let the current situation take me to another place.

I made it through security and onto the plane in enough time to send a couple of text messages before the plane pushed back from the gate. *Dena, are you still coming to Gary's tonight? Hey baby, leaving Phx should be there by eight.*

"Please make sure all cell phones are powered off at this time," the flight attendant announced.

I read the two replies, *Yes and OK baby see you then, be safe,* and then powered my phone off. The plane was surprisingly not full. I sat toward the back and had the row all to myself.

I untied my scarf from my purse handle to cover myself from

the cold, put my book in the seat back pocket, got my iPod in position for when I heard the announcement "we have reached ten thousand feet and it is now safe to use electronic devices..." and stretched out across all three seats. I dozed off before the wheels of the plane left the ground.

"So you're Mia? Hi, I'm Nina." She extended her hand.

I extended mine. "Hi."

"So what's going on with you and Gary? Are y'all dating? Are y'all just lovers? What's going on?" She adjusted her blouse.

"Why does it matter to you?" I frowned.

"I want to know because you know we used to date."

"Yeah, I'm aware of that. So why does what he has going on now matter to you?"

"Because I want him back and I'm going to get him. We need to raise our son together, not separately."

"Oh, really now?" I grunted.

"Oh yes, really." She nodded with confidence. "And you better step off before you get hurt. Just bow out gracefully and you'll be okay."

"Bitch, you have lost your damn mind." I said calmly and turned my head.

"Who you calling a bitch?" She hit me in the back of the head and pulled me by my hair. "You don't know who you messing with!"

I squatted and used my elbow to hit her in the stomach. When she doubled over in pain, I grabbed her into a headlock and held on tight until she stopped struggling.

I woke up, eyes wide, looking around, hoping that I didn't say anything aloud. No one was looking at me, so I assumed I didn't. My heart was beating fast and I couldn't wait for the plane to land.

I sat up straight, turned on my iPod, pulled out my book, and struggled to stay awake for the duration of the flight. *Where did that dream come from?* I thought.

Dena and I arrived at Gary's house at the same time.

"Hey, girl. What's up?" She met me at my car. I gave her a hug.

She sighed and tears rolled across her eyelids like a pinball gliding through the pinball machine. She looked toward the sky. "Girl, there was a note on my guest bathroom mirror this morning written in lipstick."

"What?" I said in amazement.

"Yeah, I wanted to tell you when we talked earlier but decided to wait until you got back. I don't know if it's Monty or not, but I don't think it's him." We both froze in place staring at each other.

"Sylvester?" I asked with wide eyes. "Oh my God Dena. He was in your house?"

She sighed and started to cry. "Yes, I think so."

"Dena come on now, hold it together, wait a minute. Let's. Hold on Dena, just hold on," I whispered as I tried to think of a quick plan of action. "Do you want to tell Gary? He can help."

"I don't know, Mia. I just want all of this crap to end." She wiped her face with both hands and sighed deeply. "I'll tell him. I'll be back. I need to make sure my eyes look okay." She walked back to her car.

"Y'all coming in or not?" Gary stood in the front door with his arms folded, smiling.

"Oh, hey baby. I miss you! Yeah, we're coming." I rushed

toward Gary to give him a hug and kiss.

"I miss you too." He took my bags. "How was your flight?"

"It was cool. I feel asleep. I gotta tell you about this crazy dream I had. What did you cook? It smells good in here."

"Wait and see. What is Dena doing?"

"Smart ass. She had to get something out of her car." I lied. "Is Ms. Emma here?"

"Yes, she and V are in there, T.J. and Mona—" He leaned out the door waiting on Dena.

CHAPTER 14

GARY

Dena flopped down in the chaise-lounge chair and folded her arms like a pouting five year old. "Dinner was great Gary. Damn, why do I keep getting myself into dead-end relationships? I meet a guy, start having a really good time and then he goes bananas. I guess I meet the representative for the first year and then boom, out of nowhere, he nuts up. What is wrong with me?"

I was sure she didn't want me to answer, a rhetorical question and she didn't leave an opening for me to say 'Thank You'. I poured the wine and set her glass on the table beside her, positioned myself on the stool next to the lounger and got in a position to listen.

"Monty's sick ass is becoming more disrespectful by the day." I looked at her and waited for her to continue talking, absolutely no comment from me. She took a gulp of wine and continued. "Monty is just so, ugghh, he frustrates the hell out of me. I just don't understand Gary. What is it? I have always chosen the wrong guy. I remember the mess that I got mixed up in a few years ago in

Chicago. That mess is coming back to haunt me now."

I raised my eyebrows in question. "What are you talking about, Dena?" I thought she was just frustrated about Monty's behavior.

"Somebody left a note on my garage door," she said nonchalantly, which is sometimes her M.O. when she's afraid. She sighed. "And a note written in lipstick on my bathroom mirror this morning."

"What?" I was open mouthed. That statement made me come out of a silent state.

"Yeah." She fanned her hand in the air as if this was no big deal.

"What did the note say, Dena?"

She yawned. "Something like, 'finally you come in here, remember me, Chicago 2007. We shall meet again. I'm watching you.'

"Dena, isn't that a little unnerving to you, especially with the two emergencies at your house recently?"

"Yes, Gary, especially since we thought they were dead." Her eyes widened as if she had said more than you intended to say.

"What! What the hell happened in Chicago? And who is we? What are you talking about Dena?"

She adjusted herself in her chair and looked back toward the door. "Yeah, I… uh…. I uh… I haven't told Mia but it's probably Monty's dumb self."

"You haven't told me either! Dena come on! This is serious! What if the two of you are out and some fool comes at you? Geesh, girl what are you thinking? When did you find the note?"

"I told the police. Geesh." She pouted even more. Stubbornness and inebriation was fast approaching and I know that she was getting ready for the shut-down. Therefore, I immediately stopped my interrogation. I held my head down, I couldn't believe what I was hearing.

I reached for her hand. "Dena, we really need to figure this out. Think about it and let me know where you want or need my help. I want you to be safe. Okay?"

She nodded. "Thanks Gary. The police will handle it. I changed the locks and everything. I'm not scared," she said evenly.

She thought they were dead. I needed to get this story out of her somehow, someway. I knew she can be feisty and aggressive at times but this one has gotten her a little rattled. I knew there was a lot she hadn't told me. I really didn't want to talk about that prick, Monty, but I didn't expect to hear what I heard either.

Mia walked out to the patio. "Dishes are done and all the guests are gone," she announced. "What's up? Why are y'all looking like that? You okay, Dena?" She sat down at the end of the chaise-lounge.

"Yeah, I'm good. I'm just tired. Gary gave me real talk." She took another gulp of wine.

"You sure?" Mia asked again, sounding unsure that she was hearing the truth from Dena and I was certain that Dena was not telling the truth.

"Yeah, I'm sure." Her words slurred as she took another gulp of wine.

"Okay, you've had too much to drink, off to the guest room we go." Mia instructed as she grabbed her by the arm.

"No, no, no, no. I'm going home." She giggled.

"No, no, no you're not, Dena," I said in a very irritated tone because I was mad at her for drinking too much and even madder at myself for pouring the last glass. As we walked toward the bedroom, Dena was laughing hysterically and trying her best to tell a story about her grandmother. I knew and respected her grandmother and did not remember the woman that she described shooting at men and stabbing them with ice picks. In her drunken stupor, I was sure she made it up but her bad behavior had to be learned somewhere.

We got Dena in bed and Mia surprised me when she wanted to have a conversation about Nina. She had a dream about her on the plane. She swears she saw at least three women at the airport that looked like her. The conversation was very brief and ended with me telling her, "You don't have to worry about Nina. Trust me."

CHAPTER 15

MIA

The wheels were roaring as I turned left onto Garden Heath Lane, hurrying to get me and my Corvette out of the rain, maneuvering around several cars parked along the street that was lined with mature Bradford Pears and neatly manicured lawns with flowerbeds filled with begonias, hibiscus, palms and some, just simple green ground cover. The security guards had gotten so used to me they didn't stop me anymore. I slowed enough so they could see me. They usually wave me on through unless one of them had a story to tell. Gary would let them know if he wanted them to stop allowing me into the gates. We had spent a lot of time together over the past few weeks, talking, sharing thoughts, feelings, and bodies. I couldn't be happier. I felt safe in his presence, in his arms. I felt like I could surrender, become the helpmeet, the submissive one to him. We could talk about everything, anything any time. I really needed to make sure he understood that. We had a conversation one night about love. At first, I thought he would shut down. I asked him,

"What does love look like to you? How do you express it? How do you want it expressed to you?"

He replied, "Love looks like," he paused to ponder. "First, I need to know how you want it expressed to you but my natural way is to express it by telling you, showing you either with small tokens of appreciation, telling other people, being true to you, showing affection privately and publicly. I want you to show it to me by being respectful, caring, and passionate. That's my short answer." Conversations like that with him just made me feel so good. I had waited for a man like this for a long time.

His house was beautiful, a long driveway lined with palm trees leading up to the circle drive. I usually parked in the circle and rang the doorbell like I was a guest. I never used my key and never parked in the garage unless it was raining. It was a garage-parking day.

After an extensive workout with my maniac trainer, Lamont, I couldn't wait to get into Gary's shower with the multiple showerheads hitting every part of my body. I took a quick, what me and my girlfriends call "a splash bath," which included standing in the shower and quickly giving attention to the necessary body parts. That ritual and clean dry clothes was very necessary to get you over the hump from point "A" to point "B," so mine needed to get me from the gym, through the hectic traffic on Westheimer to the Beltway to Gary's house.

I carefully pulled my car into the oversized garage beside his Range Rover.

"Easy does it, baby. I just need to squeeze by you here, this big bulky truck and all of this other stuff. I wish he'd move those bikes so I can park on the third car side over there," I mumbled as I turned the car off while simultaneously pushing the garage door button. I grabbed my bottled water, my purse, my ever-ready overnight bag, and my gym bag, leaving my laptop bag in the back seat. I finished off my bottled water and tossed the empty bottle in the trash next to the door. As I placed my hand on the doorknob, the door opened.

"Hey, Pretty Baby, how you are doing today?" he cooed, standing in the doorway with his favorite black robe covering his dark, strong 6'4" frame.

"Hey, Pretty Boy, better than blessed. How are you?" I flirted.

"I am better than blessed, too now that you're here." He leaned forward to give me a one-arm hug as he grabbed my bags and placed them on the small wrought iron glass-top table sitting in the corner of the cranberry colored laundry room.

"It smells delicious in here. What are you cooking?" My lips curled into a smile and I was still wearing a quizzical look, wondering why he was waiting for me at the door. I knew he was up to something.

"You'll see in a few minutes." He planted a honey-flavored kiss on my lips with the proper sound effects. He placed the palms of his hands on my cheeks, stared into my eyes, and then planted another kiss on my forehead, one on my nose, another on my lips and then my chin as he closed the door with his foot. I remained silent and smiled with every kiss to show my enjoyment. He caressed my butt as he slipped his warm tongue into my mouth and kissed me with a soft passionate kiss, which was interrupted by what I meant to say to myself, "I just need a shower first."

He ignored my comment and my open eyes, gently caressed my butt, and then moved his massive hands up my back and around to my double-Ds, caressing and massaging with every movement. My heart was starting to beat faster, my breathing was deeper. It felt like my entire body was pulsating, and my panties were wet.

He raised my top and then abruptly stopped, saying, "Damn, you got that bra on again."

I giggled. "Of course that's my 'bra snap' security that I will always get to take a shower before you take me right here on the laundry room floor. This was actually the extra bra that I had in my bag because the other one was soaked after the workout."

"Stay right there, let me get some scissors." He casually walked into the kitchen to search his junk drawer.

"Man, you are not cutting my bra off," I yelled with a soft chuckle. "You are too much! This bra holds everything together while I'm running, doing jumping jacks, you name it, these girls don't move. Looks like I have a uni-boob but it works for me," I said as I unsnapped my ten snap sports bra. My skin was cold.

I gathered my bags and started my walk through his beautiful gourmet kitchen complete with oak cabinets framed around rippled glass, a large black granite counter top island with a butcher block and cutting boards attached that were filled with fresh vegetables and spices, a wine storage on the end with red, white and dessert wines, and stainless steel appliances throughout. There were a couple of pots on the cook top stove with steam-filled lids. The oven light was on. I could see a foil covered pan inside. My appetite was soaring after facilitating all day at a client's office and the workout that I just had. I couldn't wait to mount one of the barstools, swing my feet and savor every bite of food art from my favorite chef.

He stood with a playful, puzzled look on his face as I walked by. He was holding a pair of red scissors as if he was waiting on me to come hither for bra cutting. I turned around to flash him with my already-exposed breasts. He dropped the scissors back into the drawer and moved with haste toward me.

I pretended to run.

"Hold on, come here," he said with a lot of seduction in his voice.

His beautiful light-brown eyes were beaming with satisfaction of what they were taking in. He didn't speak as he massaged my breasts with both of his warm hands. He kissed me passionately as he tugged on my pants to remove them. I tried stopping him again saying, "I need to take a showe—," but the pulsating had returned and I surrendered.

I stepped out of my shorts one leg at a time. He leaned down to take one of my breasts into his mouth, sucking my erect nipples and running his tongue around my areola as he caressed the other. He switched to the other breast and then pushed both of them together, continued making every part of my body want him more. He freed one hand to discover the wetness between my legs. He whispered, "I thought you didn't want it, you wanted to take a shower first? Why are your panties so wet?" He smiled and pulled his finger out and put it in his mouth and sucked it, he said, "You taste so good, girl."

My legs felt shaky. I leaned against the wall. We kissed, he sucked my lips, my tongue, as he continued to explore me with his finger. He got down on his knees and the next move was my leg over his shoulder. My legs were so wobbly I had to hold onto the counter to steady myself.

He smiled and lifted my left leg over his forearm. I put my arms around his neck to lift myself up as he lifted my right leg over his other arm so that he could hold me in a curling position. We continued to kiss, then I held on tight as he stepped back from the wall and slid me up and down slowly on his penis. It was the most awesome feeling shooting through my body.

We both climaxed simultaneously. He relaxed his arms and put them around my waist. I wrapped my legs around him. He held me in his embrace for a little longer. Our hearts were beating in rhythmic patterns. Our breathing was heavy. I felt so close to him. I laid my head on his shoulder and whispered in a whiny voice, "You make me sick."

I raised my head and looked into his eyes. He kissed me softly on my lips and said, "I love you, too," as he carefully placed me back on my feet and kissed me again.

I started gathering my clothes and my bags and headed for his bedroom. My legs were wobbly.

He chuckled, "What's wrong with you?"

"I told you that you make me sick."

I stopped, shook one leg at a time, moved my head left to right, jumped a couple of times, and started my theatrical stroll into the bedroom. He laughed and followed, watching every sway of my hips that I tried to cover with my bags.

Gary had explored every part of my five-nine caramel-colored body that was also ebony in some areas and he loved every inch of it.

I entered his room, it smelled of lavender, so relaxing. I didn't bother to turn on a light. The light from the fireplace was dimly illuminating the room. The built-in flat-screen over the fireplace was on, the volume to all of the surround sound speakers, muted. I walked straight into the bathroom, which was decked out with all brown and white colors. The shower lined with brown tile and chrome fixtures. It looked good against the bold colored accented red wall.

His bedroom had a relaxing and warm feel. As I put my hair

in a ponytail, he started the shower and stepped in, I washed my face and brushed my teeth. I joined him in the shower for another love-making session that ended up with wet hair, heavy breathing, screams loud enough for the neighbors to hear, and eventually lukewarm water. He hurried to wash the soap off and stepped out of the shower so that I could finish my shower with the remaining water before it was totally cold.

When I stepped out of the shower almost ten minutes later, he awaited me with a big white plush towel.

"Thank you, baby. You're so sweet."

"Anything for you, my dear." His eyes were piercing in a good way. He wrapped me in the towel and guided me to the king-sized bed outfitted with red and yellow rose petals covering the white sheets and down comforter. The lamps perfectly centered on either nightstand were dimly lit. Several candles were burning throughout the room.

"Baby, when did you do all of this? I didn't notice when I walked through?"

"Today."

"Okay, Smarty."

He was silent as he sat down on the end of the bed and slowly and carefully dried all of the remaining water from my body with a look on his face that showed his approval and admiration of the feast of his eyes. He dropped the towel to the floor and tenderly glided his fingers across my skin. He turned me around and planted a kiss in the small of my back, then my butt, and my thighs. My body was starting to tingle all over again. He turned me back around and kissed my stomach and then wrapped his arms around me and buried his face in my abdomen. He held me for a few minutes and then let go after he kissed my stomach again. "Lie down," he instructed gently.

I obeyed. He walked into the bathroom to get my favorite shea butter, smoothing it on everywhere my body would take it, using firm strokes, and giving special attention to my feet. I relaxed and fell into a light sleep. I opened my eyes when he removed his touch and replaced it with a soft white 600-thread count sheet. I sat up slowly on my elbows.

"I'm sorry. I didn't mean to fall asleep."

"You couldn't help it. I thought I was going to get dessert before dinner but you fell asleep on me." He gently tapped my leg and said, "Stay right there. I need to finish preparing dinner."

He was a fabulous cook, which is much more than I can say for myself. I tried but I am nowhere close to his caliber.

Again, I obeyed, because working out and great sex made me sleepy. I quickly drifted into a muffled, snoring sleep. I started to dream, a weird dream. I dreamt that a lady was yelling at me "… did you really think that getting married was going to make him love you? My gosh, you dated him for six years, what makes you think he wanted to get married all of a sudden. He either loved you or he didn't and believe me he didn't. He's showing you that. You took him from somebody else. You shacked up forever, gave him the cow, the milk and everything for free and then you think that gettin' married was gon' be different, so you gave him an ull-di-ma-dem."

When I opened my mouth to speak, I felt a soft kiss and then a tongue going in and out my mouth in a mischievous motion. I opened my eyes, Gary had straddled me wearing only a towel and was starting to kiss me singing, "Wake up, sleepy head."

I felt his flaccid inches, lightly touching my stomach.

I smiled, stretched, and yawned. "What time is it?"

"Thirty minutes after you laid down, Pretty lady."

"You have such a smart mouth and I love it."

"What were you dreaming about? Your expression seemed intense."

"Oh wow. This older lady was yelling at me, I guess calling herself giving me advice," I said nonchalantly.

"Giving you advice about what?"

"Cheating, taking somebody's man, about my living arrangements and marriage." I avoided direct eye contact. *What do all of these dreams mean? I'd hate to have to find this girl and just jack her up for good measure.*

"Okay, baby. We won't get into that now, we can discuss that later," he said as he was stepping on the floor, determined not to spoil the evening by rehashing our two week old first and only argument we had since we started dating.

For some reason, perhaps my upbringing, I didn't want to live with anyone outside of marriage. It was amazing that I could do everything else "outside" of marriage but living together was considered way out there for me. Gary and I had spent quite a bit of time together, but there was still a fear in me. I was afraid that if we moved in together our bad habits would be revealed, not accepted and then there goes a split.

He reached for my hands and gently pulled me to my feet. He enveloped me in his arms and just held me for what seemed like eternity. He kissed the top of my head and rubbed the back of my neck. "Am I gonna have to stop you from going to sleep? Your dreams are getting out of control." He kissed me again. "Look, you're my girl. We're going somewhere with this. You know that, right?"

"Yes, I know." I stared into his eyes. I felt a rush of warmth cover my body.

He placed his hands on my shoulders, looked into my eyes, and rubbed his hands up and down both of my arms. "Let's go eat."

He dropped the towel from his waist and put on his robe. He reached for my matching robe and helped me to put it on. I tied my robe and slipped my feet into my slippers. I placed my hands in my pocket. He pulled one of my hands out of my pocket, clasped his fingers into mine and we walked toward the kitchen.

My eyes were starting to fill with tears as I remembered that argument. It brought back memories of my parents and how I didn't want to disappoint them nor did I want to disappoint the man that I loved. I was determined that my parents memory would win this one. I looked up into the ceiling as we were walking, to hold back the tears, a communication technique that I learned in a 'Communication Skills' class when I first started my career. I prayed, *Lord, help me. I prayed for this but don't want to mess it up. I know, I'm already messing up. Just please have mercy on me. I just need some guidance.*

By the time we made it down the hallway, past the game room, the media room, through the family room and finally back into the kitchen, I was back to normal. He pulled the bar stool out for me and assisted as I hopped up and sat down.

"Thank you baby," I said in an appreciative monotone.

He had already prepared our plates, brown rice with mushrooms, baked chicken breasts with garlic herb sauce, sautéed vegetables and water to drink.

We finished dinner while discussing a totally different topic: the pros and cons of being an entrepreneur.

The rain had ceased, the sun returned with a bright orange

vengeance, slowly disappearing in the west. After dinner, we sat out by the bowed-shaped pool in the thick cushioned lawn chairs, drinking Shiraz and Gary with his cigar. At this point, we just existed as we listened to the sounds of "Calming Piano."

PART TWO

NO RELATIONSHIP WITHOUT DRAMA

CHAPTER 16

MIA

I woke up at five a.m. reminiscing about the night before and how I didn't want the night to end. This man lying next to me is a beast. I lay snuggled underneath his armpit, my leg bent across his body. He was still in the REM sleep, the muffled snore was alive and well. I stretched out and then eased out of the bed, careful not to wake him. Though I enjoyed every minute of last night, I was a little too tired for another round.

I was preparing for my morning run when my cell phone rang. My attempt at being quiet hadn't worked because Gary woke up and started preparing to go with me. I walked into the other room because I knew that I was getting ready to hear an earful that Gary did not care to hear, especially if it was a sob story about Monty and since Dena and I told him about Chicago, he'd been rather quiet when it came to any kind of drama.

"Good Mernin'. Good Mernin.'" I joked.

"Hey, Girl," she said in an exasperated sigh.

"What's going on?" I said in a "oh what is it now" tone.

"I gotta get out of this relationship." She began to cry.

"Dena, what happened now?" I was instantly irritated because I was so sick of Monty.

"I caught him again. He took all of my pictures down."

"What? What pictures? What are you talking about?" I said.

"Can you just come over here?"

"Dena, I'll be over there before noon. I have some things that I have to do this morning."

"Okay, I'll see you later then. I need your help, Mia," she snapped.

She worried me, tremendously. She can be from one extreme to another. One minute she can be on top of the world and at the bottom the next.

"All right, I'll be there," I conceded. "But I still need to run first." I had learned to stop dropping everything to get to Dena and it turned out to be nothing because she always took him back anyway and I end up with the bad name, "Single-angry-female."

I hung up the phone and sat on the steps in the media room. I placed the phone on the floor, put my face in my hands, and began to rub my forehead with my palms.

"What's going on, Babe? You sound irritated," Gary said putting on his running shoes.

"Sorry, I tried to get out of your way so that you didn't have to hear that this morning. Yes, I am irritated. That was Dena. That asshole, Monty has done something else that's causing her to want to move him out, again. I feel so sad for her, almost guilty. Dude is in, and then he's out, traveling here, job here, job there. She has suffered a tremendous amount of stress dealing with him."

He looked at me and said nothing.

I kept talking. "I do feel bad for her. I mean, I'm so happy that things are going so well for me, finally! But here she is, in one bad relationship after another, well actually hanging on to a bad one. And she is always giving this idiot more chances, giving more than she's willing to lose. I think she really cares about him, though. She has always wanted a good man, but it seems that she keep choosing the wrong one. And I —"

"Maybe that's the problem, she's choosing," he interrupted.

"Come on, let's go." I stood to walk out the door because he has no pity for Dena at times. He thinks she should dump Monty and move on, abruptly. I didn't want to get into a tiff with him over something that was neither my business nor his. "Why do we do this?"

"Do what?" He looked puzzled.

"Allow ourselves to be pulled in to the drama. But that's my girl, I gotta help."

"Well, there's your answer."

"All relationships have drama to some extent but damn, this one is dangerous. As I think of it, all of her relationships have been drama-filled."

"You know how I feel about him. I think she can do so much better."

"Have you ever told her that?"

"No."

"Why?"

"Because she hasn't asked for my advice. Are you going to Dena's after we run or before?"

"After. Why?" I sat down on the bench in the hallway to put my shoes on.

"I just want to know, because I'm going with you."

"Why?"

"Because babe, they are always into some shi—crap and you

get pulled in, and I don't want you physically hurt trying to help her and she doesn't seem to want to be helped. You know how he is. If that ne— if he hurts you, I swear I'll—"

"Gary, he's not violent. He's a cheater. You should probably be worried about him and what I'll do to him." I stood up and jumped a couple of times to ensure I tied my shoes just right for the run.

He grunted and smirked. "But what if she's trying to do something to him and accidentally hurts you? I just don't know, accidents happen."

I stepped toward him and reached up to hug him. "Look my dear, I am so flattered that you care so much about me. I am so blessed to have you in my life. You know I waited many, many years for a guy like you. I deserve this, and I'm happy that I have you, you are just what the doctor ordered, someone to protect me and love me for me and I thank you for loving me so well and being my most favorite person in the world to hang out with." I kissed him on his lips. "And I mean that with the seriousness of sincerities."

"Whatever, Mia. But that's my role, to protect and serve you."

"I know, right. But I am serious though." I stood in the pantry trying to decide which protein bar I wanted. Day by day, I have lowered my guards to let him in closer. But that confession just dropped them totally.

I grabbed a banana to go with my protein bar, a bottle of water, and then kept moving toward the garage. He grabbed a protein bar and bottled water.

I continued talking. "I mean, what would I do if you started acting up on me?"

He simply said, "Kick my ass to the curb and keep it moving."

He reached around me to open the door.

Within twenty minutes, we were at the park. I was preparing for the Nike Women's Marathon in October with Team in Training for the Leukemia and Lymphoma Society. "Every day a little bit of running and every weekend the long runs. You ready for this?"

"Yep, I'm ready."

"Thank you again for running with me. Your reward is waiting on you in heaven."

He shook his head and got out of the truck.

I committed to the requirement of raising money for the cause. Gary didn't commit to raising money but he committed to running with me as I trained for the grueling 26.2-mile run.

I got out and met him at the front of the truck. "You know I am blessed to be able to run because the little boy that I'm running for can't run and I can only imagine that he's going through more pain than I will feel after I'm done with my run, mastering the marathon-shuffle, a walk similar to that of Red Foxx on "Sanford and Son." Like this." I demonstrated the walk, legs stiff and rocking from side to side.

He laughed. "You're crazy, Mia."

"They told us that this disease is the number one killer of kids up to age thirteen. That little boy is my motivation. I hope that one day they will find a cure."

"That would certainly be a good thing."

We walked over to the Team in Training banner with the rest of the runners and walkers. They told us the direction for the day.

We stretched as a team, and everyone went on their way. We ran ten miles in less than two hours. We stretched again and then left.

During our ride home, Gary asked, "Who is that one lady that's always staring at me?"

"Baby, I don't know, there are new people that join us every week. Did she say something to you?"

"Heck no, she's not new. She's just staring all the time, with a big cheesy-ass grin on her face." He imitated her. "Kind of creepy."

I giggled. "She's too old for you. Maybe she has a daughter or niece or something."

"I don't care what she has, I wish she'd stop looking at me. I don't want to be hooked up with nobody's daughter or niece."

I chuckled and playfully punched toward his jaw, "You betta catch you an older woman, boy."

"Stop!" He shrugged his shoulder. "Keep it up, you'll be running by yourself."

"Whatever." I waved my hand at him. "Oh, baby remember, we need to stop by Dena's."

He didn't comment, he just turned into Jamba Juice.

Ten minutes later, we got back into the truck and was at Dena's house by nine-fifteen.

I rang the doorbell. Dena answered quickly, her eyes were swollen and red. I immediately hugged her and she began to sob. Gary stood there and then touched her shoulder in an attempt to show his softer side.

"Dena, where is he?" Gary asked as he started looking around.

"He left, begging me to let him stay." She wiped her tears.

"Dena, did he hurt you?" Gary continued to drill her.

"No, but he's mad because he said I'm not listening to him and that I don't understand."

"Let's go sit down," I said.

Gary started walking with me. His cell phone rang, and he answered. "What's up Pops?" He knew it was his dad. His dad usually called every Saturday morning at the same time and his mom always took over the conversation.

Dena and I sat down on the plush black leather sectional sofa. She curled her feet underneath her body, and she began to tell me what happened. I sat attentively and prepared to listen, trying my best not to judge, but I was mad as hell at Monty and at her for putting up with him for so long.

"You know I've suspected that he's been cheating for over a year now."

"Suspected?" My tone was critical.

"Well, I've known and I'm just tired. I had a business trip at the beginning of last week. The story that I told him was—I was supposed to be in Seattle for two weeks. I called him and he was never here or he just never answered the phone. He never answered his cell phone either for at least a couple of days. He claimed that the battery had died. He's such an idiot, that 'battery dead' lie, the worst one in the book. Lysa said that she drove by to 'check on' the house for me and saw his car. She said she was suspicious after seeing him at lunch with another woman the same day that I left so she drove by for three days straight, Tuesday through Thursday, and saw his car and sometimes a car parked behind him. He's so stupid, he never parks in the garage because he doesn't have a garage door opener, as if that's the only way to get into the garage. Dumb ass. Anyway, long story short, Lysa called me and I came home 'early'". She put both of her hands up to make the quotation symbols in the air. "He never knew that I was not staying away for two weeks. I just told him that. He has been messing around with one of our sorors. He had her in my house, Mia! He claims he thought I was cheating!" She began to cry again.

"Does she know you and that you are a soror, not that it matters?" I asked.

"No, he told her that this was his house. He removed all of my family pictures and all of the sorority pictures from the living room."

I looked around the room at the emptied walls with picture hangers. She continued talking and I suddenly felt guilty that I didn't skip my run to come to console her. It was much more serious this time around, than it had been in the past.

"She didn't know that he was living with me. I don't know what he told her about sleeping in the guest bedroom. Well, anyway, when I arrived back into town, I called Lysa and she came over with me and the girl was here."

"Dena, why didn't you call me?" I felt slighted that she called Lysa and not me but then again that was probably best. Lysa is sometimes a little bit more level-headed about things like this. She has definitely had enough practice with some of her sisters and friends.

"Because I didn't want to bother you and Gary."

"What! Uugghhh! Go ahead, finish the story." I didn't like that reason.

"She was standing in the kitchen drinking out of my damn cup, in my damn robe and he was walking down the stairs. Naked!"

She paused after the last statement, because of my widened eyes and loud gasp with my hand covering my mouth.

She continued. "I walked into my damn house and she looked at me as if I was a stalker ex-girlfriend that didn't belong here." She put extra emphasis on the word "my" each time she said it.

"I said, 'Who are you?' She put the cup down and said "Who the hell are you, just walking up in here——," she was working her neck and everything. I grabbed the knife and started chasing her ass. She ran by me and I grabbed the robe, she was struggling to get out of it because I was trying to come down on her back with the knife. She ran out with her bra and panties on. You should've seen that look of terror in her eyes. That sorry piece of crap tried to stop me and I tried to cut his damn hand off in return. Blood was everywhere. I should have cut his penis off! Punk!"

"Dena," I said in tone that was a cross between empathy and chastising. I tried to remain calm because if I got hyped, she'd get even more hyped, too.

"What?" she snapped, "I'm sick of his shit! He has used me for two damn years and I promise you Mia, I'm gonna get his ass back! I have reached out to him. I tried to help him, gave him a place to stay, money, food, clothes, my damn heart! Ugghh!" She threw her hands in the air in frustration. "You name it, I gave it to him and he couldn't wait for me to go out of town so that he can parade his bitch through my damn house." She pounded her fist in the pillow. "That son-of-bit——, ooh I can't wait to get my hands on him! I can just see it, I'll plunge a butcher knife straight through his freaking heart and watch him die."

"Dena!" I yelled. "Stop it, you are not going to do anything. Lord, you'll have your butt in jail, and he'll still be sleeping with whoever he pleases. You'd better be glad that that knife didn't land in that girl's back. You could've killed her. What was her name anyway?" I asked.

"I was trying to, Audra Briggs," she said answering the question, her mood suddenly changing.

She went from ninety to zero in a few seconds.

"What?" Gary asked in surprise as he walked back into the living room. "That's Nina's sister."

Nina was the lunatic that showed up at Starbuck's. His ex-girlfriend. I wonder if this was some sort of plot, I thought.

Dena leaned back on the couch and sat in silence for several minutes as she ran her fingers through her hair. "Mia, do you remember that time we beat dude down when we were in college?" She said gravely.

I allowed her to divert the conversation for a moment, but I was a bit concerned by her demeanor and tone.

"Yes, I do!" I let out an embarrassed chuckle. I had not told Gary this story. He looked at me quizzically.

Dena started explaining, "Gary, let me tell you what happened." She usually loved telling the story of the "Beat Down." Well, she loved telling my part of the story because if the other part got out, her butt would probably be in jail for arson. This time though, the tone of the story was different. She told it with a slight desire to repeat.

She began, "I was becoming so terrified, every time I listened to the local news, there are horror stories of crime—*Woman Assaulted By Two Men In A Parking Garage, Sex Offenders Out On The Street, Bus Driver Raped By Passenger, Couple Gets Robbed In Their Drive-Way*—one dramatic headline after another. Although these things were happening quite a distance from where we lived, we still needed to protect ourselves. Mia talked me into taking a gun class and karate. I had recently dumped a crazy dude, so we wanted to learn additional ways to protect ourselves, just in case." She giggled uneasily.

"Yep," I chimed in as I reached over to give her a reassuring touch. "We needed it."

Dena continued as she pointed at me with her thumb. "This girl went on to finish both of her self-defense initiatives. She went on to get a black belt. I stopped at brown and I consider that certified, but I know how to shoot."

Gary smiled and opened his mouth in fake surprise at her comment. "I'm impressed. I know not to piss you off. I can't win, and Dena, the way you grew up, you probably could've taught the class. You've known how to shoot since we were kids," he tried to joke. "I'm sorry."

Dena gave a wry smile and continued, "No sirrrrr, street fighting has nothing on karate. You'd straight be torn to shreds trying to box in a karate fight, that's why I know how to shoot, it's a mind thing." She tapped the side of her head. "And Gary please, your big ass could probably take on a room full of people with guns and knives."

Gary chuckled, "Nah, not me. I'm not a fighter. Anymore. Sounds like you two can, though."

I smiled but it was a little unsettling because this tad bit of information has turned guys off in the past, usually during initial conversations when you're at the point of exchanging useless information. Well at least that was the excuse, maybe they thought the information was useful.

It had always been something with guys that I met—made too much money, too independent, too aggressive, and believe it or not, the potential of being too violent—which was why I didn't tell Gary. I didn't want him running off, too. But something told me that he wasn't going anywhere. He was not intimidated in the slightest. This brother can hang with me on any level without intimidation, leading the cause I followed and I was good with that.

The fight Dena described was the only fight I'd had in my life outside of my karate classes but this situation was slightly different. That dude tried to assault me and he was emotionally abusive to Dena. I never want to use karate, we were taught to be brave and not use karate at first, try to avoid the confrontation. Ohhhh, but if we have to, it's on and poppin'.

I wanted Dena to tell the short version of this story or just stop the story completely but she continued with so much rambling I could hardly keep up and I was there, I knew how the story unfolded.

"Long story short, we had an argument and he tried to slap me. I was so shocked because he had never done anything like that, and Mia looked at me with her eyes about to pop out the sockets like 'Oh, hellllll no!' He looked at Mia and told her he'd kick her ass, too. This girl looked at him and was all hyped by then but she just chuckled and said, 'Do you, bruh.' I know she could've handled him by herself but I had to get in on this one. It's funny, we had this battle cry back in the day, not just the sorority type signals but something more audible. We didn't need it then, it was just something we did. But, anyway, after he threatened Mia, I punched him in the face. He tried to grab me by the neck and I started punching and kicking. I stumbled and he pushed me down and swung at Mia, he obviously misjudged her because of her height and size but she gave him one to the gut. He pushed her, she stumbled backward and then she came back with the takedown, quick one-step sparring, kicking and punching. He didn't know what hit him. She stopped shortly after that. He was down—you shouldn't use karate to battle but more for self-defense. I guess we can call it self-defense. She put him on his back and we started fighting him as if we were from the streets.

Well, I am but you know what I mean. He was too shocked to fight back. He started screaming, 'I'm sorry Dena, I'm sorry', as he rolled into a fetal position."

She paused for a few seconds, shaking her head. "Man that was wild. I had to dump him because he lost his mind, thinking I was a punching bag and he was pathetic and he let a girl beat him up."

"Well, good for you." Gary walked over to sit next to me and pushed my shoulder with his fist. "Slide over, Billy B."

He smiled as if he was proud. I silently hoped he wasn't troubled by the story.

I turned back toward Dena. "You know you always tell all of my stories but why don't you tell Gary what you did to Monty's house and then felt sorry for him so you let him move in with you?"

"Oh, whatever. It wasn't that bad. At least it wasn't life threatening." She scratched her head. "Gary, I just put some dishwasher liquid in his dishwasher and washing machine turned it on with a few of his suits and suds were everywhere! And then to top it off, I put a whole thing of instant mash potatoes down his kitchen sink and you know what that did. Yep, clog city."

Gary chuckled. "You make it sound like its no big deal. I would've knocked you out for that."

"Monty is not crazy. He knows he can't handle me, not in a fight anyway."

"I was kidding, Dena. I don't hit women."

"Okay, now tell him about slicing the soles on his shoes." I reminded her since she was on a roll now.

"Oh that," she muttered. "I sliced the soles on his shoes and put them back in the closet, when he put them on they were flopping like Mr. Mouth, Mr. Mouth," she started to sing.

"Dena, I'm shocked." He looked confused.

"I'm not," she said nonchalantly. "I don't do those type things anymore because I try not to get pissed off to that point. It's been a long time and now he comes back with this shit."

I looked at Gary and whispered, "They have this love-hate thing going on."

"Dena are you okay? Do you need me to do anything?" Gary asked.

"Nah, I'm good. Thanks Gary. I'm good."

Dena was resting her head in her hands. Gary was studying Dena. We sat silently for several moments.

"So, how do you know that's who the girl was if she was running?" I asked.

"Oh shit—that," she said nonchalantly. I had a feeling that she didn't want to talk anymore.

Gary's cell phone rang again. He answered. I assumed it was Sean since I heard a male voice before Gary excused himself to talk in the foyer. I heard Gary say, "Yeah we can do that." It was very difficult to focus on two conversations so I was hearing bits and pieces of both. I decided to let Gary's conversation go and focus on Dena.

"Lysa was screaming but at the same time, that fool was running behind the girl," Dena continued. "Lysa caught up with Audra and basically tried to find out who she was, how she ended up with his ass and what he told her and yada, yada, yada." She fidgeted with her foot and swatted her hand in the air. "Lysa was trying to get her covered up and I didn't care. Bitch."

"Dena, do you think you need to cut her a little bit of slack since she didn't know that he was living with someone else, and stop cursing, gosh!"

"Hell no! Did you hear me? If she didn't know, what was all of that neck working about then? Huh?"

I wasn't the slightest bit fazed or shocked by her yelling at me but I knew when to back off.

We sat there for a few minutes quietly, our eyes staring, piercing each other. Dena finally spoke as she flopped back on the sofa with her right hand covering her eyes.

"Lysa found out that her name is Audra Briggs. She works at the hospital. She's a soror. She met asshole. Sorry, didn't mean to curse again. She met him one night when he went there with one of his boys. They've been messing around for about a year now, which was around the time when we were on bad terms, you know, the shoes slicing incident. I'll bet he brought her here every time I was out of town. He accused me of cheating. I should have, and I did. Nevertheless, when I found out that he'd been cheating, it still hurt. You know that jerk had the nerve to bring up marriage when he was on his way out. Somehow, he must think I'm desperate to get married. He yelled, *'You will marry me, you haven't seen the last of me,'* she mocked him.

She ignored all types of red flags, yellow flags, orange flags— my goodness! I didn't respond to her last comment because if he asked her to marry him, she would have said 'yes.' I sat quietly for a few moments.

"Dena, I had a dream about something similar to this situation. Sometimes dreams are to show you signs for other people. Remember we talked about that?" I said cautiously.

She nodded but didn't speak. You know I usually do not give you advice on whether to leave or stay, but I'd say this time, cut your losses. This is way beyond disrespectful. That's if you can," I said in an emphatic tone. I was worried about Dena. This was the third guy that took advantage of her.

"I do have a plan for his ass. Just you watch. It involves fire, ashes, cremation type stuff. The kind with gasoline, lighter fluid, or anything flammable, and a match. I am so tired," she said in a monotone voice. "His ass will be pushing up daisies, or should I say weeds."

Now I was really worried, she was from one outrageous thought to another. I chuckled nervously and prayed silently that she was joking.

CHAPTER 17

❧

GARY

I ended the call with Sean and I was standing in the foyer looking out the glass storm door at a couple of little girls on roller-blades. I called my parents back because the previous call somehow disconnected but my eyes were scanning the street trying to make sure I spotted Monty if he tried to come back. Mia wanted to help Dena so she tried her best to listen without judging. I wanted to help also but I just didn't want to deal with any drama or violence and at the rate they were going, I knew both were a possibility. If that happens, I'm sure I can turn back to the streets of Bed-Stuy on the corner of Presidents and Malcolm X Blvd in a heartbeat. I knew some of Dena's drama-filled history and since she and Mia were so close, I couldn't help but wonder how many stories that Mia hasn't told me. At first, I felt the need to protect Mia and I still do really, but I have no doubt that Mia can take care of herself. I tried to talk to Dena again about the comment she made, "I thought they were dead," and I got nothing.

"Hey, son! What are you doin'?

"Hey, Dad. I'm chillin. Just finished running with Mia and we stopped by Dena's for a minute."

"Is that right? Maybe I'll get to meet Mia soon."

"Yeah, maybe we can meet Miss Mia soon," my mother chimed in after picking up the other phone. My dad sighed and mumbled, "Lord, have mercy."

"Oh be quiet, Clive!" she said.

My dad sighed again.

"You will Ma. We plan to make a trip within the next few weeks."

"Oh really, that's good, baby we called to tell you…"

My dad interrupted, "We didn't call, *I* did."

"Clive!" my mother whined.

I chuckled at their banter.

"You two always make my day."

I remember the day when the back and forth bantering was not in a joking manner. I used to think that they seriously hated each other. I'm so glad that they worked through that phase.

"We know you expect it, son," they said in unison.

They were so cute together. I wanted the same type of relationship when I got married. Two people making it happen together for years, through tests and trials, they made it, together, in love. Staying power. I know many people that didn't have that, didn't even attempt it. I hoped I had it in Mia. I was willing to do my part.

"Baby, we called to tell you—"

"Hold on a sec Mom." I muted the phone, pushed the door open and stepped outside as I saw the two little rollerbladers collide near Dena's driveway. I walked over to them.

"Hey, Mr. Gary," the oldest little girl said, trying to stand and dust herself off.

"Hey, Emya. Are you two okay?"

I looked toward the end of the street. I saw their dads standing at the end of their driveway. I whistled and waved for them to come over. Both men trotted toward us.

"Hey, man, how's it going? What happened?"

As I stood there watching them get their precious daughters taken care of, I saw a car driving slowly toward us, jerking every few seconds.

"Somebody's trying to learn how to drive." One of the dads frowned.

"This is not the place for that. They need to be on an open parking lot." The other dad said, visibly irritated.

It was Nina and one of her friends. She was looking straight ahead. I pretended not notice them.

"Are y'all okay?" I playfully asked the girls.

"Yes, sir." Emya said.

"Thanks man." One of the dad's reached to shake my hand.

"No problem." I walked back toward the house.

"Okay, we called to tell you that we decided to take our children's advice, so we are planning to renew our wedding vows to celebrate our wedding anniversary in September and we want to do something really special. Do you have any ideas?" My mother's voice snapped me back.

"Hey, that's really cool. You guys, that's great, and yes, I'm sure I can come up with something, you know me. But I need to get with Vance and Jessica to see what's on their minds."

Vance is my older brother and Jessica is my younger sister. I'm in the middle. Both of them are still in New York and love it.

"Are you all up for anything that we come up with?" I asked.

Total silence.

"Ma?"

"Will you be bringing Mia with you to the celebration?"

"Ma, both of you just ignored my question. I plan to bring Mia to visit before September. So are you all willing to do whatever we plan?"

"That's good. I can't wait to meet her in person."

"OK, good, now answer my question." I paused. "Please."

I heard a click.

"Ma? Dad?"

"Uh, baby, we're gonna let you go. We don't want to run up your cell phone bill," she chimed. She abruptly hung up, I guess she hadn't figured out how bossy she wanted to be yet. They listen to their friends and relatives with cell phone issues so she thinks that everybody has the same issues with zero anytime minutes.

My dad had hung up the phone before the conversation was over. I'm sure he'll call me later. I had missed two calls while I was on the phone and had two voice mail messages, one from Nina, and one from Lynne. Two people I did not care to hear from. Nina asked me to call her, which I was not going to do and Lynne reminded me that I was to help her get some stuff out of her attic. I deleted both messages and decided I would call Lynne later. Mrs. Griffin had given up and I was glad about it.

Even with all of the drama, Dena said she we okay. Though I did not believe her at all, I didn't press her. I had walked back into the room just in time to hear Mia and Dena talk about who the chick was that Dena caught with Monty. I heard a few minutes of their conversation before loudmouth Sean called wanting to go to the driving range again. We're playing in a charity golf tournament next month and he wants to practice almost every day now.

I left Mia at Dena's house after our run, went home to change, and met Sean at Wildcat Country Club. We swung at one basket of balls after another. I judged his swing, he judged mine.

"Sean, what's up, man? Something bothering you, playa? Your swing is way off as if it's the first club you've had in your hand. You need to talk about it?" I looked at him with concern. He was swinging like a beginner, no form, no technique, just a swing.

He didn't hesitate and just started talking immediately after I asked the question. It was as if I had pressed *Play*.

"Man, I went online, to Holly's online page and I think she's seeing someone else."

He pulled out his driver, walked back over to set up another swing, positioned himself, pulled the club back over his right shoulder, and swung with way too much force. I placed my clubs back into the bag and sat down on the bench. I figured there wasn't going to be much more of this after he started the conversation anyway and I didn't want an accidental hit in the face with a club from all of his erratic swinging. After his initial statement, I remained quiet, deciding to wait until I heard more. I thought he was enjoying the escapades with the 'classroom mom' but I do know that men can be territorial. I guess the way I looked at him made him change the entire tone of the conversation.

"Man, some dude was saying a lot of inappropriate stuff to her." He paused. Eyes narrowed, waiting in anticipation of a response from me. "Aren't you gon' say something?"

"What do you want me to say? I'm just listening."

"I don't know, man. I know you're thinking that I'm cheating on her so why should I care."

I grunted, raised my eyebrows, scratched my head. Even though it wasn't itching. "Naw, that's not what I was thinking."

"Well, what the hell are you thinking, man? Come on, now!"

I chuckled because I knew he was not frustrated at me but at his own situation. "Have you asked Holly about it? Sometimes people want things to seem as though they are, when they're not, just to get your attention."

"Yeah, but I know she wanted that stuff to show because she has to approve all comments before they show on her page."

"Why don't you talk to her, man? She might have wanted you to see the comments just to get your attention."

"What? She had my attention!" He shouted. "She was the one that didn't start planning the wedding as if she didn't want to be with me. I'm done." He pouted. And I was shocked that he was pouting. I'm just glad he didn't do the lip protruding and arm folding part of it.

"And you were the one that stopped having sex with her because you were enjoying that classroom-chick so much, pretending to be mad."

Sean was a good guy. He has been a professed monogamist since I've know him—until now. He was always very committed to whomever he was dating. I guess my comment left him speechless because it took him a moment to speak.

"Man, I was not pretending. I am mad at her." He used his club to push grass back into its place. "But I love Holly."

"Do you? Really? Does she know that?"

"She should."

"Why?"

"You always hit me where it hurt."

"I'm not throwing any punches, Sean. I'm just asking a question." I gathered my bag and hoisted it onto my shoulder.

"I guess I need to talk to Holly and then break it off with Wendy, huh?"

"Oh, is that her name?" I chuckled.

He smirked as he put his clubs in the bag. "Man, let's go to the gym."

I stood at a distance waiting with my bag on my shoulder. "I'm good with that, I need to check on Mia and Dena first."

I was trying to determine if he was really into Holly. As he put his clubs in the truck, I tried to study his facial expression and body language. I put my clubs in, changed my shoes and headed for the gym. I didn't say anything to him but I thought about trying to hook him up with Dena, but I dismissed that thought from my mind as soon as it entered, for various reasons. He has too much drama, she has too much drama, and that may end up being more than what I bargained for. We've already had that happen to us. Mia and Dena's friend, Lysa and my boy, Ronald were sneaking around together and no one knew. Mia always joked about them getting together. She thought they would be a cute couple. I never said a word about them getting together because I let grown ups do what they do without any coercing from me. Anyway, one Sunday after church, drama ensued. Even after a very good service, with a message that was more than a feel good but an action-oriented message. We wanted to eat Italian so we went to a spot on I-10. We were discussing our goals for the remainder of the year, and how we could help each other achieve them. Lysa and Ronald disagreed on a couple of topics, the conversation got heated then Lysa threw the entire basket of bread, and poured the oil and bread crumbs into Ronald's lap before standing to leave.

Mia yelled out, "Lysa Mitchell, what is going on with you?" I was surprised that Lysa behaved that way because she was usually an even-kill personality. Nevertheless, the entire scene was only a show for the group, as later on, Ronald went back to Lysa's house and did what sneaking grown ups do. I've seen Lysa's car at his house several times. He lives in the subdivision not too far from where I live and I sometimes take that route home. So, she could've planned her little show so they could leave early and that's exactly what they did. I usually don't miss much.

I decided not to say anything to Sean about Dena. If he were interested, he would let her know.

Just as we were turning the corner near 24-Hour Fitness, my cell phone rang. It was Lynne again. I answered saying, "I'm sorry Lynne. I'm on my way now."

"Okay, I was just checking." She beamed.

"Be there shortly." I pressed *End*.

"Man, I need your help. Lynne needs me to get some boxes out of her attic."

"Yeah right, Lynne is still trying to hook you up with her daughter. She probably put the boxes up there just so you can come over and get them down. Watch she'll have lunch fixed and everything. Matter of fact, Lynne probably won't even be there."

"Man, be quiet. No, she's not." I said nonchalantly.

We arrived at Lynne's house within forty-five minutes and just as Sean predicted, Lynne had left to go "to the store" and December said her brother had already taken the boxes from the attic. I smelled something cooking that was not pleasing to my nostrils. Sean stood there looking as if he wanted to die laughing.

I rubbed my hand over my head. "Okay, December, well tell your mom I stopped by."

"Oh well, do you want to stay for lunch, Momma will be back shortly."

"Nah, we just finished eating." I lied as I rubbed my stomach. "And I have somewhere else I need to be, shortly."

She started walking toward me smiling, I guess she was trying to look seductive. I turned to walk out the door. I had to push Sean because he was just standing there. We walked out, got in the truck and Sean laughed so hard he actually had tears running down his face. "Man, this shit made my day! I told you!"

I chuckled slightly but I didn't find it as funny because the joke was on me.

❧

Three weeks later a similar scenario played out. Mia and I ran in the morning, I dropped Mia at Dena's, Sean and I went to play golf and was headed to the gym. My phone rang as we were getting in the truck at the golf course.

"Honey, um, how long before you're back at Dena's house? We uh, need you. We have a slight emergency. My goodness." Mia sounded like drama was about to ensue. Again.

"What's the emergency? Never mind, I'm on my way. Fifteen max, baby."

"Okay, hurry, please."

I placed the phone in the cup holder.

"Man, we need to stop by Dena's. They have some type of

drama going on."

"I bet it's with Mr. Monty."

We weren't at Dena's house ten minutes before Monty showed up. He had threatened to come by to do some bodily harm to Dena. I didn't feel like fighting today.

We were standing in the driveway, trying to understand the full story when he drove up, hopped out of his car and headed straight toward Dena yelling, "You gon' give me my stuff or I'll kick you're a—."

I stepped in front of Dena and Mia. "Wait a minute, hold on, Monty. What's going on?" He reeked of weed and alcohol.

"This Bitch owes me for…" His hands were flailing all over the place.

Dena reached around me and threw a punch that grazed his jaw. "Who are you calling a bitch?"

"Dena, stop it!" I was a bit surprised but I don't know why because I have seen Dena battle several times growing up. I used my elbow to try to keep her from throwing another punch.

Mia grabbed Dena. "Dena! Cut it out. Let Gary and Sean handle it. You don't want your neighbors all in your business."

Dena calmed down without a struggle. She walked a few feet away and folded her arms defiantly. I was holding Monty at bay as he was still trying to get around me to get to her. After he saw that wasn't going to happen, he threw a punch at me. It landed on the right side of my chin. That pissed me off. I grabbed him by his shirt collar at the opening of the buttons to hold him steady and landed a punch right in the middle of his forehead. His head bounced back like a bobble-head. I held him up, I didn't want him to fall because I had something to say to him and I didn't want to yell it out. The blow made him dizzy. He shook his head.

I leaned in and growled in his ear, "Look, you little punk ass mothafucka, if you ever swing at me again, I'll do way more than punch you."

His eyes widened.

"Now get your ass in your car and get the hell away from here."

I pushed him and he stumbled toward his car.

"You haven't seen the last of me, Dena," he said with hands flailing in the air again as he continued to stumble toward his car.

My hand ached. I turned to Dena. "What the hell do you have that belongs to him? You need to give it to him."

"He's lying. I don't have anything of his. This punk was living with me."

"You still sleeping with him? You sleep with him since you put him out? Why would he just come back over all of sudden Dena? What did you say to him?

Silence.

I let out an exasperated sigh, "You need to stop messing around with dudes that want to beat your ass, Dena."

"What? I've never let a guy beat my ass."

"Well, you sure as hell choose the ones that try. Damn!" My voice had elevated slightly.

"It's okay to date someone that is not in the same profession or on the same financial level as you are but you definitely need to choose the person with the right character and values that's not trying to beat you down every chance he gets. A man is supposed to protect a woman and love her. Do you get that? Damn, I don't know why that's so difficult for y'all to understand. But then again, this situation does involve Dena Thomas from Brooklyn." I glared at her. "I'm sure you said or did something that was ultimately disrespectful, which only fanned the blazing fire that

Monty already had burning but that's still no excuse for him to try to hurt you. You two should definitely stay away from each other, I don't care how good you think he is in bed. Trust me, there are other guys out there that would treat you much better."

I couldn't believe I was giving a lecture. I tried to soften the look on my face slightly but to no avail. At this point, the etched frown was too deep. Dena was like a sister to me and I would never want to say or do anything to hurt her.

"Dena, look, I care about you, you know that." I paused for another try at softening my facial expression. It still didn't work. "I got your back, you know that, but you can't keep provoking this man Dena." I paused, looking at my hand. I hit that fool too hard, now I'm in pain. "Mia and I are leaving for New York next week. If you have anything that pops up, call the police. Please. Don't try to handle things yourself, okay? Or call Sean if you have to."

"Yeah, you can definitely call me." He walked over to hug Dena. He and Mia stood in silence during most of the altercation but I'm sure both of them were waiting on their turn when and if necessary. I'm glad they didn't have to "show up" for this one.

"Thank you, Sean. Thanks, Gary." She reached for a hug and whispered in my ear. "You're worried about me but you need to make sure you keep Mia away from your crazy aunt. When you get home, you don't want your childhood history to turn into a disastrous lie."

I pulled back and faked a smile. "You're welcome."

I walked over to Mia, hugged her. "You okay?"

She nodded.

I kissed her gently, hugged her into a tight embrace that neither of us wanted to let go. I kissed her again. "I'll see you in a couple of hours."

"Okay."

Sean and I went to the gym and played a few games of basketball with our usual smack-talking crew, Postway, Larry, Mack, Drew, Jr., Hicks, Holmes and an older-cat named, Sonny. They looked forward to the game every week.

There was a group of girls huddled around the information desk when Sean and I were walking out. They stopped their conversation as we walked by.

"Hey, handsome."

We greeted them politely and kept walking. I don't need to entertain any distractions and Sean didn't need any more.

CHAPTER 18

❧

MIA

Gary's assistant, Lynne, did the searching and made all of the reservations for our trip to New York, including hotel and air. She was very helpful sometimes. That's why I felt guilty when I had to ask her to change my flight reservations again because I was trying to please a demanding lack-of-planning client. I had done a weeklong leadership seminar for them recently, and she asked if I would be the keynote speaker at luncheon for a non-profit organization where she was chair of the board. What she failed to tell me was that she had already scheduled it and printed the programs. In covering her tracks, she didn't time my acceptance with the program committee so she forgot to confirm with me. It was irritating but when duty called, I went. It was more exposure for me at events, even with my hormones out of whack and my period late. Here I was doing something that I said I would never do, put my health on the back burner. Gary kept telling me that he can take care of me so that I don't have to accept that type of invitation where people try to take advantage of me, but I refused his offers. I had to do it for me.

"Hi, Lynne, I hate to bother you, but I …"

"Then don't," she interrupted me. "Just kidding, Mia," she followed up with a semi-non-joking tone.

I hesitated for a moment because I was a bit appalled by her comment. My impression of her was quickly changing. Many thoughts went through my head. Maybe she wanted to joke since Gary was not there or maybe she was serious and felt she was Gary's assistant and not mine, although Gary had volunteered her services to me for small things like scheduling appointments, making airfare, hotel and rental car arrangements. He bragged about her keeping him in line but I did not hold her in the same high regard because the bottom line is, she messes up my stuff. He told me that she wanted him to date one of her daughters but he thought that desire was over so he didn't think her mistakes were intentional. I'd always retort and say, "Maybe it's because she's old."

I know some mothers are relentless and sometimes outright ruthless when they are trying to plan their daughters' lives. My mother was the opposite. She allowed me freedom to date whom I wanted as long as he wasn't using me as a punching bag. Lynne was a nice lady but I couldn't let her slide with that little funky comment. If I let that little slip-up ride then there will be more in the future, so I retorted.

"I see you got your broom started this morning." I paused. "Just kidding, Lynne," I said in the same tone as she did.

She pretended to laugh. "Girl, you are a riot. You're just like my daughter. How can I help you?"

I grunted because I knew good and well, I was nothing like

her deadbeat daughters. "I need to change my flight." I decided at that moment I needed the confirmation number so I could change the flight myself so she didn't mess it up. Intentionally. "Do you have the confirmation number?"

"Oh, I can do it for you. What's your credit card number?"

"What? It's on Gary's card and I don't have that information, Lynne."

"Hold on, let me check something. I think I remember Gary telling me something about that."

I shifted my weight from my right foot to my left. *What the hell, is she talking about? This old lady is about to make me cuss! She made the reservations for Gary weeks ago. She has a comprehension problem.* I heard her long and ugly manicured nails tapping on the keyboard. I heard a few clicks of the mouse.

She was taking so long to respond and I was beginning to think she had started surfing the internet while I was holding on. "Did you find it?"

"One moment," she said curtly before I could get my sentence out.

I balled my fist and squeezed my eyes tightly shut. I could not wait to tell Gary that he had a crazy rude woman for an assistant.

This menagerie went on for about ten minutes. "Lynne, you know what, I'll find it. I'll just call Gary when his flight—"

"Oh here it is." She cut me off again. I heard her shuffling through papers.

I scoffed but did not say a word. *Now I know she's crazy.* When I mention Gary's name she acts as if all is well. And why is she now shuffling through papers after clicking and surfing the net a few seconds ago with those ugly nails. She gave me the confirmation number as if she was uneducated. "Pah, pah, P, bah, bah, b, dubyah, R rah, fo' nine." I guess that meant the number was PBWR49.

"Thanks Lynne." I hung up before she could say anything more. I had to end the call before she continued with all of that foolishness.

She was really putting on a show, trying to sound and act slightly senile and incompetent so that I wouldn't ask her to do anything for me. She succeeded because I'd do it myself before I have her mess it up.

CHAPTER 19

❧

GARY

I had to stop by my office to drop off some files to T.J. before going to the airport and Nina had me rushing for my flight because she brought some drama that delayed me. She had followed me to my office, parked behind my truck, and caused a huge scene, which involved building security. It was so embarrassing. I know I shouldn't have but I confronted her about driving by Dena's when Mia and I were there after our run a few weeks ago.

Lynne has started to make too many mistakes in her duties. I had to redo every plan that she made for our trip to New York. This was not like her. She had always been very meticulous about my travel arrangements, checking and double-checking flights and hotels before I got there. The hotel she booked for me was hideous; my cousin Sam had confirmed it. The website had the consumer reviews and she ignored it or booked it on purpose. She'd been acting differently since I asked her to make the reservations for Mia and me, and she never mentioned the bogus-box-trip that I made to her house and she was not there. I didn't want to hear her lie, so I didn't bring it up either.

I checked my voicemail as soon as the plane landed. Mia had left a heated message that I could barely understand because the signal was not good. I heard her heels clucking against the pavement then bits and pieces of a sentence, "Lynne… crazy… she…was….had… me on hold…the in..net…rude…broom. Call me. Love you, bye!"

I wasn't sure what that was all about but I was sure I would find out later.

I originally planned for Mia to come up at the same time as me but I was glad it didn't work out that way. I really needed to make sure that my feelings toward my family were as in tact as I thought. I arrived in New York two days before Mia was scheduled to arrive. My parents tagged along with Sam to pick me up from the airport. Sam owns a car service, called The Starz Limo. There are nine vehicles in his fleet all with license plate *Starz1* through *Starz9*, one stretch Hummer and one Cadillac Escalade. The rest were Lincoln Towncars. He had several drivers but he drove sometimes depending on the client. He also helped his buddy repossess a few autos from time to time. Sam, the businessman. The way he behaves sometimes, you'd think he had at least two felonies, but ironically, he had none. He was cool. His demeanor and appearance sometimes caught people off guard. Both my parents love him dearly and so do I.

My dad hugged me. "I thought Mia was coming with you." He pushed back, looked at me, and pulled me into another embrace. A feeling of guilt wrapped me like a blanket. I felt horrible about all of the days, weeks, months and years that I wasted being upset with them because they kept such a big secret from me. I would have been probably be a lot further along in the healing process, maybe totally over it and not thinking about it all the time. But they never stopped loving me and never stopped showing me that they loved me.

"Oh, I forgot to tell you guys, she's not coming today."

"Well, is she coming at all?" My mother chimed before dad could speak again.

"Yes ma'am, she'll be here Thursday. Duty calls. She has to speak at a luncheon tomorrow."

"Oh, well that's good. I can't wait to meet her." My mother squeezed me and continued to rub my back.

I must admit, it felt good to be home with them.

"I know Ma, you'll get your chance soon. You want to see pictures?" I asked sarcastically.

She perked up, "Well yes, do you have some?"

Sam laughed. "Yahmean, he better not be walking around with pictures of his girl in his wallet."

"As a matter of fact, I do have one in my wallet."

"What? Man, you getting soft, you've been hanging around Sean too long. You need to move back here, yahmean."

My dad came to the rescue. "Man, G-Matt is getting old. He needs to find someone and settle down and you do too, Sam. Just because you and Tammy didn't work out doesn't mean you can't find someone else."

"I know that's right, Clive," my mother said, determined not to be left out of any conversation.

I handed my mother a couple of pictures of Mia.

"Oh, Gary, she is beautiful." She cocked her head to the left. "How'd you meet her?"

"Ma! What do you mean? You act like I can't—."

"Let me see that picture," my dad and Sam said at the same time.

One of the pictures was one that Sean snapped. Mia had a very big smile, arms around my neck, with her cheek pressed against mine. The second picture was a head shot professionally done, black and white.

"Sam, you watch the road, son," my dad ordered.

"I got the road, yahmean! I'm trying to see this be-yuu-tiful woman that G-Matt snagged."

"Yeah, she is beautiful." My dad handed the pictures to Sam.

I could not believe them. They all pile into the car to come to the airport. They want to see pictures. I show them like a dummy and now they are 'ooohing' and 'ahhing' as if she's a new car.

"Dude, she is fine!" He started dancing while he drove.

We all laughed as I leaned forward and snatched the pictures from Sam. "Man, give me the dang pictures."

I had to take a look at the pictures myself. I truly adored Mia and was not embarrassed to say, I missed her already.

My dad whispered with a straight face so that my mother wouldn't hear. "You're ready to get married aren't you, Son?"

Sam's phone rang and my mother was busy trying to hear his conversation, her head was moving back and forth.

"I don't know for sure but I think so." I paused. "Dad, she is an extraordinary woman. I need to talk to you about some things."

"I'm sure she is, Son. You talked to V.?"

I found that strange for him to ask that question. I sometimes felt like he and V. are in a competition of who gets to assist me first.

"Not in detail. He asked the same thing you just did, last night.

I didn't say much because I wanted to talk to you first." I found myself justifying as if I can't make my own decisions, although I know I am capable and I will. But with my parents being married for almost forty years, I would expect that they know what to do more so than V., who's divorced, single more than he's been committed, and getting ready for a second go-around of marriage with Ms. Emma. However, I get a lot of advice from V. I respect him.

He patted my leg. "We'll talk before you leave."

"Talk about what?" My mother turned around in the seat. "Gary, you know that girl came by last night to see if you had made it to town?"

"What girl, Ma?" I said nonchalantly as I checked my text messages. Nina had sent three.

So u think u can ignore me now, huh?

I hope ur satisfied.

Don't make me hurt her?

"That Tracy girl," she said in disgust and turned to face the window again.

"Oh." I looked out the window because I didn't want to comment nor did I want to see Tracy. She was my "son's" mother. I was the idiot because I didn't ask for a DNA. "Who told her that I was coming?"

"I don't know, there's no telling because I've been telling everybody. I was so excited," she muttered. My mother sounded as if she was disappointed in herself. She knows the drama and heartache that Tracy, her mother, and my aunt put me through during college.

I grunted. "That's okay, Ma." I tried to reassure her that it didn't matter who she told. I was not thinking about Tracy and I was contemplating how I was going to respond to Nina.

I was at my parent's house for less than two hours when I heard three loud knocks at the door. My dad, Sam, and I were sitting in the living room laughing and joking as we normally did when I get home. We were waiting on my brother to arrive. "That's probably Vance knocking that loudly," I said as I got up to open the door. To my surprise, it was not Vance. It was Tracy. And my smile turned to a frown.

"Hey G-Matt, how are you doing?" she said with excitement as if I invited her. She reached for a hug.

I immediately put my hands up to block her, gently grabbed her wrists, and pushed her back. "Hey, Tracy."

"Why you gotta act like that?" She folded her arms and pouted in her usual manner when she didn't get her way. It irritated me back then and it's irritating me even more now.

Her face looked the same, but she was dressed like a ghetto queen. She had on tights with one of those balloon-looking dresses that was tight around the thighs and was never flattering on any woman. She also had an awful-looking long, red and brown weave that needed to be washed because I could smell it.

"What do you want, Tracy?"

"I just stopped by to see you because I heard you were gonna be in town. I haven't seen you in so long. It's been years."

"Really," I replied in the driest most nonchalant tone that I could muster.

"G-Matt, why you acting like this?" She smiled and tried to

reach for another hug. I pushed her away again. *This fool must be on drugs.*

"Look, Tracy, I did not come home to see you. I came to be with my family," I said calmly.

"I am your family. I'm your son's mother." She twirled her finger through her matted weave and then folded her arms across her chest again. "You know, he would be eleven years old now."

I looked at her in disbelief but didn't speak. I just glared. She was always the type that tried to hit where it hurt and then pretend to console you afterward. Her comment obviously brought back many memories full of drama and hurt feelings. Her entire family was nuts and like a young idiot, I fell into the trap.

Without my parents' consent or knowledge, her mother paid me to take her daughter out with one rule: whatever happens happens. I was a horny teenager, willing to make some money. I had no emotional attachment to her, I took her out a few times, things got going. She wanted to impress her mom that she could keep a good man that she met on her own, not knowing that her mother set it up. We did it, she got pregnant and the next thing you know, after seven months of morning sickness, cravings, and bedrest—all filled with drama—I was a daddy. Little that I knew, the joke was on me. I did not know but her mother knew she was messing around with a very abusive deadbeat guy that she was sleeping with. I was good in football, so she thought that I was headed for a successful career and wanted her daughter to experience a "good life" versus a life of torture and poverty. My ignorant aunt assisted her with the lie. Although Tracy's mom did not care for me, she figured I was better than the deadbeat that Tracy was sleeping with. Again, I say, I was stupid.

She stood at the door waiting on a reaction from me so I gave her one, I gently pushed her back. "Bye, Tracy." I closed the door and locked it.

Tracy's mother and my aunt, my dad's sister, were behind the whole debacle, as they were in every bit of drama that ensued in our family. Every detail from wanting some of the money that I did not have to accusations of rape and assault. I feel like things spiraled downhill after I found out that I was adopted. My aunt has never shown any love for me. She'd always try to have my best friend, her son Jai, and I compete against each other in everything. I'd always win and I think she hated me for it. After the car accident, which Jai caused, she blamed me for letting him drive. He blamed me for saving his life. Tracy's mother and my aunt were best friends and anything that they can concoct together to destroy someone they did it, or they tried it, and my parents hated them for it. Just recently my parents welcomed her back into their home after all of these years but only because my grandmother begged them to. I was headed for an extended stay in jail until Tracy admitted she was lying about the whole thing. I was exonerated in the end. After all of that drama, I had absolutely no words for Tracy, her mother, or my dad's sister ever again.

Tracy knocked again as I walked back to sit down by my dad.

"You okay, son?"

"I'm cool."

He got up went to the door. "Tracy, please leave my house."

She turned and stomped away after she saw Sam appear in the doorway behind my dad.

"So, how have you been, son? I see female drama continues to follow you."

"Yeah, Nina and Tracy, two major mistakes from my past."

"I'll see you guys later, yahmean. Call me G if you want to

check out a spot later." Sam was still standing at the door. He sensed the need for my dad and me to have a moment.

"You're not seeing Nina again are you?"

I frowned. "No, she just popped up after I started dating Mia, talking and acting crazy. I'll handle it, though."

"Just be careful, son. You don't want to get yourself in no trouble."

"I won't."

My dad and I talked about several different topics from politics and our support of President Barack Obama to sports to all of the infidelity among the celebrities then to me getting married one day. I spoke of the pros and cons of my relationship with Mia, what I thought the future would look like, being equally yoked, children, finances, and anything else that I thought was appropriate.

"Dad, does Mr. Henry still own that jewelry store?"

"Yeah, same place it's always been. His son works it more now since he's been sick."

"Really? What's wrong with him?"

"Old."

I chuckled. "I need to go see him for a couple of items."

"For what?" He gave a big smile. "I was in there the other day." He whispered.

"A birthday gift for Mia and maybe something else that's long lasting," I kidded my dad.

He knew that I would eventually want a ring for Mia and Mr. Henry can make exactly what I wanted. He made my mother's twenty-fifth wedding anniversary ring for my dad and probably the original ring, too.

"When is Mia's birthday?" he said with raised eyebrows.

"You're looking at me as if you don't believe me, her birthday is Saturday," I chuckled again.

He looked at me and smiled, patted my leg as he got up from his seat. "Well, looks like there's going to be a wedding soon."

"Y'all still shooting for September for the anniversary celebration?"

"Nah, you know your mother. I think she wants it Thanksgiving weekend. That's why I went to see Henry."

I shook my head and smiled.

I had calmed down enough so I called Nina.

"Hey, Gary. How are you?" I could tell she was smiling as if all was well with us.

"Look, I don't have time for pleasantries. I'm responding to your text. You know, I don't play games and I don't like drama. Your idle threats will get your ass in trouble. I promise you. Stay away from me and lose my number." I said firmly.

"I wasn't giving any id—" She huffed.

"Stay away from me. Bye, Nina." I interrupted her and hung up the phone.

My mom cooked one of my favorite meals, yams, fried chicken, greens, macaroni and cheese, deviled eggs and peach cobbler. We ate and reminisced about old times. Sam came back, Vance and Jessica came by with their families, and it really felt like old times again. I had a blast playing with my toddler nephews and nieces, three boys and two girls. Jessica and my mother could not stop loving on me. On one hand it was flattering but on another it was way over the top and almost embarrassing.

CHAPTER 20

MIA

I thought I was scheduled into Newark Airport just as Gary's flight was but somehow my flight was changed to New York. Lynne was up to one of her tricks again. I arrived at LaGuardia shortly after eleven a.m. Gary was a little perturbed about it but I didn't know the difference in distance since I didn't live in the area.

Gary said he'd meet me at baggage claim. I miss the days before September 11th when you could step off the plane and run directly into the arms of your loved one.

We had several conversations during my trip. I had told him about how rude Lynne had been to me on the phone. We laughed at the message that I left on his voicemail and he said he would talk to Lynne about it. I ended the conversation with, "Tell Lynne, that I should be a convicted felon. I just didn't get caught." As usual he laughed at my comments not knowing that I was half joking.

I was doing as he instructed, maneuvering my way through

all of the travelers, trying my best not to go into a full sprint. I was too excited and my heart was racing. I was ready to see him. My huge rectangular leather brown bag and matching Carlos Santanas are keeping me from running. So I tossed my hair back over my shoulder, head held high and strutted my way toward my final destination. As I was coming down the escalator, I saw a man that was slightly larger but similar stature as Gary with a long beard, no mustache, somewhat scary. He was wearing a white shirt, long slim tie, black and worn black pants, the usual outfit of a car service driver but was standing out over all of the other drivers in the area, one, because he was much bigger and taller and two, because he was standing a lot closer than the others. He had a tent card that read M. Matthews. I walked past him, making eye contact, but no connection. I was expecting to see Gary any minute. As I was standing in front of the carrousel waiting for the buzzer, the red light starting blinking to let us know that the bags will be coming soon. I was looking for Gary because being without him for two days, made me very anxious to see him.

Mr. Big and Tall walked up to me and tapped my shoulder. "Excuse me Miss, is your name Mia?"

"Yes," I said with a hint of irritation but ready to defend if I needed to. His tap was a little bit firmer than I'd like.

He proceeded to grab my elbow saying. "You need to come with me, your bags have already been picked up and ..."

"Hold on! Please stop touching me. Who are you?" I was ready to take his big behind down.

Gary walked toward us laughing and immediately took over the situation. "Wait, wait, Sam. You're way off script."

I jumped into Gary's arms, hugged, and kissed him, forgetting about Mr. Big and Tall for a moment.

"I missed you so much," I said with enthusiasm.

"I missed you too girl." He returned the sentiment as we hugged and swayed. "This is my crazy cousin, Sam."

I turned around scanned him up and down for a few seconds, extended my hand. "Hi, nice to meet you," I said a little embarrassed.

"Yeah, good to meet you too," he said as he laughed.

I tucked myself underneath Gary's armpit. I felt so safe in his arms.

"I missed you so much." He squeezed my shoulder.

"Me too baby. I needed you." I said as I hugged him tighter.

"Really now? Well I'm all yours for the next few days."

He was very protective, not possessive just protective. Paranoia had begun to set in quite frequently. Unfamiliar territory, a big black guy tapping my shoulder, grabbing my elbow, he was about to get it. I don't like people in my space and unfortunately, it happens more than I'd like. During the luncheon yesterday, the usher passed a hardly legible note from someone that read, *Hi Miyah, I REELLY enjoyed your speach! Can we talk sometimes? I REELLY need talk to you.* The note had no name, no number, just a bunch of misspelled words. I waved to the usher and asked, "Who sent this?" He didn't know. After the luncheon several people came up to talk to me, some asking about my story, others needing advice.

"We've been hanging out most of the morning and had to slip away to the airport to pick you up because everybody wanted to come. Mom, Dad, Vance, his wife, and Jessica wanted to come. So we left the house for breakfast around seven knowing that your flight was expected to land after eleven. They didn't need to come." He flashed a smile. "We devised this skit to see what you would do. The outfit that Sam was wearing was a tear-away that he used when he used to strip at parties years ago. That's why it was so tight."

Sam tore away the outfit when we got to the car. I gasped because I didn't see it coming. Gary thought it was very funny. He and Sam are two of a kind, jokesters. Sam put the luggage in the trunk as Gary and I got into the back seat.

"I hope you'll remember this when I get you back. Payback is a motha." I playfully said.

"Enough about me and Sam. How was your luncheon?"

"It was good overall."

My head rested on his triceps as he pulled me close, our fingers intertwined. As I was going on about my day, he was looking at me, then occasionally looking away, but said nothing more. He asked about my speaking engagements just to be polite because he certainly wasn't as focused on what I was saying as I wanted him to be.

"There were a lot of women, a lot of people. I—"

In the middle of my sentence, he put his hand on my chin, raised it up, and planted a slow, soft kiss on my lips. That was my cue to be quiet and ride.

Within thirty minutes, we were on the expressway, headed toward our hotel on Lexington Avenue with the Hip-Hop sounds of Hot 97 pumped up loudly. Sam dropped us off for me to freshen up and get refreshed. I was so happy to see Gary. I couldn't believe how we behaved after being away from each other for only two days. Since I wasn't in town yet, he stayed at his parents' home until I arrived. The bellhop brought our bags to the room. Gary tipped him and closed the door.

"This hotel is really nice. Lynne actually picked a good place. I can't believe it with that stank attitude she has."

"No, I really picked a good place." He frowned.

"Oh, well you have just won some extra brownie points with me," I said as I stood there and admired the room and decided not to say more about Lynne.

My mouth had already been agape in the hotel lobby. Sometimes I amazed myself. I have stayed at very nice hotels in my travels in Corporate America but I still silently awed at the ambience of every new place I go.

"Trust me, by the time the weekend is over, I am going to get a lot of brownie points." He hugged and kissed me all over my face as he usually does.

"Oohhh, wow! I can't wait to see what you have in store."

The next couple of hours were history. Good history.

Sam returned to pick us up in four hours. Gary's mother, father, brother, sister and nephew had called several times just checking to see if I had made it. He told them that my flight was delayed. He and Sam had concocted that story, too. When we finally arrived at his parent's house in Long Island, it appeared that we were at a family reunion. All of his aunts, uncles, and cousins were there. He had told me about each person, who to avoid and whom I'd probably get along with. I hugged a lot, shook hands, felt stared at the whole nine. Gary's dad had grilled so much food that was very tasty. We ate, laughed, and talked. He had a very accommodating and friendly family.

"Mothers and fathers look out! Hide your daughters. And

your sons, because this fine man G-Matt is on tha—loose!" An exaggerated voice came from behind Gary.

He turned around and was pulled into a full embrace by a guy wearing shorts, sandals, and a golf shirt with beautiful, shaved and toned legs, it was his cousin, Jamie. Gary had told me that I would like him. He was hilarious. Jamie was one of the family members that he actually wanted me to meet. He is definitely an example of living life to the fullest. He worked and lived in Manhattan. Jamie was an over-the-top gay guy that did not care who knew it. He made great money as an accountant, dressed immaculately, and had the busiest affluent social life that anyone has ever seen, attending scholarship galas, fundraisers, and just lively parties that his cronies invite him to.

Despite Jamie's choice, Gary still respects him because he's family. He allows Jamie to talk to him about anything except sex. He did not want to hear about that, at all. Not from Jamie. That's where he drew the line.

"What's good, man?" Gary grabbed Jamie into an embrace the way guys do.

"G-Matt, dude, I haven't seen you in so long." He stomped his foot. "I miss you being around here. You should come up to visit more often."

"Nah, dude, you need to come visit me." Gary shook his head. "This is my girl, Mia."

"Boy!" He smacked his lips. "Stop playing calling me, dude." He fanned the back of his hand toward Gary.

Gary chuckled. He was convinced that he was not born gay but his mother pushed him that way with the unisex name and the way she used to treat him when they were younger. She always wanted a daughter but after her second son, she had an emergency hysterectomy. I guess adopting was not an option either. The colors that she used to buy for him and his brother, the sports that she wanted him to pursue, and even allowing him to put a relaxer on his hair. His brother went totally in the opposite direction, a gigolo. You can't choose your family nor can you choose what they do.

"Well hello, Miss Mia. I heard so much about you, girl and you look fabulous, honey!" He reached for a hug.

"Thank you, Jamie. You do, too!"

"Girl, I know, honey!" He smacked his lip-gloss covered lips.

He rubbed my back and ushered me over to the chair away from the crowd.

"I heard so much about you, and you are just as beautiful as I've heard."

I widened my eyes. I was flattered, actually. "Thank you, Jamie."

"Girl, so how long have you been dating my cousin?"

"Since March, April, some time in the spring." I looked upward trying to remember exactly.

"Oh." He grabbed his mouth. "I guess strong independent woman don't remember dates just like men huh?"

"Ouch that hurt, Jamie." I pretended to be offended.

"Girl, that's good, though! I am so happy for him. He has been through so much and he deserves a good woman. He is really a good man, too. Strong and confident. That's my cousin," he said as he looked across the yard to Gary talking to Sam and Vance.

My mind started to wonder how much Gary had not told me. I expected some things because of his previous comment—"before we made any major decisions, I will eventually tell you everything you need to know." He felt most of it was just history, no bearing on anything, especially decision making. I wasn't sure about that when he said it but I agreed. So, I planned to do more listening than talking.

Jamie was very pretty for a guy. His hair was cut low, almost identical to Gary's, very neatly trimmed facial hair, light brown eyes, very slim build but lean and muscular. His dark brown skin was flawless. He's the type of guy I would look at and say "Now why, Lord, another one of our gorgeous black men not available to the black woman. Why Lord? Why?"

"So what did Gary tell you about me?" He slapped my leg and laughed.

"Just that I would probably like you, enjoy talking to you," I lied, kind of. Gary had told me a little bit more about the affluent men that he dates and his requirements but why would I mention that.

"Oh!" He put his hand over his mouth as if he was shocked that anyone that he knew would knowingly, not talk about him.

"You're funny, Jamie."

He tapped my knee. "My cousin, my cousin! He is my hero, though. I remember Gary, Sam, and Jai used to tease me about being gay or 'soft.'" He gestured quotation marks in the air. "Until one day, two guys jumped me after school. That was a horrible day for me. I wanted to end it all for me and a few more people." His mood changed slightly but he kept talking. "But Gary was right there for me. I was sixteen years old and my 'man' at the time had dumped me for a girl." He gestured his hands in quotation marks again and continued. "He said he wasn't gay anymore. I cried all day long, honey. I remember I was sitting on the back of a park bench." His shoulders dropped as he took us both back almost fifteen years ago. "And these two dudes just didn't like what they saw I guess, a gay dude crying, so they jumped me. I was holding my own though." He smiled. "Gary was walking toward us but didn't know it was me until he got closer. He started running and yelling and then here comes Sam and Jai from somewhere, girl I don't know where they came from, we were fighting like crazy." He chuckled. "We beat their asses', girl. It was four dudes but only two of them were jumping me, the other two jumped in when Gary got there. But Gary didn't care, he was trying to save me, honey. His cousin. You don't mess with blood. That's why it hurt my heart when we found out…" He paused. "Never mind. My cousin is my hero, honey. He always teased me that I got my heart broken and my ass kicked in the same day. He's so crazy and you know when Sam gets started, he doesn't stop until somebody is almost dead or hurt pretty badly or something, honey. He is crazy for real." He widened his eyes.

I smiled but remained silent and just looked at him with a hint of sorrow for him and a hint of excitement for Gary saving his life. "You know my cousin never judged me for being gay. He just always said 'you can't choose your family, it is what it is' and I agree with that because love makes a family. So as long as I'm not bringing a bunch of drama, he's all right."

He tapped my leg again. "Yep, that's my cousin, girl. Know this, he will go to great lengths for you if he cares about you. Trust me on that!"

Gary walked over to us. "What lie are you telling her now, Jamie?" He pulled me from my seat. He sat down and pulled me into his lap, never looking at me but had his eyes fixed on Jamie halfway joking but still wanted to know.

"Nothing. No lies. Just the truth about why I adore you so

much. You saved my life and I will go to the end of the earth, telling people about it. Ev-verybody doesn't appreciate when someone saves their life but I do! Oh, I didn't tell her about that time we got on the elevator and these two thugs got on. They looked me up and down and I grabbed my belt. Do you remember that? Remember you asked why I grabbed my belt and I told you that I was about to spin around, turn into Wonder-Woman and fuck them up, honey!" We all rolled laughing.

"Man, you are nuts. I do remember that." Gary laughed.

Jamie jumped from his seat leaned in quickly and kissed Gary on his jaw. Gary tried to move out of the way, as I fell off his lap but to no avail, Jamie landed the kiss right below the eye.

"Man, you know that's nasty right? Don't ever do that again!" He pretended to be mad. "Got me dropping my girl on the ground trying to dodge your bull."

Jamie ignored Gary, hugged me, and walked away. "Mia, it was good meeting you, girl. You take care."

Gary's cousin T. came over for an introduction. Gary had given me a summary on her and Sam. He introduced us and walked away to answer his Dad's calling to play flag football. He kissed me on my cheek, pushed T.'s head, and said, "I'm watching you."

She replied with "Whatever, negroid!"

Sam had given me a briefing about T. Her real name was Tammy. She wanted to be called T. She was Sam's ex-wife. They divorced because Sam cheated. He said he cheated because T. was too needy, not supportive and wanted him to do so much for her before she would give him sex. She complained when he made money and when he didn't make money. She didn't do anything for herself at home, always tried to make him feel guilty for having a life. 'Sam can you get me this? Sam can you get me that? My head hurt. My leg hurt. You didn't do this right. Can you do that better.' And so on. He said the other woman that he cheated with made him feel like a king.

While T. didn't go into detail about any family stories as Jamie did. She mentioned she wish that Jai and Gary could go back to old times. "Gary is my boy, you know? I got so much love for him. Jai is my cousin too but he can be an ass sometimes."

I asked, "Is Jai the one in a wheelchair?"

"Yeah, G-Matt told you about Jai?"

"Well yes and no. I truly don't know how much there is to tell, but what I remember is that he is in a wheelchair from a car accident that they were in together and that was about it. He said that he doesn't know if Jai will ever make it to Houston but he had his house built with him in mind. Extra wide doors throughout the house, guest bathroom with wheelchair shower, wheelchair ramps, things like that."

"Oh yeah, I heard about that." She looked as if she wanted to say more but she didn't so I didn't question anything. She changed the subject to shoes. She complimented mine and I complimented hers. She told me that Mrs. Matthews and Gary's sister, Jessica were going shoe shopping later. She said she would hang but she had to work later.

"I need to go with them, but wait a minute, you're T. so are you Sam's ex-wife or is there another T.?" I felt a little bit silly switching the subject back to the family so abruptly, but she answered with no problem.

"No, there's not another T. It's me." She nodded her head continuously. "Yes, Sam, and I used to be married." She rubbed her hands across her legs. "That boy is a fool. We're better friends now, though. I was young and naïve. Now I'm old, educated, and sophisticated."

"I know that's right."

"I finally got past my issues and the insecurities of thinking that if I kept all of his attention on me he wouldn't cheat. Well, I was wrong." She twisted her face. "But I forgave him. We live and learn."

I smiled. "Re-marriage?"

"Hel…heck no!" She rolled her eyes and smiled, "I'm not crazy! Like I said, young and dumb. Now we're friends and it's best to keep it that way. I travel too much anyway, flying all over the place. Becoming a pilot has put a strain on trying to maintain a relationship."

"I hear you. All the more reason to get with someone you already know and care about. Just kidding." I teased her.

She gave a wide smile.

"So you're Dena's cousin?" I continued as I was trying to connect all of the dots.

"Yes, girl, that's my cousin," she beamed. "That's my girl! She hasn't been home in a while. How's she doing?"

"She's doing very well." I lied.

"Me and that girl have been in so much trouble together. Whew!"

"I can only imagine because we have, too," I said as I thought about some of the trouble that Dena caused and some that I caused.

"Really? That's wild. Gary and Dena left and said F— New York. They hardly come back to visit."

"No, I think they both love this place, there are a lot of memories. I hear them talk sometimes when they get into a zone and the 'yahmeans' and 'that's what's ups' complete with hand gestures, start flying."

She laughed, "Wow, those two are my dawgs, yo." She lightly pounded her fist in her hand. "Wow. That's what's up. So you're from Arkansas right?"

"Yes. Pine Bluff."

"Did you like it growing up there?"

"Well, since I didn't know anything different, I guess so. I mean, I appreciate all of my experiences or lack thereof but I'm glad things turned out the way they did for me. My parents raised me in the south. It was either Pine Bluff or Detroit. They chose The Bluff."

"Yeah, well be glad you didn't have to deal with fighting every day and dodging bullets."

"Yeah, I'm glad that's not my experience."

"Hmph." She sighed as if she was remembering her childhood.

Gary, Jamie, Sam, Vance and Jessica joined T. and I. Gary sat down in my lap and pretended he didn't see me. T. laughed. "Boy get your big butt off that girl."

We all stood and since Gary put his arm around my shoulder, Sam did the same thing to T., and Vance followed suit and put his arm around Jessica. Jamie put his arm around Sam and Gary and started singing. "We are the world, we are the children, we are the ones to make it a brighter day for you and me…." We all laughed. Jessica said, "What song is that?"

"See, baby girl, you need to know your black history! Okay? Boo-Boo, you're too young, okay?" Jamie sang.

"Whatever Jamie, I do know my history. And in my history, that song didn't go like that!"

We laughed.

"I'll sing with you, Jamie." I encouraged.

"Naw, I won't dare bless them now."

"Thank you," Gary whispered.

"What the hell is going on over there?" Sam scowled as he looked toward two women who pushed past Gary's uncle and were headed in our direction. "G-Man that's Tracy and her momma."

T. slipped out of her shoes and said, "Don't worry about a thing, G. Jessica and I got this one, man."

"Not before me," Jamie chimed in.

"No, T. and Jamie, nobody's fighting today, put your shoes back on," Sam commanded.

Gary never moved his hand from my shoulder. I wondered what the heck was going on? And who is Tracy and her momma? Sam, Vance, Jessica, Jamie, and T. had built a human wall in front of Gary and me.

"Gary, who are these women?" I whispered, because everyone around us had taken on a battle stance in a matter of seconds. None of them knew that I could whip both of them in a flash and go sit down and have lunch without a problem.

"I'll tell you later, don't worry about it. I got you." He kissed my hair.

What? You got me. What the hell? Okay, Mia, let it go. Obviously, this has nothing to do with you.

Sam and Vance started walking toward the women. Gary squeezed me tighter.

I heard the motherly looking woman say, "He's not gon' dis my baby, just 'cause he got his lil' girlfriend in town."

Okay now I got it, this is one of Gary's ex-girlfriends. Looky here. Okay Mia, pay attention to everything around you.

"Look, you need to go on. I don't want to body slam your ass. You know I will," Sam sneered.

"You not gon' body slam nothing here!" the older lady exclaimed. She tried to hit Sam and then T. and Jessica were all over her in the blink of an eye.

The police arrived a few minutes later and took both women to jail for disturbing the peace. As quickly as the altercation ensued, it ended and I still had no answers. Gary's mother had called the police before the women arrived because they had called her house prior to coming.

The music started to play and Gary's entire family did one line dance after another, just partying as if nothing just happened. I thought the south was the line dance capitol of the world but they had it on lock. I tried my best to join in and forget about the incident but I kept my good eye on the street just in case another nut decided to visit.

After most of the family left, his mother, her sister, and Jessica wanted to go to the store, supposedly to a shoe sale at a store not too far from the house. Of course, I wanted to go especially when the subject was shoes but I was a little bit afraid of potential drama from some other woman that Gary used to date and I felt I didn't quite know if they'd have my back if drama ensued. I wanted to stay at the house with Gary also just to be with him and possibly get a few answers to some questions. They insisted that I go and promised that we wouldn't take long. Gary didn't insist that I didn't go, so I went shoe shopping. What's a shoe-aholic to do in a situation like this?

His mother was something different. She talked about sex

more than we did. She talked in the car, in the store, in the car again on the way from the store and at home. I couldn't figure out if all of this talk was because Jessica was having problems in her marriage or if she was just a horny sixty-something year old that enjoyed that particular discussion topic.

As Gary and I walked into the kitchen, I overhead his mother talking to Jessica again, "At our age we still have great sex. It doesn't have to stop because you have children. Besides, my children are grown and we've never stopped even when they were here. You just have to make time for it. Don't give up, girl." I tried to turn around and go the other way but she said, "Oh Mia, honey come on in here, you need to hear this for when you and Gary get married."

Gary pushed me toward them, laughed, and walked out of the kitchen. I was sure my face was beet red, I was so uncomfortable. I know I heard my heartbeat through my ears. I was now face-to-face in the conversation. I didn't have the car window as a distraction. I didn't have the rack of shoes to distract me. I had to look at her and listen. Looking at the cabinets and decorations on top would have made me look slightly silly so I sucked it up and focused on what she had to say, which was basically *have sex often when you're married.* I would had never had a conversation with my mother on the subject.

Gary allowed me to suffer for a few minutes and then walked back into the room to inform me that Sam was ready to take us to the hotel. As I was walking out and saying my goodbyes, his mother called out, "Mia! Enjoy those shoes girl."

"I will," I said, grateful for the escape.

Sam was being a very good chauffeur and I didn't mind at all. He pulled into the drop off area at the hotel, got out, and opened the door. Gary handed him some money. "Thank you, sir."

Sam glared at Gary. "Come on, man. Don't play like this, not again."

"It's a tip."

Sam walked over and put the money in my hand and gently pushed me away from the car. "Here you go, Mia." He rushed to get back in the car. "Got you!"

I looked in my hand and looked at Gary confused. I tried to hand it to him.

"Keep it, he gave it to you. We've been at this since I got here. He refuses to take money from me."

I folded the one-hundred dollar bill and slid it into his pocket. "Just accept his blessing, dude."

We stopped at the bar for a cocktail, to people watch and to chill. He was very affectionate, hugging, kissing, looking into my eyes, and pressing his forehead against mine. Not saying much but intently staring. He usually acted like this when we hadn't seen each other in over a day or if something was bothering him. I could imagine the incident from earlier was bothering him but I decided not to say anything unless he brought it up and the feeling in my gut was telling me that he wouldn't.

Maybe he was making up for lost time, I didn't question it I just enjoyed it. I loved him so much but I never told him because I was afraid it would change things between us. *I questioned myself—Do I want to tell him that I love him? What if there is a real issue to the crazy woman showing up at his parents' house today? What if there is something to the dreams? What if? What if? What if? But, I'm already in love, what do I do?* I just didn't want to scare him away with that word by blurting it out too soon, like scratching the needle on a record.

"You know I found out why Monty came over to Dena's pissed off." This thought was totally way off base to what was going on at the moment, but I needed to distract my mind so I just blurted it out. "I don't think she's still sleeping with him."

He didn't respond, just a look, waiting on the follow-up. I kept talking, "He wanted his Wii, PlayStation and iPod, all of the gifts that she bought for him while they were dating."

He rolled his eyes and pulled me close, "Listen. I." Kiss. "Don't want." Kiss. "To talk about." Kiss. "Dena." Kiss. "Tonight." Long Kiss. "Okay?" He stared into my eyes. I melted. Kiss.

I flirted. "I bought you something today." I flipped my thinking back to another episode of the shoe-shopping trip with his mother, aunt, and sister. "They were speaking liberally about sex when we went shopping during the entire trip, as we walked through the intimate apparel department on our way to the shoe department. I'm serious the entire trip, released all inhibitions, your mom had none whatsoever. I had picked up a slamming pair of candy apple red four-inch stilettos with a peep-toe. I knew that you'd really like the shoes. But for some reason I felt the shy role and said, 'I couldn't walk in these for long.' Your Mom grunted, 'Who said you had to walk?' I gasped and said, 'Okay, well I guess I'll get 'em then.' She said, 'You'd better, I know Gary would like them and Mia, my son is so in love with you girl' and she gave me a one armed hug. I'm telling you Gary, I was continuously embarrassed by the direction of our conversations and truth be told, I wanted out. They made things more bearable when they started talking in general about women needing to let go and have fun, especially in their fifties and sixties, and not specifically to me or Jessica.

He responded with, "That's usually a topic of their conversation."

"Sex doesn't have to stop at any age," his mother chimed. I guess she felt the need to talk about it because she let it be known that she wanted me to have Gary's baby when I talked to her on the phone prior to arriving in New York. I can usually have a sex conversation with the best of them but it was just something uncanny about having the conversation with my boyfriend's mother.

"So, what did you buy?" He changed the subject.

"Shoes."

"Really?" He signaled the bartender for another gin and tonic.

"Yes," I ignored the sarcasm and sipped my drink.

"Will I like them?"

"Of course you will."

Gary and I stayed downstairs for a moment longer. We people watched, finished our drinks, and then retired to the room. He immediately walked into the bathroom and closed the French doors. Five minutes later he emerged wearing a white robe. He walked over to the nightstand and attached his iPod to the radio. "Loving after dark," the seductive male voice said.

"I guess we'll listen to the radio then since loving after dark is on." He mocked the DJ's voice. "I thought you said you bought a pair of shoes for me?"

"Oh, I did! Well, actually your mom insisted that she pay for them and they were expensive," I explained as I removed the shoes from the box. "I was kind of embarrassed about her paying for them for me."

"You need to calm down, it's no big deal." A big smile covered his face, "Ohhhhh." He picked one shoe up to examine it. "Mom is cool, she really enjoys that type of stuff, buying things for people."

"Uh yeah, she insisted and Jessica cosigned, quite a conversation today. According to her, these will get her the grandbaby that she's been waiting for from you."

"Are you serious?" He continued to smile as, he sat on the bed, pulled my feet into his lap, rubbed them, put the shoe on my foot. "Nice. I like." He admired it a moment longer then removed the shoe and placed it back into the box. "I told you my mother has no shame. I can talk to both of my parents about anything. They're cool like that."

"I see, but how are we going to tell her about my issues?" I said as I tried not to show the sadness in my voice. The sadness was not about his parents' relationship but in the disappointment of my medical condition that might require a little bit of work to have a baby. "But, baby, you know it's more than just having sex. I have fertility issues. I will beat this fibroid thing, folic acid, fish oil, jade eggs and anything else that I hear will help dissolve them, I will try it. I just don't understand why they keep coming back after surgery. Well, there are other options but all end in a 'maybe' for pregnancy."

He stood and gently grabbed my hand and led me into the bathroom. "Mia, my mother likes you and don't feel pressured about a baby. She can wait, trust me. And she does not want you to feel pressured by her comments."

The conversation ended when we stopped beside the huge garden tub filled with water, bubbles, and red rose petals, and lined with white votive candles. He placed both of his hands on my face and leaned in to kiss me.

"It's only been two days, but I miss my ba-by," he sang.

It felt good.

He rubbed my face, caressed the back of my neck, and kissed

me again. He undressed me as I stood there like a kid and then he took his robe off and we stepped into the tub. The water was hot but tolerable. "Would You Mind" by Earth, Wind, and Fire started to play in the background. I exhaled and leaned my head back against his chest. He put his arms around me, kissed my neck with tenderness, smelled my hair, and just held me. Quiet.

He whispered in my ear and said slowly, "Mia, I admire you and I love you so much."

I know that my mind should have been on him only but I couldn't help but complete a quick compare and contrast of my past relationship to him. I was struggling, trying not to be totally attached, because I was just waiting on the ball to drop on me just like a past relationship that ended in way too much drama. And after Tracy and her mother showed up, I just had a gut feeling that something drama-filled would come from that, too.

Gary was just too good to be true. My grandmother and her best friend used to tell me that I should never give a man all of me. When I was younger I just listened but when I got older, I used to say "Grandma, but doesn't the Bible say that you should be submissive to your husband and love and cherish and respect and all of that good stuff." She'd say, "Honey, I'm not talking about the Bible right now. I'm talking about you and how you need to guard your heart, young lady. 'Cause if you don't, he'll crush it and then you'll have to stab him in his. Hmmph. If you just happen to find one that you got to have, then let him find God in your heart, Miss Lady since you brought God back in it." My grandmother had two sides. She and her best friend told my sister Desilyn and me how to treat men but she and my mother introduced us to Christ. Desilyn is my only sibling. She was saved, sanctified, Holy Ghost filled, happily married with children, and a dog.

I sat quietly for a few moments longer, said a prayer, hoped God listened since I was sinning, as Gary continued to kiss my neck, my hair, my cheeks. I inhaled and then exhaled very slowly. *Despite what Grandma says, I love this man and I love the fact that he continuously finds ways that makes me speechless.*

I turned around, got on my knees, and then sat on my heels. The cushioned pad in the tub helped support the pressure on my knees. I was very careful not to knee the jewels. I looked into his eyes, and then embraced him. I felt guilty and I didn't understand why. I needed this—to be loved, to feel loved, to feel special.

"I have loved you from the day we met. I really thought that this was love at first sight. But because I was so guarded, so behind the walls that I had put up, I wouldn't allow myself to feel it. I didn't open up. I really love you, too."

"I sensed that," he said, "And since I'm no longer guarded, I felt I needed to let you know how I feel, and I didn't say it for you to say it back, I said it because I mean it."

The tub was large enough, so we took advantage of it, along with the shower.

After we got out of the shower, he dried every inch of my body and performed the ritualistic rub down with Mango Shea Butter as he did more kissing than moisturizing. He glanced at the clock. 12:07. He rolled off the bed and walked over to his bag, his penis bobbing as he moved across the room. He had no shame. He was so sexy.

"You have the cutest butt. Just so sexy." I flirted.

"Mia, stop it," he said shyly and came back to the bed and sat down.

"Well, you are. I'm serious. Just speaking the truth."

"Anyway, I have something for you that I want you to have."

He handed a card that played the song "Greatest Love of All" when I opened it. Tears started to fill my eyelids but I held them at bay. He handed me a second card that had a preprinted "I love you, do you love me, check yes or no." My mouth opened in amazement.

"Where did you find a card with this in it? How cute!"

"Don't ask questions, just read." He smiled and handed me another card.

This continued for five more cards filled with humor, songs, and sentiments. After I opened the seventh card, I was still as excited as I was on card number one. I must say, his efforts were very commendable. He was absolutely adorable. The seventh card played the song "Love Calls" by Kem. Now I think this one was made especially for me. Tears were rolling like condensation on a window. I hugged him tightly, I kissed him, I pressed my forehead and nose to his, and then I kissed him more.

"You are the most adorable man I've ever met."

"It's complete. We have been dating for seven months today or somewhere near today so I decided to get seven cards. I would've gotten the number for your age but… you know," he chuckled, "I didn't have that kind of time."

I playfully slapped his arm as I wiped away the tears. "Watch it now!"

"No seriously, they all fit so well for us, so I bought several."

He finally placed a small box in my hand. My heart started racing again. I couldn't believe it! I was so excited. We were sitting in the nude, my mouth agape with a big smile on my face. I opened the box and there were Platinum Four-prong one-carat diamond earrings.

I panted because I knew the earrings cost a lot of money. Better than G color and no visible imperfections. Yes, a lot of money. Wow!

"Oh my, Gary, these are beautiful. Thank you so much!" I stared at them and looked back up at him. "You are just so awesome." I hugged him repeatedly, still in shock. "Thank you so much, Gary."

I was happy. Before he revealed the box, I was silently hoping that it was a ring, although I was not sure if I was ready for marriage. But, when I saw the box, it was too wide for a ring box, so I calmed myself.

"Sam and I stopped by this Old Cat that we know named, Mr. Henry, he owns a jewelry store. I saw the earrings and wanted you to have them, so I bought them." He observed me for a few moments. "Happy Birthday, Mia."

"Oh, thank you! And just think, I thought you forgot," I chimed.

In the past weeks, I had been trying to prepare myself for the big let down, to be mad that he had forgotten my birthday. I wanted to ask many questions just to be nosey but thought better of it. I didn't want to appear too anxious to get married. So I just enjoyed the birthday moment.

"Hold on there's more." He handed me a card and a big box with a few pieces of lingerie.

"Thank you so much, Gary." I pushed the box to the side, reached over to the shoebox, slid both shoes on at the same time, pushed the lingerie box to the floor, and we went on to act like the little rabbits that we were at times.

❧

The next morning I woke up singing, *It's a beautiful morning*, as I did a cat stretch and then snuggled into him. We got up, showered, dressed and went back to his parents' house in Long Island for breakfast. His mother called it my 'birthday breakfast.' Gary had given a few tidbits of information about me. She and Jessica had prepared bacon, sausage, eggs, hash browns, pancakes, biscuits, grits, and rice laid out buffet-style. Mrs. Matthews let her southern roots come out. I enjoyed every bite.

Gary and I finished our breakfast and went to the basement to watch TV and chill. I offered to help with the dishes but his mother and sister wouldn't allow it and I didn't object, especially since domestic chores were not my thing, I was good at it only because I didn't like a nasty or junky dwelling. Immaculate living was what I liked. My home nurtures me. It was clean, peaceful, and very organized, which kept my mind clear and focused.

The weekend's purpose was to meet his family, put faces with names and as he informed me last night, to kick off the month-long birthday celebration.

Gary sat on the sofa, pulled me on top of him, and started kissing me.

"Gary, stop! What if someone walks down here?" I whispered loudly. My nipples started to beam like lights through my blouse.

"They won't." He kissed me again.

"Gary, stop it. What if they hear us?" I tried to resist but continued accepting his kisses.

"They won't." The look in his eyes had me mesmerized. His tongue danced in and out of my mouth slowly. He traced my lips with his tongue.

"Baby, please." I begged and pretended to cry because I knew that I was too weak to resist him any longer and I didn't want to ruin my reputation before I started.

"Okay, I'll stop," he conceded. "But you are in trouble when we get back to the room." He flashed a mischievous smile. "Scary ass."

"I'm cool with that." I kissed him on his forehead. I sat down beside him as he grabbed the remote and prepared to channel surf. My body was heated from the inside out and he was as hard as a tree branch. We sat in silence for a few moments. We did this often, just enjoyed being in each other's presence. I leaned over and laid my head on his shoulder to take a quick nap. He put his arm around me, which allowed my head to land on his chest but that can present an uncomfortable position for an extended period, so I slid down to place the back of my head on his thigh. I woke up to a loud female voice.

"Hey, G-Matt, you down here?" the female voice said.

"Shit!" He sounded disgusted. "That's my dad's youngest sister, loud mouth and messy as hell. The one that I told you I'm not quite ready for you to meet, but I guess you will eventually. I'm surprised she didn't show up yesterday with Tracy and her mother."

"Hey, baby, how you doing?" she said loudly.

Gary hesitantly hugged her.

"You don't have to act like that, boy. You look good. I haven't seen you in so long, how many years has it been?"

Gary's mother made her way down the stairs quickly. "Mia, how you doing down here, Miss Birthday Girl? Is Gary taking care of you?"

"Yes, ma'am. We were watching TV."

"The TV was watching her." He cracked a smile.

"That's fine, sweetheart." She stood next to me then pressed her cheek against mine and rubbed my arms as if she was trying to warm me from the cold.

Something was not right, she came down those stairs to protect. I could feel it. I don't know if the protection was for me, Gary, or both. She quickly ushered the aunt back upstairs without an introduction. She looked back at Gary with one of those looks that I remembered from my mother: "Momma got your back, baby."

"What was that all about?" I asked as we walked back to the sofa. I sat and looked around the room waiting on an answer. The basement was finished nicely. Industrial carpet, full bar with really nice leather swivel bar stools, eight-foot pool table in the center with the oversized sectional sofa that was sitting against the wall, plants and trees outlined the corners of the room with pictures of different actors and movies on the wall. His Dad was a movie buff. A fifty-two inch flat-screen TV was mounted on the wall.

He let out an uncomfortable chuckle. "It's a long story. A college story that I need to fill you in on when the time is right. She and her son, Jai and her friend, Tracy's mom in which you saw yesterday." He paused and looked at me with furrowed brows. "Do you mind if I tell you another day? I don't want to spoil your birthday."

"Okay. That's fine baby, but is it bad?" I said as I looked into his eyes, trying to see if I could tell how bad it was. I made a mental note: "Nina, Tracy, now a college story."

He looked away and rested his face in his hands.

"Trust me. One day you will know everything you need to know. Trust, I won't hold anything from you that will keep you from making the decisions that you need to make about your life and your future with me. Please trust me on that."

Now he's said this to me before but what does it mean, really? I wondered.

"So does that mean that I can't ask questions to clarify what Jamie and T. said?" I said hesitantly.

He rubbed his head. "I prefer you didn't since I don't know what they told you nor do I know where our conversation will go from there and I truly don't want to suck up all of the time on your birthday talking about my history. This is your first birthday with me and I don't want to spoil it talking about my sad history." He tried to sound calm but I could tell he was slightly irritated.

"Okay, but both Jamie and T. thinks you walk on water. They love you, and they think you're cool. I promise."

He smirked.

I sat there but soon resumed my position on the sofa until Gary said, "Let's go, I need to show you this place."

He dialed Sam's number. "Dude, I'm on my way out there."

We caught the Long Island Rail Road, then the 'A' train to Sam's place on Hancock Street. He was one of several family members that stayed in the Bed-Stuy area. We went for a walk so that they could give me the history of this small city within a city. We passed through tree-lined blocks of gorgeous brownstones and other buildings that showed the talents of the people that built them. It seemed somewhat serene. They told me that the area was primarily African and Caribbean American and at sundown, I would see neighbors sitting on each other's stoop playing cards, dominos, checkers, or just bantering back and forth. Kids were playing in the streets, balls, scooters, and two of my childhood favorites, double-dutch and hopscotch.

Sam was narrating the tour in his lovely Brooklyn accent, filled with 'yahmeans' and 'sons'. I couldn't help but think if some of the guys back home were giving a narrative tour, one would hear 'Knowamsayin' and 'Man.' "Mia, you should come back next year on the July 4th weekend for the International African Arts Festival. Yahmean?" His voice sounded like Busta Rhymes.

"Hmmmm."

They'll have so many vendors with African arts and crafts and live bands. You'd love it, Yahmean?"

"Sounds fun."

"Or." He pressed his fist in his hand as if he was trying to convince me. "It would be even better if you came in November for the Home Tour Bed-Stuy Brownstones. My place will be featured."

"Wow, Sam you're big time huh?"

"Nah not me." He blushed. "G-Matt told me that your place is hot to def, yahmean, you got that lil' interior decorator thing goin' on."

"It's cool. I do aught." I smiled.

He chuckled.

We made our way around several blocks to a Caribbean restaurant on Atlantic Avenue for a late lunch. We sat and I listened to them talk and reminisce for a couple of hours while I asked a lot of questions. I could just sit and listen to them talk all day. I love the way Gary flips his dialect back to Brooklyn. I guess it would be very difficult not to while talking to Sam.

"Yeah, MiMi this is my boy. Oh sorry, is that name only for G-Matt to use?"

"You're good."

"But yeah this my boy yahmean, I'll die for him yahmean. I

wish he would've never left Brooklyn."

He spoke as if Gary was not sitting there. Gary played with his straw in his glass, looking down, quiet, occasionally taking a sip.

"But I know the two of you couldn't meet if he was still here. Had to get out." He rambled. "But now that he met you, yahmean, y'all can move back here."

"No." Gary mouthed.

They looked at each other with total devotion in their eyes, like brothers.

It was very interesting to watch someone that was always protecting me, get protected—His parents, his brother, his sister, and now Sam.

"Did he ever tell you that he was a balla for real? Real talk. This dude excelled at any sport he played. Lotta people didn't like that. Yahmean. He was fierce on the court, on the field, in the street, yahmean, you name it my boy could do it."

I looked at Gary. "Really now?"

"Don't believe Sam," he said playfully.

"Martial Arts." He pointed his thumb toward Gary.

"What? You didn't tell me that, even when Dena told you about me. Are you keeping secrets?"

"I told you, don't believe Sam." He tried to act modest. "Yo Sam, this is your black-belt right here."

"Yo, word? Now that's what's up." Sam giggled and looked at me.

I started shaking my head, "No, I'm not a...I'm no..."

"Whatever, girl. You can wax somebody when they get out of line? Had I known that I would've turned you loose on them yesterday."

"Nah, we weren't having that," I protested.

Gary grunted.

"I know, man, I had y'all, you know? Then T. and Jessica were all in the way." We laughed because T. and Jessica got crunk in a matter of seconds.

"Yeah, Mia, this man is a maniac, will fight anybody, anywhere, anytime." Gary explained.

"Don't believe that Mia, I'm a teddy-bear." A mischievous smile covered his face.

"I bet." I smiled back.

When we left the restaurant and began our walk back to Sam's place, Gary asked if I wanted to walk or catch a cab since we had walked quite a ways. As we discussed the distance, my cell phone rang, instead of answering his question I answered the phone and moved my fingers in the motion of walking. Gary grabbed my hand as we began our stroll.

"Hey, Dena! Yeah, I made it fine. I'm sorry I didn't call you… Oh. Well. Yeah. Okay. Okay. What's up?"

Gary and Sam continued to talk until a short stubby dirty guy approached us. I didn't hear everything the guy was saying because I was trying to listen to Dena and listen to their conversation at the same time. I was unsuccessful at their conversation because Dena really got my attention.

"Some lady at the gas station approached me and asked about you today. I couldn't figure out who the lady was but she was trying to act as if the two of you were good friends. I think she said her name was Jane, Janice, June, or something with a 'J'."

"Jane, June…" I tried to remember someone by that name. I couldn't remember anybody that I knew personally. However, I was a little startled by this because of the encounter from the luncheon earlier this week, I remember the lady said her name was June.

It was becoming difficult for me to hear because of Sam, the guy and Gary. So I tried to step away from them but Gary gently pulled me back. I pressed the Bluetooth closer to my ear and adjusted the volume to hear Dena continue. "Dena, speak up I can hardly hear you."

"This broad wanted to know where you lived, how often you do speaking engagements, what you like to do, your birthday, just a bunch of damn stuff, I didn't answer any of her questions. I was actually shocked that she asked me this stuff. Damn that's not the type of stuff you just hop out of your car and ask somebody at the doggone gas station. Just pissed me off. She got pretty upset, too, said I was being a 'stuck up bitch.' I started to flatten her ass right there." I could hear Dena shuffling through papers.

I was feeling nauseous. "So, how did you leave the conversation?" I asked, worried.

"I got in my car and left. I don't have time for that damn drama. I got other things to do, but not because I was afraid but because I didn't want to end up in jail since you and Gary are in New York and not able to bail me out quickly."

I chuckled at her last comment because I really knew that she has no shame going there when she needed to.

She said, "People will learn, one day. Speaking of learning, Gary's ex-girlfriend bumped into me yesterday at Startbuck's and I almost spilled my coffee. She tried to act as if it was an accident but I know it wasn't. She's hating, I know it. I got something for her though. You just watch. She'd better be glad I was in a hurry."

"Maybe it was an accident."

"Whatever. She almost got slapped to sleep. Monty called today begging me to let him back in. I told that punk to kick rocks. I got a man!" She changed the subject abruptly.

I laughed. "Dena, you are so crazy, and who is your man?"

"Remember Dwight from the range a few months ago?"

"Yeah," I said with excitement.

"We lost touch for a few but now he's back and we've been hanging just trying to see where it goes."

"That's good. I'm so happy for you." I cheered.

"Yeah, me, too, but anyway, girl, Monty tried to play the sob story about his heart and he can't breathe without me. I was like, well shouldn't you be dead? And isn't the purpose of the defibrillator to shock you when you stop breathing, when your heart stops? I told him to go back and get an upgrade because technology goes obsolete quickly, since he needs his shocking, he needs to check into that."

"Dena! You are so mean!" I whispered-loudly.

"I know, I try my best. I hear they are loving you lots up there."

"Yeah, they're great."

"Okay, well, have fun, Sissy. I'll see you in couple of days." She abruptly ended the conversation.

"Okay." I sighed.

"Everything is going to be fine, Mia. I promise." She could tell I was worried.

I sighed again before speaking. "I know."

"Okay, love you, bye." She hung up.

"Bye," I said to a dead line. That's my girl, but now I'm scared for her and me.

I noticed that the conversation between the guys had started off with pleasantries of long lost friends but it was turning into a slight altercation. Gary pushed me behind him. Sam forcefully stepped toward the man.

"Man, what the hell you gon' do with that toy ass gun?"

"I want some money," the man tried to explain. "I need some money."

"Well, motherfucka that's the wrong way to get it," Sam growled. He punched the man and knocked him to the ground, stomped one of his knees, on his hands, and was getting ready to kick him until Gary stopped him.

"Sam! Come on man. What are you doing? It's not worth it!"

Gary was trying to stop Sam, while at the same time trying to keep me behind him.

The man screamed in anguish as Sam stood there, twisted his foot on his hand as he called someone. He gave them our location and then said "Hurry up!"

I was in shock and trying to figure out what had just happened and who Sam was talking to like that. Turns out, it was a cop, his brother.

I stood there looking scared, confused and feeling mildly sorry for the guy. Before the cops got there, Sam was acting as if he was making sure he'd never use his hands again, until Gary grabbed him, pushed him away, and said, "Chill out, Son!"

Sam jerked away slightly. "I can't believe this mothaf—oohhh, trying to rob us with a freakin' water gun no less. Yahmean? Man, can you believe this shit? I oughtta blast his ass. Yahmean?"

"Dude! Keith will handle it! Chill the fu--, chill out man!"

Sam chilled but not before saying, "This is bullshit, Son!"

His brother arrived with his partner within a few minutes and put the man and his water gun in the back of the car. It took a short while to get statements from Gary and Sam, which gave Sam enough time to settle himself.

I heard Sam say, "This dude rolled up on us and asked G. for some money, saying he heard he was rich now, a big time NFL star. When Gary brushed him off, he got belligerent and shit. I thought he was drunk, he sure as hell smelled like it." He turned away and spat on the ground. "We were getting ready to walk away until this fool pulled his jacket back to show his lil' gun. I noticed the red plastic clip on the gun."

Gary interrupted Sam's story. "Sam would have done the same thing if the gun was real. He acts like that concealed weapon license in his pocket will keep a bullet from penetrateing him. A real bullet can take you out, man." He turned to Sam.

"Tell me about it. Sam, you do need to calm down, Son," his brother said.

Lord, what have I gotten myself into? I felt the vibration of my phone in my pocket. I pulled it out, tapped the screen a few times, and read the text message. "Hello, Mia, I'll be in town this wknd wud like to see u 2 rekndl sum old times. I really miss u."

A flash of heat rushed over my body. "Please, Lord, not now." I whispered as I quickly deleted the message and tried to erase the thought of that relationship that should have never happened.

After the incident was over, Gary put his arm around my shoulder and whispered, "I'm so sorry, Mia. This has been a wild trip. I promise you baby and trust me on this, you have nothing to worry about with me."

"No problem. I'm cool," I lied. I was flustered from his incident and flushed from mine. I was worried about my own situation that I had not told Gary about and apparently, he had a couple of things he needed to share with me. Past was soon to meet present for both of us.

Sam put his arm around my shoulder from the other side and said, "I'm sorry, Mia."

I looked up at him and smiled nervously but I knew he was only mimicking Gary. Gary playfully pushed his arm away.

We started our walk toward Sam's place in silence. I was in shock and really afraid to ask questions in fear that opening such a new wound would definitely cause turmoil. I certainly did not want to see those two rams lock horns. Sam was furious but trying to hide it. He started scrolling for a number in his cell phone. I was just ready to get back to Sam's place, Gary parents' or best of all, my place in Houston.

Gary kissed my cheek in an attempt to soften my mood and his. It was working as it always did. I sometimes wondered if my love for him clouded my judgment about things regarding him. I let it go and as usual, just enjoyed the moment.

I closed my eyes briefly and opened them when I felt Gary's arm clinch me tighter. I saw a big black Great Dane running toward us, barking. Looked like a barking pony. I ran behind Gary, back to the front of him and behind him again, and back to the front screaming hysterically, trying to leap into his arms. I was terrified. The owner of the dog had allowed too much slack in the leash, which resulted in the dog getting away from him. He caught the leash before the dog reached us. He had to wrap the leash around his arm quickly in order to snatch the dog back. He was apologizing profusely and saying "gentle giant, gentle giant." The dog was only being playful but I don't play with dogs, I'm too afraid.

Gary and Sam stared at the man with anger in their eyes. He held up his hand as if to beg, "Please don't hit me." He looked at me. "Ma'am, I am so sorry, so sorry! Are you okay?"

I nodded. "Yes."

The man backed away until he was out of arms reach and then turned to trot with his dog again.

"That damn gentle giant was gon' get a cap put in him," Sam yelled.

Gary pulled me into his arms, with my face buried in his chest, rubbing my head. "It's okay, it's okay, he's gone."

He pushed me back to look into my face. He smiled, "You auight?"

I was slightly embarrassed, with tears running down my face. "Yes." I nodded. I didn't know if it was the dog that had me hysterical or there was too much going on at the moment.

He pulled my head back into his chest. Hugged me. Rubbed my back, rested his chin on top of my head. "It's okay baby, its oh-kay."

Gary said, "Sam, it's cool. Let's just go."

"I'm cool." He kept messing with his phone.

Gary joked with Sam. "Were you scared, man?"

"Hell nah. I had something for his ass."

"Really? Out here on the streets in front of everybody? You had something for him? Man, these people would stone your ass for messing with a dog."

Sam shrugged his shoulders but didn't respond and started talking into his phone. "Yeah. Man, where you at, Son! Get me on Atlantic. How long? I need you to hurry up? Yahmean? In a minute." He ended the call and shoved the phone into his pocket. "I should have crushed that mothafucka too or better yet, just shot him," he mumbled.

"Sam!" Gary said firmly and then turned to me. "Mia, you see what I mean? This fool is crazy, I always have to try to keep a level head when I'm with him. When he goes off, it's on. This fool will have everybody in jail." Gary sounded frustrated.

Silence.

We had walked two blocks from the restaurant.

Sam said, "Man this is too much, I'm getting one of my drivers, Aspha, to come get us, Keith had already hit him up. Mia, I'm so sorry that I'm trying to give you a tour of my city that I'm so proud of and all of this bullshit keeps happening. I'm sorry." He moved his hands with every syllable.

He walked over to hug me. "Yahmean?" He patted Gary's shoulder. "I'm sorry, G-Matt, I should've given her a tour in one of the cars instead of walking but I wanted her to get the full experience."

Gary shook his head. "No problem, dude. You know I know how it goes around here but you do need to mellow out some."

"I know I do and I will."

We continued to walk until we arrived at a bench to sit. Gary pulled me onto his lap and put his arms around me. Rubbing me. Looking at me, tenderly. He was really good at public displays of affection and didn't care who saw it. I was still mortified from the dog and was definitely enjoying the attention. I leaned over, put my head on his shoulder. My phone vibrated in my pocket again. I knew it was from that past fling again. His name was Brock, S. Broderick Coleman. I knew that he would keep sending messages and calling until I answered. He was controlling that way. We were seeing each other casually a few years ago and one day he just vanished—no call, no text, no nothing. I didn't find it odd until after a few weeks had passed and I had tried three times to contact him with no response. I just deleted his number from my phone and moved on.

Sam said, "When we get home, I can't let you catch the train back, I'm taking you home."

"Cool."

I rested my head on Gary's shoulder. I felt my phone vibrate in my pocket, again. I couldn't wait to text back.

CHAPTER 21

&

GARY

The rest of the evening was uneventful. I woke up early the next morning, trying to get my thoughts together so I could tell Mia about me because as much as my family talked and all of the drama that had been poppin' off everywhere, I definitely needed to tell her before they did.

Mia stretched and yawned. I pulled Mia into my arms. "Good morning, Sunshine."

She groggily said, "Good morning, dude," as she fell over on the bed in an attempt to go back to sleep.

I turned the TV on, starting flipping channels to find ESPN. After several sports updates, the anchor started talking about President Barack Obama's athletic abilities, which I intently tuned into then to the New York Marathon.

Mia sat up and joined me with her back pressed against the black leather cherry wood trimmed headboard.

"Hmmmm."

I said, "Don't even think about it."

"Don't think about what?"

I didn't answer her and she didn't continue to question. We sat through that story and a few others. My mind was racing trying to think of a good introduction to tell her about my college nightmare with my cousin, my aunt and her messiness, my "kid" and just my life in general.

"Baby, we need to get moving, pretty quickly," I said to allow her time to get it together. She had experienced quite a bit of Brooklyn and I questioned whether it was worth it or not to tell her. I kind of felt like it was really nothing and it didn't matter if I told her at all. I decided to wait a little longer but I will be the one to tell her.

The phone rang in the room twice and then my cell phone rang.

"Shit, who is this?" I said as I reached for the phone. "Hey. I will. I said I am! Bye!"

My brother really liked Mia. He thought she was the perfect woman for me. I didn't see him talk to her that much; I guess he got his feeling from the excitement that he saw in me. Vance and Jessica said they had never seen this type of excitement in me about any woman that I had dated. He was bugging me to tell her everything from my perspective before things got turned around to a disaster as his did a few years ago. Although I didn't think my story could touch his and the amount of drama it caused. He did not tell his fiancé before the proposal that he had a thirteen month old and my aunt told her with special added effects. His fiancée then, wife now, was so mad at him for at least a month. She eventually got over it and forgave him for not telling her. He has not spoken to my aunt since. And since then, he has become quite the worrier about everything. I honestly didn't think that

THE BEST I HAVE TO OFFER

Mia would care one way or the other about my history but I know if my aunt told the story, it would have definitely been totally different from the way it actually happened. In a nutshell, it would have been a damn lie.

I flipped more channels and remained silent.

Mia was in the shower. My phone rang again. I looked at the caller ID. It was V. I didn't answer. I checked the voicemail as soon as I heard the chime. I noticed that I had three voicemail messages. One was from Lynne. "Hey, Gary, this is Lynne. I have a favor to ask of you. My daughter needs an escort to this ball that she's going to and I thought maybe you could do it since you're not married. I thought about asking T.J. but he's married and you two are the nicest men that I know that I would want to take her out. Call me and let me know." She paused. "ASAP." I looked at my phone in utter disbelief. I deleted the message with no intentions of calling her back. She had to be joking. I wanted to throw my phone against the wall but decided against that quickly. My destroyed phone would hurt her none. The second voicemail was from Nina with another one of her idle threats.

V. said, "Hey G-Man, when you come back, I need to see you. It's about Mia."

I called him back immediately, but didn't get much information because V. didn't want to give much over the phone. That pissed me off but he said something along the lines of a man and a woman came into his restaurant asking about Mia.

I sat stunned by all three messages. I quietly surfed more channels, just a motion, not paying attention to anything because I was mad as hell.

CHAPTER 22

∽

MIA

Gary went from resting and quietly watching TV to rushing to get back to Houston. I felt like I was in a sprint from the moment I put my foot on the floor. He said he was just ready to go home since he had been away for almost a week. We woke up, sat in bed for a few moments. I watched him flip channels, we showered separately, dressed. Sam picked us up, we headed to his parents, had lunch at a bistro in downtown Long Island and Sam insisted on taking us to the airport.

Our flight landed in Houston at six fifteen p.m. to overcast skies, with a beautiful sunset, darkness was imminent. The Houston humidity welcomed us with the beads of sweat around my hairline to prove it. Gary had checked his voicemail as soon as the flight landed. He mumbled something about Lynne being crazy. Now that, I already knew.

"Should we get something to eat while we're here?" I said as I was about to trip over his bag looking back at Pappadeaux.

"Nope."

"Why? I'm starving. I'm about to black out."

He looked at me confused. "Because tonight is date night, Mia. Remember? Talk Sweet? V.'s place?"

"Oh. I forgot."

He shook his head and chuckled. "Ginko Biloba or whatever it's called."

I swatted his arm with the back of my hand as he ushered me onto the moving walkway. We maneuvered around all of the focused business travelers, returning vacationers, and construction while idly chatting, trying to keep the conversation light, non-threatening, non-probing. He was acting very distant on the plane. He held my hand but drifted off to sleep a couple of times, his mind preoccupied. Our conversation had been brief. I said, "I got your back, baby." He said, "where'd that come from?" I said, "whatever is bothering you." He leaned over and kissed me and said, "Thank you, baby. But there's nothing bothering me. I'm just chillin'." So, I just listened to my iPod, gazed out the window, and thought about my parents as I sometimes did while in flight, there was something about the clouds that caused that.

Gary was the perfect gentleman as always, guiding me onto the elevator first and the escalator. In the baggage area, he pulled the bags from the carousel as I watched and cooperated with every move.

We arrived at our vehicle only twenty minutes after getting off the plane. I asked, "Is that limo tint on your windows?"

"Close," he said as he put the luggage in the truck.

"Is it against the law? Is it on the front too? It looks lighter," I continued to quiz.

"Nah, the dealer did it. It better not be against the law." He opened my door, I got in and he closed the door.

As he walked around the truck to get in, I rambled through my purse quickly. Gary got in and cranked the truck, turned on the air, plugged his cell phone into the adapter and flipped the radio to the old school station. There was a gas commercial on, so he pressed the CD button. "I Choose You" by Willie Hutch started to play. He hummed and sang every other word to the song. *Perfect timing.* He placed his hand on the gearshift and I placed my hand on top of his.

"Wait a minute, honey," I said as I looked around for people coming to the adjacent vehicles. None.

He looked at me quizzically. "What's up? What's wrong?" He started looking around also.

I pressed the "Repeat" button, smiled a naughty smile, got up on my knees, and leaned in to kiss him as I rubbed his crotch. He was speechless. He just moaned. I had never done anything like it before so I was sure he was a bit taken aback. I unbuckled his belt and fumbled with his zipper. I pulled out the sanitizing wipe that I had already opened as I continued to kiss him and sucked his tongue. He gave in, I could tell because he had an erection. I pulled it out and wiped up and down the shaft, simultaneously pulled out the chocolate runner's gel that I had in my purse and followed the same pattern all the while still kissing him. I actually amazed myself sometimes.

I whispered, "I've wanted you since we left the hotel this morning."

"Really, why didn—" He became speechless again as I took him in my mouth and used my hand to make gentle circular motions. He rubbed the back of my head and moaned, he called my name. I brought him to a near climactic state.

I rose up. "I love chocolate."

I continued to stroke him. I raised my dress and moved over to straddle him. My left leg was stretched toward the passenger seat and my right leg was wedged between the door and his leg, resting on the seat. He was tall so the seat was already in a reclined position. I got instantly wet from his touch so no problem there. He had asked earlier why I chose the halter dress to fly in, I just simply said, "I have a jacket, plus you got me covered if I get cold." I had planned for such a time as this. I wore the strapless dress for easy access to my breasts and although the dress reached my ankles when I stood, it was easy access from that end too. I moved up and down on top of him, very slowly. He held my hips and assisted in my movements. We kissed. He pulled the top of my dress down, took my breasts in his mouth, and nibbled from one to the other. I moaned and let out loud noises of pleasure as my body tingled all over. Even with the air on, sweat beaded on our foreheads, on my chest, on our stomachs. We were hot. We came in unison. I lingered on top of him until the explosion in my body subsided.

I kissed his face, whispered in his ear, "You should really try to resist me."

I carefully dismounted him and winked at him. He stayed in his position, wiped his forehead with the back of his hand, and leaned his head back on the seat. "Damn!"

I pulled out a wet towel from my plastic bag, wiped myself, folded the towel and wiped him. He sat there and watched as I continued to pull out wipes and other sanitary items to clean us. I offered him a wipe for his mouth, his hands. I used the bottled water that I purchased at the airport to rinse my mouth. I squirted water in my mouth, swished it around, opened the door spit it out, did that twice, did the same thing with the hotel mouthwash, opened the door again, spit it out.

The song "I Choose You" was beginning its fifth repeat.

He said, "Damn! Are you prepared or what?" as he watched me apply lip-gloss and blot my face with my powder puff.

I popped my lips, blew him a kiss. "Yep, preparation meets opportunity." I zipped my bag and threw it in the back seat. I flipped the mirror closed. Leaned over, kissed him again, "Okay, I'm ready. Are we going to Talk Sweet? Well, let's roll."

He nodded his head, and then mumbled, "Your ass ain't goin' no-where." He continued to look at me with pure admiration and a little bit of surprise.

"And you ain't either."

My cell phone alerted me that I had a new text message. I pulled out my phone. *Mia, where are u? Y haven't u responded to any of my msgs? Did I just see u in the airport? Call me.*

I squirmed in my seat, leaned my head back, and looked out the window.

CHAPTER 23

❧

GARY

It took us over an hour to get to the restaurant because there was an accident on 610. I was still determined to have a good time with Mia because I felt like she deserved it. Mia was as good as it gets. A genuine, intelligent, independent, caring, loyal, respectful, fun, down-to-earth woman. Lynne was up to something that she had all of sudden felt the need to turn up the heat on. She left another message while we were in flight that I did not tell Mia about: "Gary, this is Lynne. I think you need to watch Mia. I saw her laughing and flirting with that trainer guy that comes to the office sometimes. I forgot to tell you about that when I left you a message earlier and she was rude to me the other day. Call me, bye." Again, I was in disbelief. I did not have time for drama.

I hoped I had enough energy to eat and socialize. After Mia's surprise, I was spent. I used to come to Talk Sweet alone before I met Mia. I had also been there a time or two with a couple of dates. My favorite table when I was alone was in the corner near the bar facing the street so I could watch the weather, the people, the traffic or just to think. After I started bringing Mia on a regular basis, V. moved us to a more private booth closer to the back with high-backed, dark fabric, cushioned seats. He said the booth had a better feel for a couple and I agreed. Every time we walked in, he'd hold both of Mia's hands, look her up and down, he'd hug her lightly and place his cheek against her cheek and kiss the air and say "Hello, beautiful." We'd do the one arm, slap on the back hug and he'd whisper to me, "This is the one, I can tell." Mia always heard him, which I think was his intent. I would always smile and say, "Man, you are out of control." We started going to Talk Sweet after dating for a couple of months. We shared a lot, talked for hours, trying to get to know each other.

Our usual server, Miranda came over to the table to get our drink orders. "How are my two favorite customers today?"

"Good." Mia and I chimed one after the other.

"Great, what can I get for you? The usual?"

"Ah, yeah, that would be great." I concurred.

She left to get our drinks and Mia looked down at the menu, gently biting the corner of her lower lip. I couldn't help but stare at her. I had told her that I loved her before she ever told me. That was quite a shocker. *Is it time for me to settle down?* I beamed inside. She was an adorable, beautiful, and extraordinary woman, imperfections and all.

Miranda returned with our drinks and looked at Mia, "Do you like chocolate?" as she sat the drinks down.

Mia glanced and me and I at her. "Yes, absolutely, why?" She wore a smile.

"We have this new dessert that I want you to try."

"Okay!" Mia agreed.

"We're celebrating her birthday tonight so put a candle on top of whatever it is," I requested.

When she walked away, Mia and I started grinning like two horny teenagers. Mia covered her face with the menu.

V. had walked over. "It looks like you two are having a good time."

"We are, we really are," I said.

"Mia, you'll really like that new dessert."

"Thank you. I can't wait to try it." Mia smiled.

"And Happy Birthday, I'll have to get you something."

"Ahh thank you, Mr. V.," she sang, "but you don't have to do that."

"Yes, I do. Any woman that my son loves is a daughter to me."

Mia looked confused but smiled again and said, "Thank You, Mr. V."

"Who said I love her?" I joked.

Mia slapped my hand, "I know you do, you just told me," she teased, "He loves me Mr. V."

"I know he does." V. cosigned.

We chatted for a few minutes about our trip. Mia had so many questions she wanted to ask. She didn't say it, I could tell by the look in her eyes. She was organizing her thoughts and would execute as soon as she felt the time was right.

"Mia, can I borrow G-Matt for a minute?" V. rested his hand on my shoulder.

"Sure, I don't mind at all." She took a sip of her wine.

Miranda sat down to replace me almost before I got up, just to chat it up with Mia. She darn near sat in my lap. I pretended to stumble out of her way as I followed V. back to his office. They laughed.

"Sit down, son," he said in a serious voice.

I sat slumped in the chair with my arm resting over the back but sat up straight as I remembered V. never allowed slouching when you're not in a recliner in front of the TV or intentionally relaxing. He used to preach to us, "Young man, during a conversation, you need to sit up straight and look the person that you're conversing with directly in the eye. Nobody will listen to a slumped down man with no confidence." Truth was I was full of confidence but my energy level was not that high at that moment and slouching was comfortable but I understood where I was, so I sat up straight.

"What's up, V.? I stopped by tonight because of the voicemail that you left."

I couldn't read him. So, I was anxious for him to just tell me what was going on.

"Son, I'm concerned about Mia." He was sitting back calmly in his seat with an inquiring facial expression as if he was trying to read me. He leaned forward, bounced his pen on the desk and sighed. "There was a man and a woman that came in here on Thursday looking for her, asking a lot of questions about both of you. I pretended not to know that much about either of you. They even started asking my wait staff and different customers until I asked them to leave. They've been watching because they knew that the two of you come in here often. I thought maybe they'd come back but they didn't. "

I sat up attentively and leaned forward in my chair. "What? When? What did they say? What did they look like?"

"I didn't recognize them. The lady claimed that she wanted Mia to do a workshop at her company. I asked how she knew to look for Mia here. She never answered that. She left a bogus card, after I asked for it, for Mia. I had Emma to dial the number to check it out. It was disconnected. G-Matt, I've seen mess like this in my day, and I think Mia is being stalked. Maybe you, too." He waited on me to contemplate what he had just said.

"Did you get their names? Where's the card?" My elbows rested on the desk. I wiped my hand down my face and squeezed my temples.

"Yes, like I said, but I believe they're bogus." His voice strained as he slid the cards across the desk. "I've already made some phone calls. I have a couple of friends, in the surveillance and other businesses for when I need something handled. They're already checking on some things for me."

"For what? V., what are you not telling me?" I could only imagine where he was going with that comment.

He changed the subject. "Dena was in here yesterday. I started to tell her because that guy that she used to date, Monty, I saw him talking to them in the parking lot, but I didn't want to frighten her. He came in, ordered to go, and left."

We sat in silence, looked at each other.

"What should I get her for her birthday? What does she like?"

"Who, Mia?"

He nodded slowly.

I rubbed my face. "Books." I was confused because he kept changing the subject like someone in the back had a remote control aimed at his mouth.

"Son, let me ask you something, have you told Mia that I am your biological father?"

I looked at my hands. "No, not yet. What does that have to do with this?"

He didn't speak he just stared past me, coldly. I felt like crap. So I kept talking. I felt the need to justify. "I plan to tell her soon,

I just haven't taken the opportunity. The time hasn't been right. I haven't told her any of my history. It almost came out while we were in New York. I'll get to it."

He stood. I stood. We walked toward the door. I think he was pissed but I wasn't sure and I didn't care, really. He was the one that led me on for years, now I had to be rushed into confession when I was barely getting over the anger myself.

I didn't want to frighten Mia with the news that V. had somewhat shared with me. He had his buddies on the case and didn't want me involved but I needed to figure some things out, make some decisions on my own.

I walked casually back to the table to keep from appearing too anxious. Mia had ordered for me. I sat down grabbed a fork, blessed and started eating my food. I know Mia was dying to hear what V. wanted, so I shoved pasta in my mouth, one fork full after the other to keep from talking as it gave me time to think but eventually I spoke. "Mia, do you love me?"

"Of course I do."

"Yeah, I love you, too."

The entire wait staff at the restaurant interrupted us and V. came to our table with a chocolate cake, not a slice, but the whole cake. They sang *"Happy Birthday."* Miranda chimed in, "We put one candle because we didn't know your age so we'll let you choose, twenty-one, thirty-one, or your first birthday with Gary!"

"Thank you all so much." She stood to hug all of them and she leaned in to kiss me before she returned to her seat. "Thank you, baby."

The staff returned to their previous posts to continue their duties.

"My pleasure, Mia," I said as I slid another box across the table to her.

"Oh my, goodness, Gary another gift," she chimed like a little girl and clapped her hands together. She opened the gift and her eyes widened.

"Here, let me help you put it on."

I assisted her with the bracelet, made sure the security clap was closed. I definitely didn't want her losing it with all of the moving and shaking that she does.

"Gary, oh my, I can't, I just, I don't know what to say." She got up from her seat, and sat beside me. She leaned in to hug me. "You're the greatest man ever. You know that, right?"

"I try. Look, I told you that I love you, you're the perfect person for me. It's your birthday, and I want to make it the best month long birthday you've had, in a while anyway. This is how I do things, sweetheart, not a show. This is it."

She was snuggled against my arm, I could feel her heartbeat racing. She sat there for a while as I continued eating, then she moved back to her seat.

After we finished eating dessert, Miranda came to box the remaining portion for us to take home. I started the conversation again. "Yeah, as I was saying earlier, I love you too, so much, and I want to spend a lifetime with you. I know that there are some things that we need to work out before we get married but I really think that we need to revisit our living arrangements sooner than when we'll get married."

Mia and I had had this conversation before. I had shared with her that I need to see how we mix under the same roof. She wanted to talk about it and pray that we would mix well under the same roof after we were married. To me, her view is tainted because we spend most of our time together and we've already had sex so many times, we can't begin to count. When I said that to her, she'd retort and chuckle, "I told you if it wasn't for fornication, I'd be darn near perfect. I pray about that all the time, though. I'm gonna cut you off one day. Just you watch." She has such a tainted view. Cute. But still tainted.

"Mia, we will get married, that's if you want to but I think we should live together sooner than later."

She dropped her shoulders. Mist formed in her eyes. She looked afraid. "Why do we have to go there, Gary? We are having a great time. What did Mr. V. say to you?"

"Mia, what do you mean, why do I have to go there? You act as if this is some type of conspiracy. I've been trying to talk to you about this since the beginning of our relationship and you never want to talk about it," I tried to whisper but I was too excited and it came out a little louder than I intended.

She looked at me, confused. She put her fork down. "Why are you yelling at me? Is that why I got all of these gifts?" Her tone was inquisitive. She sat back and folded her arms. "Okay Gary, let's talk. You first, what do you need to tell me about your past that you keep avoiding?" She tossed her napkin on the table. If I'm not mistaken, I think she had a little neck working going on with every word. "Don't start with me when you have a bunch of shit you need to tell me."

My eyes widened. Damn, now she had to go there. I shifted in my seat, narrowed my eyes at her. "Mia," I paused. I looked down at the table, wiped my hands down my face and looked at her, trying to maintain control because I was not pissed at her. I was scared for her and wanted to protect her. From what? I didn't know. I saw V. in my peripheral view, which certainly helped me to keep my emotions in check more than ever. I was pissed at the fact that someone was potentially trying to stalk her. I didn't want to push her into a corner by appearing too protective. But the way I approached it, who could blame her? I should have approached this conversation totally different. I continued, "I told you that I would tell you," I paused again, "Okay, okay, Mia, I'm sorry, I'm sorry." I held up both hands to surrender. "Look, let's start over."

"Yeah, let's." She showed a slight temperature change but she was still irritated. "I'm sorry for being so snippy. Baby, I know we can be unstoppable together. I can see us making things happen. I dream about it all the time but living under the same roof without being married, I just don't …"

I reached for her hands to soften the mood. I rubbed the back of her hands with my thumbs. I got up, moved to her side of the booth, put my arm around her shoulder, hugged her, and pressed my head against hers.

"I got you, baby. I promise. I promise," I whispered in her ear. I kissed her hair.

She remained silent. I could tell her mind was racing.

I tried a different angle to keep the conversation going. "Okay, baby, have you talked with Dena?"

"Yes, why?" She sounded concerned.

"When?"

"When we were in Brooklyn and Sam was beating that guy down."

"Oh."

I sat in silence, waiting on her to tell me more. I knew there was something else to tell but I knew she would not offer any more because she felt that I wasn't offering enough information. This was quid pro quo for her. I didn't want to interrogate her in public; we had a lot to share so I suggested we go home.

I waved for the waiter, tried to pay the check. V. had taken care of it.

"Let's go, baby."

"V., hey, thanks, I'll call you later man. Take care."

I hugged V. as we prepared to leave.

"All right, G-Matt, let me know what's up with that situation we talked about," he whispered in my ear. He let go and reached to hug Mia, kissed her on the cheek and winked at me, ensuring she noticed. "Miss Mia, you take care of yourself okay? Keep this man out of trouble," he tried to joke. I don't think he told me everything because I was with Mia. I couldn't wait to get home and distract Mia so that I could call him to get the rest of the story.

As we were walking out the door, Ms. Emma was walking in with gift bag for Mia. "Hi Mia." She beamed with joy. "Happy Birthday, honey!"

"Thank you. How'd you know?"

"Don't worry about it. Just open it." She handed the bag to Mia and clapped quietly.

Mia pulled out the contents of the bag to find two fifty dollar gift cards from Barnes & Noble. "Oh my God, my favorite." She squeezed Ms. Emma. "Thank you."

V. and I just watched the two of them.

"Man is her love language gifts or what?" I joked with V.

He chuckled.

"Yes." Mia fanned her hand at me.

"And so what?" Ms. Emma said chastising. "She deserves everything she gets as a gift."

Ms. Emma treated Mia like a daughter and Mia certainly loved her like a mother. Although we knew no one could take the place of her mother, she turns into a little girl when she talked about her parents. Mia was appreciative and grateful and that's what I loved about her, the small things made her happy, and the fact that she could turn her mood on a dime. One minute we were pissed but in the presence of others, we showed the love that we have for each other and not the feelings from the disagreement that were having at that moment.

We rode to my house in total silence after making some abrupt moves to leave the restaurant. I knew danger was not far away, and I was going to do everything in my power to stop it.

The occasional chime on Mia's phone, indicating a new text message was the only sound I heard. She replied to several with a frown on her face.

CHAPTER 24

⤠

MIA

I sat there tapping the screen on my phone, thinking. "*Is Sylvester back and stalking us? Dena told me that she thought Sylvester was back. I am a little afraid of what appears to be happening. Brock is back. Is he the stalker?*

We didn't say much on the way to Gary's house. So, to take my mind off our issue, I replied to a couple of text messages. One was from Brock. I made a mistake responding to him because he kept replying. He had sent eight messages over the past couple of days. I was getting irritated and the longer Gary and I were silent, the more upset I became with him. He and Mr. V. were acting really strange. He pulled into the garage, got out and came around to open my door. As we walked into the house, his phone rang, he answered and walked into another room. I didn't like it because I couldn't figure out what they were up to. I had enough going on without them adding to it and when there was silence, I conjured up my own drama-filled story in my mind. My cell phone chimed again. I read the text: *Mia I really want to see u.* I deleted the message and dropped the phone into my purse. I sat quietly and waited on Gary. He walked back into the room, his phone already in the holster.

"Gary, I need to talk to you."

We sat in the kitchen at the bar, side by side. He rested his elbows on the counter and listened.

"Talk to me, Mia. I'm all ears," he said.

"Remember the luncheon that delayed my trip to New York?"
He nodded. "Yes."

"Well, during the luncheon the usher handed me this note that was hardly legible from someone." I handed him the note.

He looked at it, frowned, and read aloud, "Hi Miyah, I REELLY enjoyed your speach! Can we talk sometimes? I REELLY need talk to you." He looked back at me and mumbled, "Horrible spelling."

I continued. "No name, no number, so I waved to the usher and asked who sent the note. Of course he didn't know. After the luncheon several people approached me, some asking about my story, some saying thank you, some enjoyed the presentation and others needing advice. You know the normal stuff that I go through after a presentation. I did notice a lady standing back, watching and waiting until the crowd cleared. As I was gathering my bags, she approached me. I extended my hand to introduce myself. She extended hers. It was a very weak handshake. She mumbled her name, *June,* and dropped her head. She didn't say much. Her eyes were darting back and forth; she wouldn't look into my eyes. She was fidgeting. I was a little scared to be honest, but I kept it professional, you know, kind of friendly. She said she wanted to talk to me about her situation. I tried to get some more information from her about it, but I couldn't really. What

I did get was—she said she wished she was like me, she wished that she had what I have, the ability to speak like me. You know, something similar to this happened to me before but this one was a little different. Usually it feels more positive because it's coming from a younger girl with drive and ambition. This was somewhat weird. This woman didn't look even remotely qualified to speak in front of a crowd, but I guess looks can be deceiving but that handshake scared me. Clammy." I shuddered.

I paused. He held my hands. I continued, "When Dena called me, she told me about some lady that approached her at the gas station, asking a lot of questions about me. She wanted to know things like, where I lived, what I enjoyed doing, my birthday etc."

"What?" He rested his head in his hands, exhaled. "Why didn't you tell me this sooner? Who was the lady at the luncheon? Did your description match Dena's?" He got up, walked into the pantry, and pulled out two bottles of water.

I started rambling. "I don't know who she is, Gary. So much was going on since I arrived in New York, I decided to wait. I was trying to tell you, but you didn't listen when we were in the back of the limo with Sam and I haven't spoken to Dena since we got back. I…"

"What?" His head spun around as if it wasn't attached to his body. "What do you mean I wouldn't listen? Mia, you make me listen to something like this! I can't believe you haven't— I'm calling Dena." He pulled out his phone, his large fingers glided across the buttons. "You've had plenty of time to tell me since then. You just didn't want to."

I was irritated and he was really getting on my nerves yelling at me.

"Dena. What's up? You busy? Hey, I need to talk to you."

He put the phone on speaker.

"About what? Where's, Mia? Are y'all back?"

"About Mia, she's right here. Yes, we're back.

"Hey Dena," I chimed with more of a grimace on my face than a smile because I was being interrogated. I needed some moral support.

"Hey, Sissy. Gary, why are you sounding so serious?"

"Because, Mia just told me about your gas station confrontation and I need to figure out what's going on. Who was this lady?"

"I have no clue, who she was. She just popped up and started asking questions while I was pumping my gas. She asked a lot of questions about Mia and got mad when I didn't give her any information. Ain't nobody worried about those haters." She tsked.

He sighed heavily and looked toward the ceiling. "What's going on with you? Any more notes?"

"No, I used to think it was Sylvester but now I think its Monty's dumb ass."

"What makes you think it's him?"

"Because, Idunknow, I just know." She sounded nervous or preoccupied.

"Nah, I don't think it's him," he said matter-of-factly. "Who is Sylvester? Is this the dude from Chicago?"

Silence. I looked down at my hands.

Dena sighed. "Why don't you think it's Monty?" She sounded defensive. "Sylvester is an old friend."

"You care to explain who this old friend is?"

"I'll be there in a sec."

"Okay."

He placed the phone on the counter, opened the bottle of water, and drank the entire contents. He put the bottle in the trash, folded his arms, and leaned against the counter. He stared at me, not in anger or irritation but with concern and love. He walked over, wrapped his arms around me, and exhaled deeply. He rested his chin on my head then pressed his cheek against mine. I closed my eyes and wrapped my arms around his, I was scared.

He whispered in my ear, "Don't worry, I got you."

CHAPTER 25

✄

GARY

D ena walked in dressed as if she had just stepped out of a boutique ad.

"You look nice," Mia and I said in unison.

"Thank you both," she said as she rambled through her purse. "Look I only have a few minutes, I'm meeting Dwight at ten."

"Damn, who is Dwight?"

"A new friend." She pulled out a flavored cigar.

Mia shook her head and handed her a glass of Shiraz.

"Let's go out here." I ushered her and Mia out to the patio. I did not allow smoking in my house.

She sat in the low-back contemporary-styled Italian leather chair that I had just sat outside for conditioning in preparation for a major brainstorming session with myself. Cigar in hand, she lit it, twirled it around the flame until she got the desired amount of smoke. Mia and I watched and waited on her to start talking.

"Ready when you are Dena," I urged.

Right leg crossed—never inhaling, blowing circles into the air, her four-inch black patent-leather stiletto rhythmically swinging from her foot.

"Gary, believe or not, I have secrets. I had planned to go to my grave with this one but—anyway, here goes, I will be brief—this happened in Chicago. Sylvester, a guy I used to date, mess with, play with, yada, yada and his wife were laid out. Gone. His wife was sprawled out on the chaise-lounge and he went down after the gun went off." She paused. "Hit his head on the wall." She looked down and then stared straight ahead.

"He should have known, I am not to be messed with. I told him that, numerous times. I told him that I learned how to shoot—I'm licensed to carry—self-defense— you name it, and he still tried me! You know, I've been told that I'm just like my grandmother. Do you remember her? I'm telling you, people will learn—one—day. I mean I feel like I'm following in her footsteps. She didn't take crap from no one, especially my mother when she tried to drop me off at a fire station. She beat my mother down about that. I guess I was a little unruly back then and my grandmother was the only one that could handle me."

"Dena!" I said in a stern voice to get her back on track.

She sat up straight, tapped the cigar in the ashtray, staring at it, she crushed it, picked up the wine glass that Mia handed her when she walked in, and took a slow sip, allowed the taste to linger on her palette for a moment. She swallowed, leaned back again, took a deep breath, exhaled through her nose, and stared at the ceiling. Mia sat perched on a bar stool, her back erectly postured. I leaned against the bar, arms folded, listening cautiously. I'm sure all of the feelings and memories of that evening were crowding her mind. She fidgeted in her chair.

"That was it."

"Dena, that's it? I said incredulously.

"Yep. I messed with a married man. I didn't know he was married until that day. His wife was abusive to him. I could tell because they argued about it while I was there. I knew he was involved in some shady stuff in some form or another but, I didn't ask about it. I knew he wasn't making the amount of money to fit the lifestyle that he was portraying. I was just enjoying the ride, literally." She let out a soft giggle. "He and his wife had some illegal activity jumping off. He volunteered some information. I didn't intend for it to go down like that but it did. You know, I never heard anything about them again, absolutely nothing about the story. I guess because they covered it locally and I left immediately—went back to Dallas. But I'm past that now. I'm sure they're fine or they could be dead. That was years ago when I first moved to Dallas. I dabbled with that for a short time against my better judgment and will, suffered minor consequences and scars, and moved on. Dealing with him was hazardous for my health."

"What kind of dealings did he have Dena? What information did he volunteer? You act like this whole thing was just nothing, a fluke." I gestured. I really didn't like her casual attitude.

"Well. It was really. No big deal." She shrugged her shoulders and looked at her watch. "I have to go. Mia, can fill you in on the rest." She stood up, looked down, smoothed out the wrinkles in her black pencil skirt, picked up her black purse, and started her casual and slow stroll toward the door as Mia and I followed, she stopped, and turned around, "You know what? I'm never smoking again."

"Good," Mia said in chastising tone.

This woman is crazy. I thought.

She hugged Mia, gave her signature wink and left.

I looked at Mia in a bit of surprise. I still had a lot of questions.

Dena left and we walked back to the kitchen, I paced the floor, mind racing, Mia turned her chair around looked at me. She dropped her head, sadness and fear flooded her eyes.

"Honey, I have more to tell you. I know it's not my story to tell but she gave me the permission to tell it now."

I sat down on the barstool next to her, preparing to listen.

It was amazing that I told her I loved her and then all hell broke loose. Lynne was attempting to wreck our relationship but I'm not even close to entertaining her nonsense and Nina was a freakin' loose cannon that bounces in and out at will and now Mia and Dena have a history of this Chicago escapade.

"A few years ago, Dena was messing around with this guy, Sylvester. I think they met at work. They hit it off pretty good, started playing around, trips together, secret escapades and everything. I knew she wasn't serious about anything long term. I thought maybe it was because of the long distance. She went to Chicago to visit him. One night at dinner as she was making the plans to go, she offered a few details to Mario and me." She rubbed her hand across the counter as she spoke.

"Who is Mario?"

"Mario is a mutual friend that was into her. He was a cop. He told me that he was concerned about Dena dealing with this guy because he looked familiar and he thought he was a scam artist or something. Mario had met him one day when he saw them at lunch. Dena, Mario, and I were all friends so we talked about our relationships a lot." She paused for a moment as if she was trying to make sure I was keeping up with the story. "As I said, Dena had told us about this trip while we were at dinner one night. Mario asked his private investigator friend, Dottie, to follow Dena to Chicago. Dena didn't know it but I did, Mario didn't want Dena to be mad at him. So, his friend followed Dena to Chicago and I tagged along, same flight, but I did this without any of them knowing." She smirked. "Mario, gave me all of Dottie's flight information, not knowing I would use it."

I narrowed my eyes but didn't speak. So, I see she had a bag of tricks too.

"Dena and I always give each other details of flight and travel arrangements so that someone will know our whereabouts. Anyway, I arrived at the hotel where they were staying, checked in, and asked for a room on the third floor as Dena had told me on a voicemail."

"So, Dena did know you were coming? Oh, never mind. She left the message because she was just giving you an FYI of where she was." I folded my arms. "Keep going."

"Okay, so anyway, we try not to go above the fourth floor in a hotel. I heard that the firefighter's ladder couldn't go higher than the fourth floor of a hotel. Don't know if that's true but I believe it. So anyway, I digress." She fanned her hand in the air. "When I got off the elevator on my floor, I heard yelling coming from the end of the hall. Apparently, Dena and Sylvester were on a rendezvous and Ari, Sylvester's wife, showed up and confronted them. Lucky for me, I saw Dottie slip into the room and I rushed down the hall toward the room and used the same method she did to get in."

"What method did she use?"

"It was simple actually; she stuck her foot in the door before it shut completely. So when I saw her entering the room, I was luckily close enough to run and catch it before it closed."

"Hmmph, so, how did you get there just in time? And why didn't somebody call security or at least report a loud noise?" I adjusted myself in my seat.

She hunched her shoulders. "I don't know, they just didn't. I guess no one heard it since the yelling was brief. Dena said it happened so fast."

"Oh." I nodded as my mind was racing with so many questions. She paused to give me time to process the information. It sounded like a soap opera. "Go ahead. Finish." I motioned my hand for her to keep going.

"When I got into the room, Dena was shocked but glad to see me and as she said, they were sprawled out on the floor. She was face down on the chaise-lounge and all I could see of him were his feet."

"So you've never seen this Sylvester?"

"Nope. I've never seen him." She shook her head. "It wasn't a serious relationship. So really, there wasn't a need for me to meet him. Anyway, we got out of the room quickly. We helped her gather her things amid all of the roses and fruit and other crap. My room was on the opposite end of the floor. We hid out until three in the morning with Dottie constantly checking things, leaving the room double-checking again. I think Dottie was mad at me."

"What things? Checking what things?" I tapped my phone on the countertop.

"Flights, transportation, making sure no cops were there and that they were still in the room, I guess." She rubbed both her hands down her face.

"Oh."

"It was really scary. Dena was scared for me but mad at the same time because I followed her. She understood, though. She said she'd never forgive herself if something happened to me. She was distraught beyond words. We finally got an okay from Dottie and went to an airport on the other side of town. Not the airport that we flew into. "We flew into Midway and left out of—"

"O'Hare," I interrupted.

"Yes, O'Hare. That trip cost us a grip but I wanted to help my friend. So I did."

"Wait a minute, back up, what happened that caused them to be sprawled out on the floor?"

"Ari, walked in and started acting crazy. She was abusive to him, a raging out-of-control mad wife, that's why he said he cheated. She wanted to keep him, said she was sorry for being so crazy and abusive. She was trying to get them to have sex while she watched because apparently Sylvester had been secretly recording him and Dena so that he and Ari could watch it, so that she could learn from it."

"What!" I said in amazement.

"He was her first. Yes, I know it's bizarre but that's the story that he told her. So anyway, Ari had a knife, she was threatening to cut them so he sweet-talked himself close enough to her to get the knife and snap her neck, supposedly, and put her on the chaise-lounge. He then tried the same tactics with Dena and got shot in the shoulder, hit his head. Dena was scared to death because she thought he was dead and when she tells the story, she will tell you that they were dead. I, nor Dottie, thought they were especially from a shot in the shoulder. Dena decided that night, she was done with him, and hasn't heard from him since. This is the short version I'm telling you. That whole trip could have ruined my life. Thank God it didn't."

"My, gosh, this is wild. I don't know if I want to hear the long version." I was truly astonished by the entire story and quite frankly at a loss for words, but still had many questions rumbling in my mind that I couldn't quite formulate. "So nobody heard the gun shot?"

"Silencer. Suppressor."

"Wow."

"I know it sounds like the movies but this is how it went down," she explained, "I just hope this guy is not back here and trying to cause problems."

"Okay back to this lady that stepped to you at the luncheon. Describe her, please."

"She was shorter than me, hundred sixty pounds maybe, dark, kinky twist and a dead tooth in the front." She demonstrated the size with her hands. "So, what did V. tell you tonight?" She changed the subject abruptly.

"We'll talk about it later." I didn't want to answer her question. After she told the story and described the secret-admirer lady, she seemed exhausted and I wanted her to relax, especially after I alarmed her with my outburst earlier. I affectionately grabbed her hands. "Come on, you need to relax for a few minutes. Let me run you a bath." I wanted to distract her until I figured out what I should do next. I did not want to add to her fear so I didn't tell her but I had an idea about who the lady was that was asking about her but I needed to make sure before I made any accusations. But for Dena's case, I needed to know more about this Sylvester character from Chicago.

"Gary, you're being too quiet. You're scaring me, abruptly stopping the conversation," she mumbled as we walked through the living room.

I stopped slowly, turned to her, gave her a gentle hug, held her face in my hands, and looked into her eyes. "Oh, baby, I'm sorry. I don't mean to frighten you. I just need to think for minute." I kissed her forehead, held her. I figured she would toughen up and get ready for battle but instead it was quite the opposite, she started to cry as I held her. "Oh, Mia, please don't cry, honey. We're going to figure this out. Okay? I will tell you everything. I just need you to relax for a minute. Okay?"

"I know. I'm sorry for being a wimp especially after all the crazy stuff I've done with Dena but I'm getting scared. I don't know who this lady is just walking up to me, I mean what if she tries to hurt me, you know, catch me off guard." She wiped her tears. "I know Sylvester is probably stalking us. He probably has this lady doing what she's doing, somebody snapping pictures, and leaving notes everywhere. Everything is getting out of control."

"Hey, hey, hey, come on now, Mia." I raised her chin so that I could look in her eyes again. I wiped her tears.

She blinked and another tear fell. She sniffed. I had planned to tell her all about my past but we'd had enough for one day.

"Mia, you're not supposed to have the control, God does and I promise you this, with his help I will definitely do all I can to protect you from whoever and whatever. I promise you that, Mia. You will have my best in everything, that's what I'm offering you. Just let me handle it, baby." I hugged her again. "I just want you to relax for a few minutes and we will figure this out."

"Gary, what if our best is not good enough?"

"Mia, stop." I intertwined my fingers with hers and walked toward my bedroom. She sat on the bed, stared at her hands, and continued to cry. It really hurt me to see her cry.

I turned the water on to start her bath as I thought, *she has drama, I have drama, what if she's right? What if our best is not good enough?* I sprinkled Vaseline crystals for softness, rose petals, lit the candles, got towels ready, called her name and she walked in slowly. I undressed her and assisted her as she got into the tub.

I got on my knees beside the tub. "Mia, I will protect you. I promise. We will figure this out. I want you to relax. Please. I'm going to get our luggage out of the truck and I'll be back."

I left the room but not before I slightly increased the volume on the iPod in an attempt to mask my phone conversations that I was getting ready to have.

Mia's eyes were swollen from the continuous flow of tears. I'm sure she was crying for two reasons. In my efforts to protect her, I screwed up by being too aggressive and she had a fear of the unknown of people asking about her. She wanted to move in with me but had her own issues about that as well.

V., T.J., Sean, and I had a conference call. I told them about my suspicions. Our plan was to talk to Dena again since she had most of the information that we needed. V. had friends that did everything from mowing lawns to building high-rises so he called in favors to do some snooping around and T.J. was my business partner, and lucky for us, he recently set up and became Mr. Private I, a new division in our company. We are in the claims consulting business and sometimes, special investigation was needed. T.J. had gotten his Private Investigator license a few years ago but hadn't put it to use yet because of his illness. He planned to set up his surveillance at Dena and Mia's house. He said that it would be good practice for him, an expensive practice at that. We joked about having to watch what we did because T.J. was watching everything and everybody.

CHAPTER 26

❧

MIA

Gary walked back into the room as I was getting out of the tub and starting to dry off.

"Hey, wait a minute, you're doing my job. I got this." He removed the towel from my hand and started his ritual of drying me off, looking at my body with complete adoration, the towel gliding gently across my skin. Quiet. I inhaled, bit the corner of my lip, and slowly exhaled. It was not the time to get all hot and bothered but he had a soothing touch and spirit about him even in the time of a storm. He ushered me toward the bed and applied lotion to my body, he had this thing that he did with his tongue and finger that caused me to drift into a restful nap. And that's what I did.

Gary tried unsuccessfully to keep his plan from me. It was difficult to do with T.J., Sean, V. and Dena sitting there. I knew something was going on. I walked in on the conversation and all of them looked at Gary and then looked at me as if they were caught stealing something that they knew was dear to me.

"What are y'all doing?" I tried to sound casual.

Gary got up to give me his seat beside Dena.

They had called Dena and asked her to come over again. She was beginning her story when I sat down. "I don't know who it was but the truck tried to cut me off on I-10. At first I thought it was a mistake, then he tried it again. It was one of those big double-wheeled trucks."

"An 18-Wheeler?" Sean asked.

"Nah, the pickup truck with the double-wheels on the back."

"Oh," he replied.

"But I took the first exit and he kept going." She shuddered. "The wheels were almost taller than my car."

They were standing around the island in the kitchen as if we were in an interrogation room. "I've been getting prank calls in my office and at my house."

"Why do you think you're being harassed or stalked?" V. asked.

"Did you find out more about the false alarms at your house?" T. J. followed before she answered the first question. "Do you have the note from the garage?"

"No, I don't. I can find it though. I didn't toss it. And they had pictures of me on different days in an envelope with one of the notes."

I gasped. "What pictures?"

"Of the two of us at the park on the swings, at the driving range, me by myself just out and about." She tossed the pictures on the counter.

V. picked up the pictures, looked at each one, and then passed them to Gary.

"You think it's Monty?" Sean asked as he rubbed his chin.

"No. Not anymore."

"Why not?" Gary asked. "You said earlier that you thought it was Monty."

"Because I know its Sylvester. I thought about it after I left. Monty doesn't have the intelligence to do that. Sylvester was a scam artist and that's his modus operandi. And he—"

"Who is Sylvester?" V. interrupted.

"Long story."

"We have time. Who is Sylvester?" V. asked in a stern voice.

She continued to elaborate on her relationship with Sylvester and about the trip to Chicago. She never told them that I was there. They were throwing one question after another and she did not flinch. She managed to calm herself. She stood her ground, but I know the anticipatory anxiety was getting to her. She was tough as nails but I was still nervous for her and for me.

If it was Sylvester, then who was the lady at the luncheon and who was in V.'s restaurant asking about me? And why did the cop just stop me out the blue one day, just to say 'slow down'. Was there a connection or just coincidence?

A couple of HPD uniforms came over to ask a bunch of questions. They told us to stay out of it but the process seemed very unofficial. V. knew them very well. I wondered if they would do anything with the information or just treat it as relationships gone badly. Dena had reported a few things to the police over that past few months so it should have really raised some eyebrows. T.J. promised to get all of the needed equipment to set up surveillance for Dena and me. He didn't need HPD's permission for that.

CHAPTER 27

GARY

Dena did not tell the entire story about Chicago to the police and we went along with it.

Mia and I had a good night's sleep despite the circumstances. We decided to stay home the entire day since police had asked us to stay out of the investigation. I hoped they would find Sylvester or even connect the dots with these women asking about Mia. I wanted to confront Lynne and Nina just to be sure, it wasn't either of them, but I was trying to obey the law. This was where I regretted telling T.J. and V. about my suspicions because they were by the book and brought the cops in. Sam and Sean would have been down for whatever until we figured it all out.

I left Mia in the bed to rest this morning and she took another nap at four. She had slept for a couple of hours when I heard her walk by the media room.

"Hey, baby, come here. How was your nap?" I pulled her into my lap.

"Fine. I didn't mean to take a nap. I wanted to talk to you." She adjusted herself on the arm of the chair and her legs rested over mine.

"I know, baby, I know. We need to talk. I realize that my timing may be way off with all of this stuff going on but I need to tell you some things." There was no pause, I had gathered my thoughts for the past few hours so I was totally ready. "When we were at V.'s last night you said something that really cut deep, to the core actually."

She looked puzzled. "Baby I didn't mean to…"

"Sh, sh, sh." I put my finger to my lips. "Please, just, let me finish, I have a lot to tell you." I paused for a few seconds. "You asked what I am avoiding telling you."

My palms started sweating and the darkness that I had pushed to the back of my heart was exuding from my pores. For some reason, I was ashamed. I began to speak slowly.

"Well, for starters, I'm uh, I was uh." I adjusted myself in the chair. "I was adopted. Clive and Judy Matthews are not my biological parents. I was nineteen when I found out that V. is my dad."

Her eyes widened but as I had asked, she remained silent.

"V. was a uh, was a uh, a playa back in the day. He was married but messed around with my biological mother, Karen, and I was conceived. He did not know it. And, my biological mother didn't tell him until after she had given me away. She was or is an executive, professional, single, traveled a lot and was apparently not taking care of me the way she should have because she was not ready for children. My mother knew her from some of her professional associations, so my parents, my mom and dad, asked to adopt me when I was a few months old. They did it legally, changed my last name. My biological mother was an only child also, her parents passed away when I was younger. They left all of the inheritance in my name because they were pissed at her for giving me away. But they left specifics with it, certain age, no criminal activity, college degree first, house for my family then build a family. If I would have done things out of order the money would have gone elsewhere. Where "elsewhere" was I don't know, possibly to my children. The money was invested over the years obviously with ups and downs while attorneys, financial advisors, Mr. V. and my parents watched it every step of the way."

Mia reached for my hand. She still didn't speak.

"V. has always been a part of my life, giving me advice, money, taking me and my brother places but he promised my parents that he would not tell me anything unless and until they were ready because he didn't want to complicate my life any more than it already was." I stood and paced the floor as I finished the story.

"He said he would've gone to his grave with that secret because of his loyalty to my parents. Vance and Jessica did not have a clue. They were just as hurt as I was when we found out. They both said they didn't care, I was forever their brother. I was obviously mad at first and ready to get away from all of them, including V. I was away at college playing football. My family came to my games and I pretended everything was okay in the presence of other people but in private, I was totally rude to them, not talking. I was breaking and setting records on the field, headed for the NFL, until I injured my knee and that pissed me off even more."

I paused and stood near the TV, wiping dust that wasn't there.

"Karma is a motha' I shouldn't have treated them like that. I felt like I was all alone in my life with no one that I could truly trust. I came around eventually because I realized that I couldn't live this life without my family. I needed them. I loved them. I know that I led you to believe that my family is great and our relationships are wonderful, and overall it is, but finding out that they had lied to me all of my life, took a toll on me that I didn't realize would happen. I started acting out in the wrong way. I'm good now, though. I'm really good. I learned so much through the process and regret every moment that I spent being angry."

Her eyes stared at me in amazement. "Wow. Do you have any more siblings?"

"Nope, only child, mother and father had no more children. Well, not that I know of." I paused for a moment. "My son, well the kid I thought was my son…died, with my grandfather, Clive's dad. My grandfather had a heart attack while he was driving and went into a pond. The witnesses couldn't get the door open so they both drowned. That was really a tough situation. I found out the day he died that he was not my son because another dude surfaced and was grieving just as hard as I was. Tracy swears that I had something to do with his death. She got the police involved. I was investigated and everything, all the while grieving the loss of my 'son.' I moved my hands in quotation marks. "She was the one that showed up at the family gathering the other day with her mother. Tracy, her mother, and my aunt concocted a story that I assaulted and raped her because I went to her house and went off after she was telling everybody that I killed her son. I tore up a few things in their house. Instead of my aunt defending me because she knows I'm not that type of guy, she assisted them because she was mad about the car accident that paralyzed her son, my best friend, Jai."

I paused again, cleared my throat preparing to deliver the next blow.

"Also, my best friend or should I say my ex-best friend, Jai and I are no longer friends although, as I mentioned before, I did build this house to accommodate him in his wheelchair just in case you know, we make amends." My voice rattled just a little so I paused again to gather my emotions.

"He is still pissed at me because he's in a wheelchair. He feels that being in a wheelchair is not a life, and that I need to admit that I was wrong for saving his life. Obviously, I don't think that. He is stubborn, his mother is messy, and she tries to keep the fire going between us. We had been drinking but were not drunk, at least I wasn't. Poor judgment on my part, I should have been the driver that night but he said he was cool, able to drive. He went off the road and hit a tree. Luckily, I was blessed to get out of the car. The car was on fire so I struggled to pull him out, trying to save his life. The accident happened shortly after I made amends with my family and they really helped me through that. Jai's mother, the one that came to the basement at my parents' house, was totally blaming the whole thing on me, too. She said some really ugly things about me. To this day, I don't care for her ways. She and my parents stopped speaking for a long time—you know, Mia?" I stopped telling the story abruptly because it's depressing. I sat back down in the chair and pulled her back into my lap. "Everyone is dealing with something from their past, divorce, adoption, loss, abandonment, the list just goes on and on, but the key is not to let it cripple you. I didn't. You didn't. And we're better for it." I paused. "I wanted to tell you all about my family so that you will know what you're getting into as we go further into this relationship."

She looked at me with sympathy in her eyes. Silence. She traced my eyebrows with her fingers. Her eyes were studying my face, tracing every inch. She hugged me tightly.

I leaned back in my chair and fell asleep watching ESPN. My head was pounding. I didn't understand why, I had gotten almost everything off my chest. I couldn't believe it but I wanted to cry before I went to sleep thinking about my friend Jai and the sadness that overtook me when I thought about it, but I didn't.

∽

For the next few days, Mia unknowingly proved that she was the woman for me. She didn't have any scheduled appointments and all of mine were easily handled from home. So, we had plenty of time to love each other, laugh, play, and just enjoy one another's company.

One afternoon, I took a nap and woke up to Mia straddling me in my oversized recliner. Perfect. She was wearing the red pumps that she got in New York, a white patent leather coat, stethoscope, and a long brown wig. Role playing, doctor.

"Wake up, handsome man. I'm getting ready to give you a taste of your own medicine," she said with an accent.

"Heyyy, what are you doing, girl?" I was a bit groggy but pleasantly surprised. I had to adjust my eyes, at first I thought I was dreaming.

She smiled seductively. "Oh, what beautiful brown eyes you have. The doctor is here for a house call today and ready to give you some med-dicine. Didn't you say that you don't feel good?" She continued the accent and kissed me all over my face.

She unbuttoned the coat. "What can I do for you today? This is my med-dicine for you."

"Oh my." It didn't take me long to get in the mood. One look at her in a red lace bra with matching panties and I was ready.

"Let me check your heart. Ahh, your heart is beating very rapidly, sir. Let me see what I have for that."

She leaned in to kiss me, first gently then passionately as I responded to her moves. She rose up and removed the coat, a total magazine beauty. She has the most beautiful skin. I was feeling a bit down today, she perked me up by taking total control and I let her from the chair to the floor to the chaise-lounge. The doctor was working overtime. Or, should I say a mechanical bull rider dressed as a doctor.

CHAPTER 28

MIA

"Hey honey, I was just about to call you." I fastened my seatbelt.

"Is that right?"

"Yeah, because I'm settling down from all of this running around today and I wanted to talk to you."

"What have you been doing?"

I whispered in my horror movie voice, "Running from the stalker."

"Mia, stop playing, just because you haven't heard anything lately doesn't mean you get careless."

"I'm not being careless." I pouted as I flipped the visor down to look in the mirror.

The potential stalker was probably still out there but three weeks had passed and we hadn't seen or heard anything new, but my eyes were still wide open and Gary assured me that his was, too. My clientele was growing so I traveled at least once per week, ran at least three miles per day and I know I should have done more, but my body was sluggish and I was a little afraid to be out by myself, so if Gary couldn't go with me, I didn't go. I did not have any indication that someone was following or watching me but the thought was always on my mind and I did a decent job of hiding it.

Gary told me that Lynne had begun to ask probing questions about the potential stalker and me. I was not as much a target as Dena but Lynne seemed more interested in me. She told Gary that she had a mother's love for me and was asking all of the questions because she cared about me. But on a different day she told him that I was rude to her before the trip to New York and she told him that I was flirting with a dude from the gym. I did not trust her.

"What time are we meeting?" I rambled through my purse for some lip-gloss. "Can you believe it's October already?"

"We're not. I want us to ride together. I'll pick you up at six. Wear something sexy."

"I always do."

"Yeah, you're right. Okay, well, make it black." He paused. "Please."

"You mean dressy black?"

"Kind of."

"To Talk Sweet? That's a casual diner."

"It is, but tonight is special, plus we're checking out another spot afterward."

"What-ever you like," she mocked the accent of the bride-to-be in the movie "Coming to America."

We arrived at Talk Sweet, did all of our usual pleasantries with V. and the staff and after he assisted me into my seat beside him, he handed me an itinerary.

"Mia, my dear heart, this has been a really good year. We've had mostly good times." He looked at me earnestly. "I want us to celebrate by taking a trip. You think you're an athlete." He chuckled. I placed my hand on my chest in a playful surprise. "So there's a lot for us to do. Complete with horseback riding, jet skiing, rock-climbing, dancing, golfing, eating, drinking, and being you. I know this is October and your birthday is long gone for this year, but this is the last of your birthday gifts from me. I held on to it because we have had way too much drama going on."

"Really! Thank you, I need a break. Baby this is great!" I tried to maintain my composure. "Thank you baby, I really need a break. And what better way than to spend that break than with you." I leaned over and kissed him. He pulled me closer. I started scanning the brochure with wide eyes... *They say the stars are endless in... You'll witness this truth as you and your love embrace on a private balcony... with the cool Caribbean breeze kissing your faces. For couples, ... blue waters... pools and cascading waterfalls... fine dining, and an abundance of fun ... marriage license... ceremony, decorations, and wedding sites available.*

"When are we leaving? I'm ready to go now!" I gleamed.

"Next month."

"Wow! I need to check my schedule."

"I already did. No speaking engagements and I scheduled it after your marathon."

"Baby, are you serious?" My eyes danced looking at him. "Yeaahh Boyyyeee!" I reached for a high five then a kiss.

"I told you that you'll get my best and going to make you enjoy every minute of it."

"Stop it, you're making me moist." I kissed him again and

hugged him. "Gosh, man, where did you come from?"

After dinner, we went dancing at a hip-hop club downtown. We had a blast. Dena and Dwight met us there.

"Hey Dena, hey Dwight. How are you?"

"I'm good, Mia how are you?" Dwight reached for a hug.

"Dwight, this is my boyfriend, Gary," I explained.

"Mia, they've already met." Dena swatted my arm.

"When?" I looked clueless because I didn't remember Gary being out of my sight for too long.

"At the bar, baby, when you were talking to your friend."

"Oh, whatever! Dena let's sit down. Did you run today?" I asked.

"Yes, for about twenty minutes uphill." She crossed her long legs and sipped her drink.

"Really! That's good. I ran a little bit today, nothing major, just three miles, I took it easy, my stomach was queasy this morning."

"Really now? Could there be a little G-Matt getting ready to hit the scene?" She smiled, swinging her leg.

I sighed, "I don't know, I haven't seen a drop in over a month."

"Wow, has that ever happened before?"

"Yeah, occasionally." I sighed again. "Stop smirking."

"You tell him?" She motioned her head toward Gary.

"No, I don't know what to tell yet. He wouldn't be surprised. We had a protection mishap."

"Hmmm, protection mishap, huh?"

"Yep, we got carried away." I fanned my hand in the air. "I

cannot have a kid out of wedlock."

"Don't panic, Mia. It could be stress, too. And, so what, if you have a kid out of wedlock? You won't be the first. Besides, you're doing everything else out of wedlock." She scoffed.

"I know, right? I'm twisted. He planned a trip for us next month. I can't wait. I need a break. Dena, he is such a sweetheart. He is always trying to make sure that I'm okay. His mantra is *"I will give you my best, Mia, always. I'm telling you, stop worrying about things that I should take care of."* He is so adorable. I know it's been months but thank you again, Dena for introducing me."

"Girl, how many times are you going to thank me for strategically planning my best friend's love life?" She bragged.

I smiled and reached for a hug. "What would I do without you?"

"I don't know, let's not think about it, that would stress you out too much." She is such a quick wit. "You know he is kind of ready for a baby, right? And Aunt Judy is over-the-top ready for another grandchild, especially from Gary."

"I know. That's the nerve-wrecking part."

"Girl, don't worry. He is not like that. He just wants the joy of sharing it with you. He absolutely loves you and would take whatever you can give him, biological or adopted or nothing if that's what you two choose."

"Dena, you always know what to say."

"I know. I can be psychic, remember?" She winked at me.

I felt my phone vibrate in my purse. I pulled it out and to no surprise it was Brock calling again. I pressed ignore and two minutes later, he texted: *I'm in town again and I want to see you.* I deleted the text.

"Dena, don't look now but there is a man with a hat all pulled down and a woman looking and pointing in this direction."

"Where?" she said as she immediately turned around to look. She stood up and quickly headed toward them as they casually disappeared into the crowd. I looked back at Gary; he was not looking in my direction so I followed Dena. I didn't want to lose her by stopping to tell Gary what was going on first.

"Dang, where did they go so quickly?" I huffed.

"I don't know!" She stomped back toward the area where we were sitting. There was a woman standing in front of Dwight chatting away. Dena walked up to him and just stood there with her arms folded and stared at him. I walked over to Gary who had his back turned to Dwight, talking to the bartender. Our seats were already taken.

We stayed at the club until almost two o'clock in the morning and Gary called for the car service to take us home.

We went to my house. I was preparing my mind to move in with Gary so we began to spend quite a bit of time at my house, almost as if I was mourning.

I've heard older woman say that if you want to be a wife, then act like a wife. Not in a sense of giving your all to someone that you're not married to, but have a wife's mindset by handling your business, taking care of your house and all that goes with it. I didn't cook often because quite frankly, I don't find enjoyment in it, but I had started to try out some of my little recipes from the many cookbooks that I had lined up neatly in the pantry.

I didn't know exactly when I would take the "leap of faith." He stopped asking about it and said that I will let him know when I was ready. I had begun to leave a few items at his house and donating things from mine. I was really praying that it didn't backfire. I didn't feel it would, but I was definitely concerned with no ring. He was an absolute sweetheart, though. He said I could change anything in his house that I wanted, to make me comfortable. He had five bedrooms, game room, media room, and a study. I couldn't imagine I'd change anything. Well, maybe a few things, but not much. I really needed a separate study for my many books.

We discussed a *co-habitation agreement*, which meant that I was going to pocket most of my money to pay off student loans from graduate school and my remaining credit card debt, which was minimal compared to where it was a few years ago. He had no debt and was willing to assist me in paying off mine. He had the money to pay my debt but he said I needed to develop new spending habits or I would be in the same situation again. I could have paid triple my monthly credit card payment but it wasn't my desire. He didn't believe in carrying a credit card balance and I didn't care if I did. But I realized I had to change that. I was disciplined enough when I was preparing to start my business but occasionally I slipped. We did background checks and reviewed each other's FICO scores. My score was only ten points lower than his was and I was impressed.

Gary stretched out on the sofa and did his usual channel surfing of CNN, ESPN, NFL Network, Sports Center, Food Network, and then HGTV.

"Baby, I have this new recipe that I want to try on you." I said.

"Try on me? What is it? You said it like it's an experiment."

"Boy, don't act. I cook breakfast for you all the time. You like my omelets, remember?"

"Oh, is the new recipe a breakfast one?" He continued flipping channels, not really paying attention to me.

"Uh, no. It's dinner."

No answer. He focused in on the newly designed house on HGTV. I didn't worry about him not enjoying anything that I prepare because he always did. I hoped he hadn't been giving me a polite applause out of courtesy.

"Mia, you know what? I really like my house because every detail was built the way I wanted it. But, I am so willing to give all of it up to build something that you and I choose together, something smaller, bigger, I mean, whatever you like. We can sell all of the furniture and start over completely. Well, with the exception of my media room and game room, I can't part with those. If I do, it will be to get bigger and better."

"Wow, a total change of subject and I'm okay with the direction. Do you really mean that?" I walked over to sit on his lap and gave him a hug. "You are so sweet. Thank you. I'm really working with this. I gotta be honest, I'm nervous, but I'm opening up."

"I understand, but I promise, you won't regret it. Whenever you decide to make your move, I'm not rushing you by saying that. I just thought I'd let you know since I'm watching them renovate this house." He pointed at the TV with the remote.

"I think I believe you." I smiled, pressed my forehead to his for a moment. Kissed him on his nose and got up to prepare for a good night's rest. He swatted my butt as I walked away.

I walked upstairs, sat on the floor at the end of my bed to stretch. I had been working out, preparing for the marathon, stressed out, and my period was late. With fibroids, I occasionally skipped a month without a period but it usually starts as soon as the new month rolled in. It was two weeks in and nothing. Could I be pregnant? The 'what if' had been on my mind so I stopped by the store earlier to get a pregnancy test. I spent about twenty minutes stretching and then chugged two bottles of water before taking a shower trying to have a full bladder to take the pregnancy test. I knew two bottles would definitely give me more than enough to test. I stood in my bathroom looking through my cabinets wondering how I can share a bathroom with anyone with all of this stuff.

My cell phone chimed. I walked over to check the text: *Mia, I think that was Sylvester and Ari.*

I replied. *How u know?*

Thirty minutes later, there was still no response.

"I will not stress out over this, Dena." I exhaled loudly. I wanted to take the test and then show Gary the results but then I started to panic just as my brain told my bladder that it was time to release. I wanted him by my side.

"Gary!" I yelled, "Gary, baby come here! Gary!" I sat on the toilet trying to hold it but to no avail.

Gary rushed into the bathroom as I was walking out. I washed my hands.

"Baby, what is it? Why are you yelling? Are you all right?" His eyes were as big as silver dollars.

"I need you to uh, be uh, with me when I uh?" All of the stress and overwhelm-ness came out in tears.

"Mia, baby what's wrong? Why are you crying? Is something hurting you?" He started searching me for signs of pain.

"I'm fine, Gary."

"Come here, sit down, sit down. What's wrong? Talk to me. What is it?"

He pulled my vanity stool out so I could sit down. He kneeled in front of me, looking up at me, rubbing my thighs.

I wiped my face. "Baby, I'm late." I continued to wipe my face and started to ramble. "About a month a half late and I bought a pregnancy test at that little pharmacy on the corner and I was going to take it and tell you the results but then I changed my mind because I wanted you to take it with me. I guess I got scared."

He smiled. "Is that why you gave me that life or death yell?" His smile got bigger. "Mia, why the tears? Are you afraid to be pregnant?"

"No, I'm not afraid. Well, yes I am afraid. Well, I don't know. No, I'm— I don't know." I shook my head. "I just don't want you or your parents, especially your mom to be disappointed if I can't have a baby."

"Mi-yah! Baby I'm not concerned about that. You told me the deal in the beginning. Look. I love you! Okay. I don't care if you have a baby or adopt a baby, get a Baby Alive or whatever as long as we make the decision together. And as for my mother, she does not want you in any danger or stress trying to get pregnant."

"I know. I just don't want to disappoint anyone," I whined.

"Mia, I'm serious, you don't have to worry about that. Where is your faith, Babe? Love, joy, peace, patience…" he said softly as he did his signature move on me, rubbing the back of my neck and tracing down my arm, a comforting move that I absolutely loved. "Okay, now where's the test?"

"Right there with the fruits of the spirit that you're naming. We need help with several of those, that's how we're in this situation now, no self-control." I handed him the generic test.

He chuckled, "Whatever Mia, stop being ugly, you don't have any self-control. I do. You're the one always seducing me. Doctor. What kind of test is this? You think this is going to be accurate?"

He stood up.

"I don't know, that was all they had."

"Better than nothing. We can try it and call your doctor for an appointment in the morning to make sure."

"Okay." I stood up to walk to the toilet to try it again. "Gary, I am scared to be pregnant. What if I die in childbirth?"

He frowned. "What?"

"You know, from blood loss."

"Mia, stop worrying, baby."

"I've heard of it happening."

"Come here, stop it, now." He reached for a hug.

I heard my cell phone, another text message.

PART THREE

THE
STALKER
RETURNS

CHAPTER 29

GARY

Mia worked extremely hard preparing for the marathon, running almost daily, continuing to raise money for her sponsored child. As we were getting ready to leave the house I asked, "Mia, do you think you really need to do this marathon?"

If she was pregnant, I knew dang well she wasn't going to run it. We couldn't tell if the pregnancy test was positive or negative. It looked like a little bit of both so we planned to get another test. We also called the doctor and left a message for an appointment.

"Uh, yeah!" She looked at me as if to say, "you must be nuts, there's no other answer."

"Babe, I'm just saying, you've been going nonstop for two months. I used to see you stop, take a break, a weekend of nothing. You've been running around with your clients, entertaining, drumming up more business for yourself, raising money for Team in Training, dealing with me, which is actually a good thing. I think you need a break." I could tell she was fatigued.

She sighed and lazily continued to pack her waters and gels for her run. She finally spoke. "I'll get some rest this weekend. I only have to run today. Less than ten miles. I'm not trying to win the cash purse. So all I have to do is finish, no rush, just stay in front of the pacer. That's my agenda. I'm trying to get past the point where they send you on a different route or give you a medal and put your tired ass on a bus and say 'nice try'." We both laughed and giggled like two giddy teenagers. "But I'll rest on our trip."

"Uh no, Mia. You need to rest before that."

"I know," she conceded. "I was just saying."

"Mia, what if you are pregnant?" Our tones were serious again.

"I know." She pondered for a minute. "Well, I won't run, until I find out."

I left the conversation at that sentence. She still wanted to go to another shoe clinic to get fit for more shoes two months prior to the marathon so that she can get a few miles on them before the race. I had to go into the office afterward so we drove in separate cars. Despite the pregnancy drama, she was in such a good mood today. We were in a good mood. I should have known something was going to spoil it. That's just how it goes. Life definitely comes at you fast.

I picked up my phone as soon as I got in the car, dialed Mia's number since I saw her putting her Bluetooth on before she cranked her car.

"Hello."

"Hey, sexy," I said in my nighttime disc jockey voice.

"Boy, what are you doing?" I could tell she was smiling.

"I miss you already."

"I know. I miss you, too. Did you give me a kiss yet?" she said that as if she suddenly remembered that I didn't.

"Yes, I did, but if you want another one, I can give it to you."

"Okay, I want one."

I got out of my truck still parked in the garage and walked over to her car. Leaned in and kissed her. Gently. Slowly. We stared at each other as I backed away. We never hung up the phone.

She said, "Keep that up we're gonna have to go back up those stairs, buddy."

I laughed as I continued to walk to my truck. "You don't have time for that right now do you?" I was kind of hoping that she would say yes.

She didn't. She just laughed and said, "It will be better later because of the anticipation."

"Yeah, right."

We kept talking and joking until we were five minutes away from her house. As Mia was going through the traffic light on the corner of Peek and Cinco Ranch Blvd, I saw a truck speed up, swerve around a car into the intersection, and hit Mia's car. Car chase? Intentional or coincidental? I didn't know. Absolutely crazy, yes. The truck crashed into the driver side of her car. I heard Mia scream. It felt like the earth had paused. I couldn't breath. I couldn't believe my eyes as I watched Mia's car spin around to end up in the same direction only several yards away with the airbag deployed. It happened so fast. I stopped in the middle of the intersection and put my car in park. Jumped out and ran toward Mia's car. I wasn't thinking. I didn't care about the other cars. I didn't care about traffic light cameras, I didn't care about traffic jams. I couldn't get her door open. There were several people out of their cars trying to help. I ran around to the other side. I opened the door, sat in the passenger seat. All of her belongings had fallen to the floor, her purse, her cell phone, her water-fuel belt, and her iPod. It was too dangerous to pull her through. I prayed. I prayed hard. Mia was unconscious. Blood was running down the side of her face to her chest. I pushed the driver side door as the other guys tried to pull it but to no avail. The ambulance and fire trucks arrived on the scene. I was freaking out. *Is she dead?* I wondered.

I leaned over her. "Baby, say something. Mia, please baby say something."

My heart was stunned. I didn't know what to do, had I pulled her out of water, I would've known exactly what to do. I had experience there. The EMTs placed her limp body on the gurney, placed the oxygen mask over her face, and covered her nose and mouth. Still unconscious, the blood appeared to be coming from somewhere around the top of her ear, her pants and her legs were covered in blood, too. They wanted to put me on another gurney. I was headed toward the ambulance parked beside my truck.

One of my boys approached me, a work-out buddy, Windsor St. Louis, I didn't know where he had come from. He asked for my keys. I patted my pockets, no keys.

His wife yelled out. "Windsor, his keys are right here."

I had left my keys in the truck.

Windsor told me that he would follow the ambulance in my truck. He tried to assure me, "G-Matt, she's going to be okay, trust me."

I listened. He was a wise dude, maybe he was right.

Just as we were pulling away, I saw fire coming from underneath the hood of Mia's car.

When we got to the hospital, they were in full speed getting Mia into emergency. One of the EMTs yelled, "Level one, trauma activate!"

Totally panicked, I asked, "What does that mean?"

He calmly stated, "It means, this is very serious. All hands on deck."

I heart started beating faster. I had managed to call V. on my way there and he said he'd call Dena. She said she'd call everyone else. They were en route. The EMT had given me the manual oxygen for me to use on myself. I guess it helped. I dropped it as soon as the doors opened preparing to stay on the heels of the EMT pushing the gurney. They sent two ambulances to the scene but they were not needed because the truck that hit Mia's car kept going and we didn't see who was driving it.

I was usually pretty tough. I had endured fights on the block, being shot at, broken bones, all types of accidents growing up and with no tears, but this had taken me by surprise and had me full of tears. Mia was very special to me. She was different from any woman I had ever met. I desired her, totally. Extraordinary, spontaneous, independent, and intelligent, everything I wanted. I had planned to propose to her on our trip.

Windsor's wife was a doctor, OB/GYN. Her name was Wendy. They hurried into the hospital with V. She rushed around to try to find out what was going on.

V. walked toward me with open arms.

"Dad, I'm sorry, I can't do this. I need her. I guess my best was not good enough. I promised her that I would give her my best! And it wasn't good enough! I didn't protect her. Why do I keep messing up with the people that I care about?"

"I know, son. It's going to be all right." He hugged me.

Dena rushed in with Lysa, a mutual friend, and Desilyn, Mia's sister who just happened to be in town on business. She ran and hugged me, her face was wet from tears, and so was Desilyn's. She hugged Windsor. "What happened?"

Windsor explained his version, which was what I think I remembered. He said, "There was more than one person in the truck, I didn't see the driver but passenger was a guy. The truck kept going. I think it was a woman driving."

An emergency room nurse approached me and asked if there was any possibility that she could be pregnant, they wanted to do x-rays. I just started rambling. "Mia and I had been talking about her recent missed period, had a big ordeal just last night. Is there was a way to do a pregnancy test now, because she could be. You know what, just do what you have to do to make her better."

Dena, Desilyn, Lysa and V. looked at me with adoration despite all of the turmoil going on. The nurse looked embarrassed, as if she just realized that she didn't ask me in private. She motioned for me away from them to get more information. Wendy St. Louis stepped up, introduced herself to the nurse, and started asking a lot of questions. I stepped away in a daze and didn't hear most of what they were talking about. I heard them say something about an MRI would be safer. Wendy came back to me and said that Mia would be okay. It was just another attempt to reassure me, of course.

An hour of being in the emergency room, alternating between leaning on the wall, sitting in the uncomfortable chairs, pacing the hall all the while V. watched my every move. He had called my parents, Sean and T.J. to give them the news.

The doctors had given us an update. They stopped the blood from her head but Mia was bleeding internally. They were working trying to figure out where the blood was flowing from. She needed a blood transfusion. I offered to give blood, they said no. Desilyn offered they said no need again. We didn't have time to argue so we prayed and let them do what they were paid to do. This was déjà vu. I experienced the same thing with Jai, several years ago when I pulled him out of that burning car that he crashed by taking a curve too fast. I looked at my right hand that was burned during that accident.

Dena, Lysa, and Desilyn had gone for a walk. Dena was hysterical. Desilyn was calm and Lysa was just supportive. Wendy and one of the emergency room doctors came back and told me that Mia was pregnant and had miscarried.

"What!" I screeched and didn't care who heard me. Suddenly, I couldn't breath. I placed one hand on the wall to steady myself, tried to calm down. My stomach was in knots.

She continued. "She is going to be fine though. We believe that's where some of the bleeding was coming from."

She patted my shoulder as V. pulled his arm around me. I was sure she had plenty of experience delivering tough messages.

"The bleeding above her ear has stopped as well. There was a cut from her head hitting the window and there is some swelling from the impact. They're watching her to make sure she doesn't need surgery."

Her left ankle is sprained and her left wrist is broken," the other doctor continued where Wendy left off.

They delivered the bad news in a manner that I'm sure they thought was from bad to good. It was all bad to me. The only thing that would have sounded better was them telling me that I can take Mia home in the same condition that she was this morning before someone plowed her over.

"She's in a medically-induced coma to decrease the swelling in her brain. That way there's no activity and the healing can be a little bit faster," he added.

"What!" I walked away. I needed to sit down. They followed. I needed to ask so many questions but I couldn't get my thoughts to formulate into audible sentences.

V. asked, "What else do you need to tell him?"

They proceeded to tell him that they probably would keep her on the meds for a few days to see what happens. She did not have to have surgery unless other complications arose but they didn't foresee any. They will keep her in ICU to watch her.

I interrupted them because I was positive that any additional information would not have been stored into my memory anyway. "Can I see her?"

She hesitated. "Yes. Right this way."

I walked behind them, feeling like weights were in my shoes. My legs were heavy with every step as if someone had pressed the *slow* button on the DVR's remote control. I thought about how much I loved Mia and I couldn't imagine my life without her. A tornado of thoughts was twirling in my mind. I wondered how I was going to tell her that she had miscarried. *When will I have the opportunity? God, we were going to the doctor on next week! I can't believe this!*

We arrived at ICU. They said that only two people at a time in the room and for only fifteen minutes. My eyes were bloodshot from crying so much. I could not believe, what was happening around me.

I walked into Mia's room. To see someone that I love attached to tubes and ventilation was very disheartening, monitors beeping, bandages, swelling, and bags of liquid dripping including the blood transfusion in progress. My mind wandered to the words of Alicia Keys' very popular song, "…every time you hold me, hold me like this is your last time, every time you kiss me, kiss me like you'll never see me again…" In hindsight, I did that this morning, just never believing that it could potentially be my last time. I stared at her, and wiped away more tears. Her face and lips were slightly swollen.

The nurse walked in. She checked Mia's tubes, monitors, and bags. She appeared to be experienced. I guess I could trust her. My mind was racing, I didn't know whom to trust all of a sudden. "Who was driving that car, Mia?" I mumbled.

The nurse looked at me when I placed my hand on the bed. "We ask that you don't touch her until we get her heart rate, blood pressure and other vitals under control."

"Why would touching her cause a problem?" I was irritated but really trying not to show it.

She offered a half smile. "Because we believe that she is alert, although we have her on serious meds and I don't want to stimulate her by touching."

I felt like the punishment continued. "Okay, I won't touch her."

She looked as if she felt sorry for me. "Are you her husband?"

"Hmph, not yet, fiancé," I grunted in irritation that someone would actually try to take this from me. "Will you let me know when it's okay to touch her?" That didn't make sense to me.

"Sure. I'll be here for the next eight hours, so … I'm so sorry, I'm not trying to, you know."

"I understand."

She was not very friendly at first, so I needed to figure out how to ask or tell her that I didn't plan to leave this room at all. I didn't care about the fifteen-minute rule.

I stood by Mia's bed, not talking, not touching, just looking with tears flowing down my face. I had been there for forty-five minutes. They didn't ask me to leave so I didn't.

V. had called Sean and T.J. they were at the hospital along with Holly and T.J.'s wife Mona. They stood at the glass door watching me stand in one place, wiping away the tears as I allowed them to freely fall.

Holly whispered but I still heard her since the door was not closed completely. "Oh my God, is he crying?" Then she started to cry. "He absolutely loves her."

I looked toward the door.

Sean pulled her close to him. "Yes, he does."

I stepped closer to Mia's bed, forgot that I was not supposed to touch her. I rubbed her right hand with my thumb and immediately remembered, no touching. I removed my hand, slowly.

"Mia, I love you, you know that right? I'm so sorry that I couldn't protect you. I didn't protect. I let my guard down," I said in a barely audible voice.

The door slid open. Sean walked in, then T.J. while Holly, and Mona stayed on the outside. Mia met Holly and Mona when I cooked dinner for everyone at my house a few months ago. They keep in touch occasionally. Mona was more of the motherly type, which Mia can definitely appreciate and she usually just smiles at Holly and didn't say much because she couldn't seem to understand what was going on in her mind that she wouldn't start the wedding planning from two years ago. Sean reached for a hug, "Man, I'm so sorry."

"Yeah man, me, too. I can't believe this," T.J. cleared his throat, "What can you tell me, man?"

I shook my head. "I think it was intentional." I tried to keep my voice low.

V. and Ms. Emma arrived shortly after. He left to get her from work after she found someone to cover for her. She and V. walked into the room and Ms. Emma rushed toward me and hugged tightly. She walked over to the bed. She and Mia absolutely loved each other. They reminded me of a young mother and daughter.

"Ms. Emma, they said that we couldn't touch her," I whispered. I put my arm around her shoulder.

"Oh I'm sorry she wiped her tears." She removed her hand from Mia's quickly.

The door opened again. Dena appeared face covered in tears, eyes locked on mine as if she was afraid to look at Mia. I stood there until V. ushered all of the men out of the room. We were breaking the room-capacity rule big time. That left Dena, Desilyn, Lysa, Ms. Emma, Holly and Mona in the room. No one talking, all of them staring at Mia.

Holly, Mona and Lysa decided to leave. Dena stepped toward me and whispered, "Gary I need to tell you some things."

I glared at her but remained silent. I had no idea what she had to tell me but my gut told me that I was going to be mad as hell.

Day three, no sleep. All things are never as they seem. When we left Mia's room on Saturday, we went to the waiting room. V. and T.J. went into investigation mode. They were back three days later for more and believed the situation was no accident but intentional because of how all the pieces were coming together. Dena had revealed something that she had kept secret. Sylvester had been following her. He was in the club the night we went out, Mia spotted him but left abruptly and waited on her and Dwight when they left. He didn't do anything, he just watched. Dena was pissed at Dwight anyway for entertaining the lady that was flirting with him.

V. and T. J. started asking me more questions, which were quite startling to me: Enemies? Fatal attractions? Affairs? Jealousy? Envy? Deceit? I thought about Nina but dismissed it because I honestly didn't think she'd go there.

V. stopped by daily to check in. "Son, you need to get some rest." He had insisted I stay at the hospital and let him handle things.

"V. they should have something today shouldn't they? The weekend is long gone."

He rubbed his hand across his chin. "Yeah, they're reviewing the tape from the intersection. It shouldn't take as long as it's taking, it can't be more than two minutes long. I'll call back." He stepped out of the room.

"I think he's hiding something." I stood up and walked toward the door. I felt Mia's phone vibrate in my pocket. I pulled it out to see a portion of text message from someone named S. Brock C.—*Why haven't you cal...* I turned the phone off and put it back in my pocket. I didn't need to be getting upset at S. Brock C. and didn't know who he was.

Sean sat in silence, waiting on me to make a move so that he could be the accomplice. He didn't like to create chaos at all but he would finish it with a bang if we had to. We've changed. I called him Velvet, he'd called me Smooth because of how we used to get out of sticky situations, drama free. Sam, the chaos creator, was coming with my parents. He said that he will not miss the opportunity to slam whoever hurt Mia or tried to hurt me.

I was going crazy waiting. I started pacing back and forth. T.J. stopped me and grabbed both my arms.

"Gary, calm down dude, we got this! Trust me, man!"

V. walked back into the room. "Look, since I can't get the information that I want, we'll do our own thing and not involve them, not formally anyway."

I could tell by the fidgeting and the diverted eyes. He knew something that he was not telling me. "Stay here with, Mia, Son. We'll be back."

I had no energy to argue with them, so with slightly slumped shoulders, I started my walk back into ICU.

I had not eaten, nor shaved since Saturday and it was Tuesday. Lysa had purchased a toothbrush, mouthwash, towels, and other toiletries for me and refused to take reimbursement when I offered. Lysa was a good friend to Mia and Dena. She was not around a lot, but certainly there when it mattered most.

One of the nurses was nice enough to arrange one of the family rooms for a couple of nights, which was useless because I could not fall asleep.

Mia was getting better, more responses, but still not waking up. I guess she couldn't if they kept pumping the medicines in her. I had quickly developed a routine. I left her room occasionally when visiting hours were over since no one was allowed in ICU after hours except nurses and they didn't seem to be a threat. I sat in the waiting room, people watching so I wouldn't go crazy staring at Mia lying still for hours and listening to the beeps of all of the monitors. When visiting hours started again, I walked to the door of ICU, picked up the phone, said my name, heard the buzzer, the door opened and then I walked down the hall, one slow step after another until I reached Mia's room. If a nurse was in the room, which they usually were, I'd greet them, sit down and didn't say a word until the nurse left. It appeared that they were in her room every few minutes. I didn't mind that either, as long as they were doing something productive.

"Hey, Mia, sweetheart. I hope you can hear me." I walked over to her.

"At least I can touch you now, every day since you been here it's a different rule. I couldn't touch you. I couldn't talk. I could only see you for fifteen minutes. Of course, I broke that rule. I guess it depends on the nurse of the day. You know me, I was tired of all of that quickly and asked for the person in charge. Now I don't care which nurse is here, I can somewhat do and say what I want when I want."

I paused for a few minutes and just stared at her.

"Mia, I'm so sorry that I couldn't stop this. I know that I keep saying the same thing over and over but I'm so sorry."

I sat back down in the chair whispering to her. "I love you, Mia. I love you so much." I held her hand, kissed it. I pressed her hand against my cheek and closed my eyes.

I felt her body move. I raised my head and looked at her. Her leg twitched. I looked at her face to see if there were signs of impending conversation. Her leg twitched again. The nurse walked in.

I said, "Her leg keeps twitching. What do you think that is?

"It could be a number of things." She looked at the monitor and at Mia's charts. "Her heart rate is up. Let me check her blood pressure and pulse. They were all normal the last time I was in here." She muttered.

"A number of things like?"

"She could be in pain and that's her way of letting us know, it could be reflex, she could be waking up?" She pressed several buttons on the machine and the blood pressure cup started to compress on Mia's arm.

I nodded my head because she didn't sound as convinced in her answers as her body language was trying to get me to believe.

"Has she responded to you yet?" She grabbed Mia's wrist to check her pulse.

"I thought I felt her hand move but it could've been reflex, too because she didn't do it again."

"Well, you never know. In cases like this we have to wait and see. Just keep talking to her she will probably respond. If she's an affectionate person she will respond eventually." Her lips curled into a smile and her eyes were sincere.

"Okay. I will, it just feels weird to sit here talking to her and she's not responding, which is so unlike her."

"It actually helps coma patients to come back when you talk to them."

"I know, I've heard that before. I'll keep talking. She'll probably wake up and tell me everything I said."

"Yeah, you're right, you should." She leaned over the bed. "Hi, Mia, I'm Brandy. Girl you'd better wake up, there's a handsome young man standing here waiting to talk to you. Wake up, Mia," she sang softly.

I chuckled, thinking Mia would not like her that close, but I let her slide, she was nice enough, and she was trying to help.

Each day they removed more tubes and reduced her meds. She had a cast on her wrist and an ankle bandage. Her breathing was normal but she still wouldn't wake up. I know Mia's body though. I am very in tune to her body heat, reactions, feelings. She is trying to respond. I rubbed her face. I kissed her forehead. Her eyes fluttered, body twitched but her eyes didn't open, so I kept talking to her when I was alone and just holding her hand when we were not, talking to her as if she was awake.

"Lynne called in sick for two days straight. She's not feeling well. The rain continues to come. T. J. was planning to go to the office. Dena and I had talked and she offered her personal assistant, Nyla to answer phones for us if Lynne stayed out longer than two days. T.J. said he could handle the office and told me to stay at the hospital as long as necessary. Sean gave me a key to his house and said that I could take a shower if I need to. But I'm not planning to go anywhere until you leave here or show me something."

She took a deep breath and a subtle move but no eye opening. I saw a tear at the corner of her eye.

"Mia?" I held her hand.

"Mia, sweetheart, I'm right here and I'm not leaving. If you're trying to show me something or say something, I'm listening."

Nothing.

Day four. I was a zombie, praying without ceasing. Sharing time slots in Mia's room with Dena and Desilyn with very little sleep. Talking as much as I could, trying to sound upbeat and not worried. Although I must admit, it was tough but getting better especially after Mia squeezed my hand earlier.

T.J. and I had a business conference call this morning so I ventured out and went into the office briefly.

"Hey Lynne, how you doing? Were you heartbroken because I wasn't in the office the last two days?" I tried to joke but I was actually irritated that she was conveniently absent Monday and Tuesday.

Lynne was somewhat preoccupied, pensive, which was unlike her whenever she talked to me. She had been acting that way for the past few weeks.

"A lady named Tracy called this morning, said she'll see you at five."

"What? Tracy? When did she call?" My mind started racing, wondering if that fool was in town and caused all of this drama. If that was the case, I was going to jail for murder.

"She called a couple of hours ago," Lynne said in an accusatory tone and a glaring stare.

I almost felt the need to justify but I didn't, I simply said, "Thanks Lynne." I didn't want to give her too much information.

"You're welcome. You have another conference call at one. You need me to go to the hospital to sit with Mia?"

I gave her a quizzical look. I started to say "hell no" but thought better of it. "No, thanks, that's really, uh, really nice of you to ask," I said half-heartedly but wondered where that offer came from. My trust for her was slowly but surely going out the door. I still have not gotten past her messing up my travel to New York.

"You sure?" She folded her arms and rested all of her weight on her right leg.

"I'll... I'll go... later."

"So no one is there right now?" She shifted and put her hand on her hip.

I raised my eyebrows because I felt like I was being interrogated and I was confused by her body language. "Yeah someone was, is ther--, uh, no, no one is there, right, now." I lied because I knew Dena and Desilyn were there.

She leaned her head to the side and changed her facial expression to a concerned stare. "Okay, well, let me know if you need anything." She patted my arm, rubbed up and down, gave me a look that I usually get from my mother.

"Thanks, Lynne."

"Okay, well, it's almost noon. You have your conference call at one that should take you about two hours or so," she said in more of a confirmation for her than for me.

I didn't feel like trying to figure out what was going on with Lynne but her behavior concerned me. I pinched the bridge of my nose. "Yeah."

Lynne stood in the doorway, looked at me for a moment, and then walked away.

I read a couple emails, listened to voicemail, trying to prepare myself for a two-hour conference call that T.J. set up over three weeks ago about collaborating with a small company. I couldn't find the dial-in number.

"Lynne," I called out. She didn't answer.

My phone rang. I answered, "Gary Matthews."

"So I heard your lil' girlfriend is in the hospital. How'd that happen?"

"Look Tracy, this is not the time."

"What do you mean it's not the time? Don't you need comfort at a time like this. I mean from what I hear she might not make it out of…"

"Bye, Tracy." I hung up before she could complete her dumb ass sentence.

The phone rang again. I picked it up but didn't speak.

"Hello?"

"What's up, T.J.?"

"Hey man, what the hell are you doing at the office?"

"Trying to appear normal. I'm surprised Lynne was here. Didn't know if she'd show up today. I just decided to come in."

"Yeah, she called me this morning and said she was feeling

better. So I told her to come on in." He chuckled softly. I knew he didn't believe she was sick either. "Oh, well, I can relieve you. The conference call is postponed on purpose, until a later date, I wish I would have called you earlier, but I just found out. I didn't think you would even consider coming in. They don't have all of their ducks in a row and I told them I'm not wasting my time when I know coming out the gate, they don't have all of the answers to the questions that I sent them two weeks ago." He paused then started again, "I'm really going to see if I can stall them until Mia is okay because I know you want to be at one hundred percent and I need you at one hundred percent when we go in. So now, you can get out of there and get back to Mia. I'll be in there shortly."

"Are you sure?"

"Yeah, man. I told them to postpone until they can get their stuff together. I mean, I thought it was a good business venture for us but hell I'm not trying to lose my shirt in the process. So you take some time, take care of Mia. Bring her back to us."

"Thanks, T.J."

"Don't mention it. Anytime. You need to do this. Especially after you've done so much for me."

"Thanks, man. I'll talk to you later."

"Hey, V. and I might be on to something with this hit and run. But don't you worry about anything, we got it covered."

"Okay, I trust you."

"Not a problem. Later, man."

I placed the phone on the cradle. Slowly. I didn't want any specifics right then because I just wanted Mia to wake up and that's what I wanted to focus on.

"Lynne?" I called out. She didn't answer. I put my head on my desk for a second, trying to keep my emotions in tact. I had been in the office for a total of forty-two minutes.

I stood up from my high gloss mahogany desk, every piece of paper in its proper place, all of the pens and pencils in a matching cup holder. Totally not the way I left it on Friday. I'm a neat freak but not that neat. I dismissed the thought that Lynne had been in my office rambling but I made a mental note.

I walked toward the door, pulled my suit jacket from the coat rack, and put it on. I checked my eyes in the mirror. I looked fine, so I tucked the *Wall Street Journal* under my arm and headed out the door.

As I was leaving the office, my cell phone rang. It was the nurse at the hospital. Mia was responding differently. Apparently, they gave her too much of the wrong thing but her chart shows that she had not been given any medication. That was weird. It appeared that she was having trouble breathing. When I left the hospital she was fine. I had only left the hospital just over an hour ago. *What the hell happened? I knew I felt Mia grip my hand this morning but she wouldn't do it again when I asked her to, so I dismissed it, thought maybe it was my movement, but that gave me a sense of peace for today, which is why I left the hospital in the first place.* I stopped mumbling to myself when I stepped into the corridor.

I got in my truck, cranked it, and turned the radio off preparing to ride in silence. I made it out of the parking garage and decided I needed to listen to the gospel station, not much in the R&B line could encourage me the way I wanted. I pressed the radio button again as I merged onto I-10 East in the normal bumper to bumper traffic. In a hurry to wait, so I took a few deep breaths and tried to chill, calm myself, but I was pissed off. How the hell they gave her the wrong medicine, I didn't know. Desilyn or Dena should have been right there with her. Where were they? A sudden feeling of regret rushed over me. The sense of peace suddenly felt like a feeling of guilt.

92.1 FM. I turned the volume up a little, didn't need it blasting, I wasn't in that kind of mood. *"...not another second, another minute, not an hour, another day, I need you right away, I need you now, I need you now ..."* Smokie Norful continued to sing. Tears sat on my eyelids as I struggled not to blink. I gave up that battle, blinked and the floodgates were open. I wiped my eyes quickly in hopes that it would stop the tears. It didn't. I pulled into the parking garage of the hospital. God gave me traveling mercy because I didn't remember how I got there.

I leaned my head on the steering wheel as I waited on all of the cars in front of me to get their parking tickets, I wanted to pray but couldn't think of what I wanted to say. I just needed an answered prayer, so I started talking—"Lord, I need you now! I need your help. Mia needs your help. She's been through this and Your grace is sufficient in her weakness, in my weakness. She's a fighter, Lord. Please restore her, and give her everything that she needs. – Amen."

I knew I was rambling. God was probably like, "huh?" I grabbed my sunglasses. They had a very light tint but enough to shield the swollen redness.

I pulled into the parking space to the last upbeat song *"... trouble don't last, trouble don't last always, weeping may endure for a night, but joy cometh, in the morning light... don't last... trouble don't last always.* The first song, I humbled myself. I felt almost helpless. I prayed and the song that took me out was upbeat, gave me courage. I believed in my heart that Mia would show me something more, to let me know that she heard me and will respond in some way. I will accept small steps.

As I was getting on the elevator, I thought I saw Lynne rush by the elevator lobby. I stepped back to look but the person was already gone. I stepped onto the elevator pressed the sixth floor button. *Lynne is at the office. She'd better be at the office.*

My phone vibrated on my hip, a text message from my sister. *Mom and Dad will be there at 2:30, they're renting a car. G-Matt, please let them help you, they are really concerned about you and so am I, and they really want to help, call soon. Love you.* She's the only person that I know without a Blackberry that uses full words in her text messages. I pushed my Blackberry back in the holster. I looked at my watch, 10:16.

The elevator stopped on the second floor. I pulled my Blackberry from the holster again to pretend I was reading email.

Dena hit me on my arm. "Hey, Dude!" She reached for a hug.

"Hey Dena." I kept my head down. "What's going on with, Mia? She was fine when I left this morning." I tried to sound calm. I was already pissed at her for running after a man that she "thought" was Sylvester at the club and didn't tell me. It was hard to be pissed at Mia since she was helpless at the moment.

Desilyn said, "Hi, Gary."

"I'm sorry, Desilyn. Hey, how are you doing?" I reached to hug her.

"I'm good! My sister is going to wake up this trip. Just you watch."

I smiled with a glimmer of hope. "I sure hope so, that has been my prayer."

Dena started again. "The nurse asked me to leave for a few

minutes as Desilyn was walking into the room. I don't know what she was getting ready to do, maybe give her a bath or something."

I was tempted to interrogate but decided against it, nor did I tell her about the call that I had gotten.

Dena and Desilyn walked toward Mia's room with me but then decided to stay in the waiting room.

I greeted the flirty nurses, asked a few questions, tried to show a heartfelt smile but it quickly turned into a grimace when I saw Nina approaching the desk. I didn't say anything to her. I just walked into Mia's room. I started to wonder if she had anything to do with the accident or with the current issue. I found that none of the nurses knew anything more than they knew when I called. I needed a little bit more focus from them.

I did as always, stood at the end of her bed, stared, willed myself to sit down, stared at her monitor, watched her breath, chest moving up, then down. I prayed again for her recovery, while holding her hand. She had been in a coma for four days. I sat there thinking about how badly I wanted her to just wake up. I could not explain how my heart felt. After seeing Nina approach the desk, I couldn't help but have random thoughts pop into my head. *If Nina is the reason, that Mia is having issues... Lord please help me because I'm going to do something really bad.*

Dena, Desilyn, and I had spent every night at the hospital. Dena had gone back to her house only once, and she was escorted by V. and Sean because she thought Sylvester was following her.

Since we had no information on the hit and run, Dena took it upon herself to get a restraining order on Monty and stayed away from her house and office. She and Monty were so in love but hated each other at the same time because their personalities clashed big time. She was pissed because she found out from the leasing manager that Nyla was only in the office a few hours while Dena was out and the hours she was there, she was spreading rumors about Dena and some of the clients. Dena did not have time to investigate so she told Nyla to take off until she called her back. She said she didn't know when that would be.

The nurse on duty at the time walked in. Her name was Michelle, a full-figured blonde, very friendly, excellent bedside manners, and very strict about her patients. She closed the blinds on the glass door.

"Hey Gary, how are you today?" she whispered.

"I'm good. I'm good. What's going on with Mia? None of the nurses at the station knew anything," I asked, trying to sound concerned and not irritated.

She sighed. "Her heart rate went up a few minutes ago and her breathing was a little abnormal, blood pressure was a little elevated. I came in, checked her vitals and IV and everything seemed okay, breathing steadied a bit, blood pressure is finally back to normal. Despite all of this, she is progressing well, though. There is brain activity. We reduced the meds so that she can come out of the coma. According to this chart, the last med we gave her was yesterday morning. She is probably resting. Poor thing probably goes ninety miles per hour all the time. When she wakes up she can tell us if anything is hurting her, any broken bones, other than the obvious." She pointed at Mia's wrist and continued wiping, adjusting, checking the monitors and writing on her chart. "I'm gonna be honest. I don't think she needs that neck brace anymore. That's just a precaution. I can remove it,"

I nodded my head. She walked over to remove the neck brace.

"Her x-rays didn't alarm us in any way. You know, she's a fabulous lady. I heard her speak at a luncheon that I went to a few months ago."

My eyes brightened. "Is that right? She really enjoys what she does."

"Yeah, I can tell, enthusiasm oozes from her. I can't wait until she wakes up so I can tell her about it. When I saw her name on the chart and then I saw her, I was like oh my goodness, everybody in here better give her the royal treatment. Or they're gonna hear from me!" She tapped her chest in a proud manner. I wanted to tell her to keep Nina away from this room but decided against it.

"Wow, thank you so much." I was actually elated at her comments and they gave me even more hope. But I still didn't understand why her vitals were all out of whack all of a sudden.

Michelle turned to leave the room and paused as if she suddenly remembered something. "I'll let you know when the lab work comes back. Oh Gary, if her blood work comes back okay, I need to tell you something." She stuttered. She spoke almost faster than the words were coming out.

"Calm down. Are you okay? Tell me something about what? Why can't you tell me now?" I was intrigued.

She pressed her hand against her chest and took a deep breath. "There was a woman in here today. I think. Mia's monitors started beeping so I came in but I didn't see anybody so I checked everything and all seemed okay a few minutes later, I know I saw a woman walk out of her room. I stopped her as she passed the nurses station but she denied being in the room, she said she came out of another patient's room on the end. She said the patient's name correctly so I decided not to piss her off and just let her leave. But I'm almost positive she came out of Mia's room. She could've been hiding in the bathroom because I didn't check it and I know the newspapers said that this was a possible hit and run. We took blood to run tests to make sure the transfusion didn't cause it but…"

I didn't know what to say. For the first time in a long time, I was speechless. I stared at Michelle for a few seconds.

She continued and began rambling in a whisper, "I don't know, Gary. I could get in trouble for alarming you so please don't do anything yet. I don't know, just keep an eye on her and I will, too while I'm here. I'm pulling a double tonight so, I'll definitely keep an eye on her. Gosh, I sure hope she wakes up soon. I don't know…I just… I better go."

"No, Michelle, hold on wait. Please? Describe this woman that you saw."

"Well, she was about five-nine, short hair, kind of sturdy build, probably a size fourteen maybe. She was much smaller than I am. She had on flats. She had on a blue pants suit, kind of navy blue."

"What about facial features? Thick eyebrows? Mustache? Dimples? Anything else you remember?"

"Yes, she had a mole on the side of her mouth. I think she had dimples. She was actually an attractive woman. I thought it was her mother. I even asked that and she said 'no.'"

"Okay, I don't recall anyone by that description." I lied. "It's not Mia's mother. Her mother is deceased. And you're sure it wasn't her sister?

"Yes, I'm sure it wasn't De-na and Des-silyn right?" She tried to recall their names.

"Okay, thanks, Michelle."

I looked puzzled. I shook my head, because although I didn't tell her, I knew exactly whom she'd just described.

The gold padded wood framed chair sitting next to Mia's

bed didn't appear sturdy enough for my weight but was actually comfortable. It had been my napping spot. I sat down on the edge of the chair. I held her right hand in my hands and leaned my head against her hand. Thoughts of her desire to donate her organs ran through my mind. Thoughts of the woman Michelle described. Beads of sweat started to form around my forehead. I rocked back and forth in the chair. My body temperature was getting hotter and hotter.

I whispered, "Mia, sweetheart, please come back to me. I need you, baby. Please keep fighting, Mia. What's going on, baby? I'm sorry I left you again, I need…" I released her hands. I sat back in the chair, staring at her. I rested my elbows on my knees, clasped my fingers. Praying without ceasing.

"She's coming back. I can promise you that," Desilyn spoke softly as she and Dena had walked in quietly. "God confirmed that for me this morning." She spoke with confidence.

I stood to hug her. "Thanks Desilyn, I believe that, too. I don't know if I got a confirmation but He gives me the desires of my heart." I attempted to reference a scripture, didn't know if I did correctly, but I believed in it.

Dena had been mostly silent and teary. "I don't understand why God does what He does sometimes," she mumbled. "Gary, when did you all find out she was pregnant?"

"Well, never really?" I chuckled from a tinge of embarrassment talking about having sex with Mia and her big sister standing there with another scripture on the tip of her lips.

"She was so cute, upstairs yelling. I thought something was really wrong. I took the steps three at time running up the stairs to her. She had been sitting on the vanity ottoman debating whether she should take the test and tell me later, or take the test with me.

She was washing her hands when I walked in because she couldn't hold it. We eventually took the test but really couldn't tell if it was positive or negative. The test was generic so we had planned to get another one and make a doctor's appointment for some time this week." I was suddenly saddened. "Now we don't have to do that."

"I'm sorry. You all can try again." Dena tried to sound strong and comforting.

"I know."

Dena looked at Mia and started to cry again. "Come on, Sissy. Get up, please," she whispered as she gently shook the bed then ran out. Desilyn went after her.

I sat silently for a moment then adjusted the volume on the TV. Christian station... *Amazing Grace... God's Grace is truly amazing...* I couldn't control my tears again. I removed my sunglasses, wiped my eyes, put the sunglasses back on, and reached for Mia's hand again. I felt a gentle squeeze on my hand, I heard a deep breathe and then shallow breathing singing along with the song...*Goh's Gra... is truly amazing...*

I stood up in shock, slowly, eyes widened. "Mia, honey. Hey, baby. How are you?" I whispered. *Thank you, Jesus!* I didn't want to speak too loudly or move too abruptly. I didn't want to startle her. I kissed her hand. I kissed her forehead. I rubbed her face. She could barely keep her eyes open.

"Gary, are you okay?" She said in a shallow whisper.

"Huh, uh, baby uh..." I stuttered. "I'm okay. Are you okay?"

"Lord, am I in Heaven? God, you have sent me the most handsome angel. What is his name, God?" She paused.

I didn't speak because I thought she was hallucinating. I just held her hands and smiled, trying to think of who I would snap at about the side effects of the medicine that they gave her.

"Baby. Gary." She smiled.

"Mia, baby, how are you feeling?"

She closed her eyes.

"Mia?" I said gently as I tugged her hand slightly.

She didn't speak. For more than ten minutes, she didn't say anything. I pulled the chair closer and just sat there and stared at her. *I know I'm not losing my mind. She was talking.* I said another prayer.

"Gary?" She opened her eyes again.

"Yeah, baby. I'm right here." I stood up again.

"I'm in the hospi—"

"Yes, baby. You were in an accident. Do you remember?" I asked, not really expecting an answer.

"Yes, I heard all of the people talking." She closed her eyes again.

I should've called the nurse but instead I waited.

She opened her eyes and squeezed my hand. "Baby, come closer. I have something to tell you."

"Okay, baby what is it?" I leaned in front of her.

"Close the blinds and don't let anyone in here."

"Huh?" I heard her but I wanted to make sure I understood her.

"Close the blinds. Just do it. Please?" she whispered, weakly.

"Okay." I walked over to close the blinds and walked back to the bed, puzzled.

She had closed her eyes again. My gut was telling me to call the nurse but I didn't. Just in case she was preparing to tell me something about them, I needed to hear it. My heart was beating faster in anticipation of what I was about to hear. I waited until she opened her eyes again, several minutes later.

"Don't let anyone else in here."

"Okay, baby, but why? What is it?" This situation was getting weird with every passing moment.

"Don't let anyone else in here but that nurse and family and don't tell anyone that I'm awake until I tell you everything." Her voice strained as she struggled to sit up.

"Mia, whoa wait a minute, you don't need to sit up, baby. We don't know if—" I tried to keep my voice down but I was getting worried because I didn't want her to get worse by trying to do too much, too soon.

"I'm strong. I can do it, Gary." She interrupted.

"Mia, no you're not. You're struggling to speak. Baby, you're too weak." I pleaded with her.

She closed her eyes again and took several deep breaths. "I need a moment. I think Lynne tried to hurt me."

"What?" I said louder than I intended.

A nurse came running in a few seconds later. "Is everything okay?"

"I'm sorry. Yes, I got excited about the TV. I changed the channel. I'll probably get too loud looking at sports." I stood in front of the TV changing the channels.

Mia had closed her eyes.

The nurse looked at Mia's monitors. She walked over to the bed and did a few minor checks of the tubes. "She is coming back to us. I can feel it." She patted Mia's hand. "Her heart rate is a little elevated. She's coming back."

"I believe she's coming back, too."

When the nurse left the room, I walked back to the bed and held Mia's hand and waited. After several minutes, I said, "Mia, she's gone."

304

She opened her eyes and took a deep breath. "She threatened to put a pillow over my face, and she said some mean things."

"What? You have got to be kidding me!"

"No, I'm not. I laid here and pushed the button and I tried to scream but no one heard me. I only wanted to wake up when you were in the room though. I didn't hear your voice so I kept my eyes closed. I can't see, will you put my contacts in for me? And give me a mint."

"Uh, yeah. Hold on, let me… let me get your bag." I was slightly confused. Although my instinct told me some of what she was telling me, I had to slow down and try to digest the truth. I rambled for her contacts.

"Baby, please don't leave me all right? Please stay here with me until I'm ready to go home." She started to cry.

"Mia, I'm not leaving you. I'll be right here." I stopped looking for the contacts. "Calm down. Shhhh. Calm down, I'm right here. I don't think it's a good idea to put your contacts in right now." I wiped her tears and kissed her forehead. "I'm right here. I'm not leaving you."

"Okay, but baby, I don't want to go home until you get her. She is mad at you so she tried to hurt me. She said she was going to kill me to hurt you." Her voice was raspy.

"What, Mia?" I was baffled. I hated to keep asking questions because she was weak and could barely finish her sentences. But, I needed some answers because I was ready to go find Lynne and literally choke her to death.

"She said, 'I should put this pillow over your face, see how strong you are, see if you can breathe, he didn't want my baby, he's got some nerve, so I decided to hurt him without physically hurting him.'" She paused for a few minutes. I eagerly waited on her to gather enough strength to finish. "I tried really hard to concentrate on the voice. I know it was Lynne though. I opened my eyes one time but I couldn't see, my vision was too blurry, so I kept them closed. She came and was in here a few minutes, then left real fast."

"Mia, hold on, baby. I can't digest all you're telling me, hold on. I just need to… hold on a sec. Just hold on." I paused for a few minutes and just looked into her eyes. *I am going to kill Lynne.* "Just hold on. Okay, baby? Take a break, I don't want you to overdo it. I'm going to handle it. I promise."

I needed to calm down. I prayed for strength because our lives were about to change more than it already had. I took a deep breath and then exhaled.

"Let me just hold you for a second. Please. I miss you and I need to just hold you just for a second." I eased into the bed beside her trying not to hurt her. "Are you okay? Is anything hurting you? Do you feel any pain anywhere?"

"I'm a little weak. I need some protein." Her voice was still raspy.

I kissed her face again. I was amazed that she woke up talking almost as if she was never asleep. She definitely didn't have the physical strength but she was trying.

"Don't kiss my mouth. I need to brush my teeth and I need a bath."

I chuckled because only she would think about cleanliness at a time like this. "Don't worry, when we get home, I'll prepare a bath for you."

I lay in her bed staring at her for a while without saying a word. I was so happy that she was awake and recognized me but I was mad as hell that Lynne left the office and came here to hurt her.

Lord, please let this be the medicine that's causing Mia to tell me that Lynne tried to hurt her. Because I know, I'm not strong enough to let you handle this. I have to do it myself.

"I don't want to go home until you get Lynne."

"You're serious?"

"Yes, I am. I'm gonna get her. She tried to kill me."

"I know, baby. I uh, trust me, I'll handle it. I need a moment to think about a plan of action and I don't want that moment to be right now. I wanted to believe her but I really wasn't a hundred percent sure that Mia was totally coherent."

"I know I heard so many conversations. I heard the nurses talk about you. They think you're cute." She tried to rub my face but the cords restricted her movement. "I also heard..."

I interrupted her. "Did you hear me talking to you?"

"Yes, that's why I love you so much." She snuggled in closer.

"What do you remember?" I rubbed her hair, kissed her forehead softly.

"Umm, I remember you saying that I love you sooooo much, Mia, wake up, wake up," she spoke softly, "I heard Mr. V., I heard a lot of people."

"How long have you been awake?" I smiled as I tried to figure out if she was still slightly out of it or really sound in mind but just physically weak.

"Actually, I've been in and out, I think. I was dreaming. It felt like somebody kept messing with my arm. I heard bits and pieces, not full conversations because I couldn't stay awake long enough. I dreamt that they stopped giving me the drugs to see if I would wake up on my own and that I would come back soon," she rambled, slowly. "I was trying to talk but every time, nothing came out. You couldn't hear me. I kept praying to God for the strength and the right time to speak. I decided that I wanted to wait until I could tell that you were here alone to tell you. What day is it?"

"It's Thursday, baby." I continued to rub her hair. I couldn't take my eyes off her.

"Wow." She closed her eyes. "How much have they told you about my condition?"

"Mia, your accident was Saturday morning. You've been out for five days. They stopped the meds almost twenty-four hours ago to see if you would wake up on your own. You have a broken wrist and you had a sprained ankle. It was swollen but there was not a broken bone. Do you feel any pain anywhere?"

She was silent. She drifted into a sleep with a smile on her face. She looked extremely peaceful. I held her for a few more minutes. My phone buzzed in my pocket. I ignored it.

"Mom and Dad will be here soon. Their flight has already landed." I was speaking aloud but actually talking to myself because she had drifted into a nap.

"Oh, that's nice." She was awake again.

"Baby, I really think we need to tell them that you are awake so that they can check you out."

"No, baby. I want to pretend to be in a coma because I know she is coming back. She said she would. That way we can catch her. You can call one of your cop friends, to pick her up as soon as she tries something. I heard that nurse whispering about some lady to you. I'm telling you that was Lynne."

I was really concerned about her. I stood up, assisted her with getting comfortable in the bed, she closed her eyes again. I leaned in and kissed her forehead. "I'm so glad that you woke up." I was so excited about that. But, I don't know why I agreed to such nonsense especially with her random thoughts. I said, "Okay Mia, we'll try this your way."

I looked at my watch and thought, *my folks should be here by now.* Just as I completed the thought, I heard Sam. "What it do? What it do, man?" He whispered and pulled me into an embrace.

My parents trailed him, beaming with the joy of being there but so saddened by the reason they were there. We hugged and my mother cried. I, of course was holding it together really well since I knew that Mia was alert.

I hugged my parents. "Thank you all so much for coming."

Sam hugged me again and I whispered. "Thank you for coming, man. I need to tell you something."

I turned to look at Mia again to see how well she was holding up. I leaned in to pretend I was kissing her. "You okay? You sure you want to do this?"

She nodded.

"I love you." I rubbed her eyebrows. I knew she was too weak to try the little plot she had come up with; being awake did not mean strength in body.

Dena and Desilyn appeared in the doorway. The song "Never Would Have Made It" by Marvin Sapp came on the radio. *"I'm stronger, wiser, better… because I had you to hold on to…"* I was overcome with emotion so I excused myself into bathroom and gave praises to God in private. "Lord, thank You so much!" My privacy was interrupted by a knock on the door. I turned the water on to pretend I was washing my hands.

"G-Matt?" I heard Sam's voice.

I opened the door. He stepped in. He stared at me. We stared at each other.

"Man, you look like shit."

"I know I do. You should have seen me two days ago. Man it's so much going on. I had some wild thoughts thinking that Nina had done this or even Tracy's dumb ass but Mia thinks that Lynne was trying to suffocate her with a pillow."

"What?" he said, keenly. "Wait, Mia is awake?"

"Yeah, she's pretending to try to catch Lynne."

He frowned.

"Yeah, man, I'm like what in the hell? She thinks it was Lynne but Nina has been sending idle threats. I saw her at the nurse's station. I feel like I'm going crazy but the stuff that's been happening is no coincidence."

"Okay, man. I got you. Stuff like what? Just talk to me, yahmean."

"Same stuff we've talked about before. Stuff like, notes on Mia's car, notes on Dena's garage door, Nina is tripping, this hit-and-run, and a lady was in Mia's room, which I think was Lynne, too, although I didn't see her. Dena got issues with a dude she used to kick it with."

He frowned. "What dude? Monty?"

"No. Well yeah, there's always drama with him but I'm talking about another dude, Sylvester."

He shook his head. "Damn, Dena always got issues." He sighed. "So man, what do you need me to do? Take care of Lynne? Yahmean, I can do that. Nina? Or find out who this fool is that's messing with Dena."

I pondered that thought for a moment. "We need to figure out for sure if it was Lynne first. We need proof."

"Or a confession." He paused. "Well, I'm not leaving until we figure it out. Yahmean? I got you."

"And as for Nina, I don't know yet. We'll see. But thanks, man."

"We'll figure it out." He reassured me as he patted me on the back.

We walked out of the bathroom to see Dena, Desilyn, Ms. Emma, and my mother standing around Mia's bed. My mother was holding her hand. They stepped back when I approached the bed.

"Gary she's a little warm. You think she's okay?" My mother sounded concerned.

I touched her hand, her forehead then leaned in to kiss her on the cheek. "You still okay?"

She opened her eyes. I know that gesture meant that she didn't want to pretend to be in a coma any longer. I pulled back slightly. "You sure?"

She nodded. I kissed her forehead. It appeared warmer than the last time.

"Mia? How are you feeling?"

"Not good."

I didn't want to alarm her, but I wanted to yell, "Nurse! Get in here!" so instead, I pressed the nurse-call button.

Nurse Michelle rushed into the room.

"Is something wrong?"

"Yes, I mean no. She's, she's awake!'

"Oh, oh wow, let me… Hi Mia, how are you feeling?" She said slowly.

My mother and Ms. Emma, Dena and Desilyn were nestled together against the wall. My dad, V. and Sam had left the room.

"Hey Mia." Dena and Desilyn said one after the other. They were noticeably excited that Mia was awake and so was I.

As the Michelle examined Mia, my mother put her arms around my waist and gave me a tight hug. I felt relief, comfort that everything will be okay.

Mia had totally regained consciousness. Her body was feeling the pains that had now manifested themselves since she was aware. She was awake with a sound mind and yes, I am glad, but the activity of her limbs was a different story. She asked Michelle for pain medicine immediately and we knew she would need physical therapy. Michelle gave her medicine for the fever, called the doctor, and asked everyone to leave the room so Mia could rest.

Sam and my parents stayed for a week, which gave Sam plenty of opportunity to constantly disappear and talk to T.J., Sean, or V. I gave him Nina's address and he said he'd see Lynne at the office.

Mia was released a few days after she woke up because she was doing well. Even though, she could barely complete a thought before one of us was at her beck and call at the hospital and at home. I was so glad to have her back but the drama was far from over.

My mother added a little twist to the drama that I didn't expect. As soon as we got Mia home and I was alone in the kitchen, she walked in, sat down, and just looked at me.

"Ma, why are you looking at me like that?" I said inquisitively.

"I talked to Karen yesterday."

I sighed. Karen is my biological mother.

My mother kept talking as she walked over to me and slid her arm around my waist, "Gary, she is really concerned for you and she told me to tell you that she hopes Mia has a speedy recovery. I'm not telling you to drop everything and run to her but, Gary I think you should try to listen to what she has to say, try to get to know her."

"Tell her not to be concerned with me, I'm good."

"Gary," she sounded disappointed. She kept her hug tight. "Life is short, sweetheart."

"I know that Ma and I really don't want to talk about Karen now."

"I understand, but..." She stopped talking and I stepped out of her embrace.

CHAPTER 30

MIA

None of my personal belongings had been moved to Gary's house but I was so afraid to go back to my house so I planned to stay at his house indefinitely. He told me that I could have his room without any intrusions from him. I declined that offer because he was definitely the one person that I did not want out of my sight. I wanted to share the room with him.

Although I loved Gary dearly, I was somewhat concerned that the issues with these women wouldn't stop. I was going through so many emotions, there were so many people around, and I was struggling to hold them in. I knew I had lost the baby and Gary hadn't said anything about it. I wanted to scream but I knew that everyone would think that I was crazy, so I cried in silence.

Dena came over to see me. I wanted to ask her if she knew about the miscarriage but decided against it. She knocked on the door and pushed it gently.

"Hey Sissy. I'm so glad you're back." She sat down on the bed and stroked my hair.

"Thanks, Dena. I'm glad I'm back too." My eyes filled with tears.

"Sissy, what's wrong? Are you in pain?"

"No, Dena, I'm scared."

"Mia, why?" She sang as she reached for a hug.

"Dena, I'm scared somebody will try to hurt me again. Is it safe to be with Gary anymore? Or will I always have to look over my shoulder because a crazy lady from his past will show up?" Out of all the emotions, rolling around in my head that one came out.

"Mia, now that is nonsense, girl. Gary absolutely loves you and he will go to his grave trying to protect you. You know that! Now, stop saying that! Breaking up is not an option. No." She moved her head from side to side.

"He can't protect me twenty-four hours a day. I can't even stay at my own house, Dena." I whined as I leaned my head against the headboard.

"Mia, come on now that's because you're not physically at the level you need to be."

"I really believe it was Lynne but what if it was Nina?"

"Mia Simone Nixon! Now stop it! You need to take a nap." She started pulling the covers and preparing the bed for me to take a nap. "I'm getting out of here so you can rest. You're talking crazy. He loves you. And just between us, I'm going to find Lynne and handle her. If I can get to Nina, I'll handle her too!"

"Dena, don't do anything crazy."

"I'll be fine, Mia. I just need to ask some questions."

"Dena, what are you going to do?" I sighed.

"I don't know yet. But I can guarantee you neither of them will like it." She winked and walked out the door.

I scooted down, got underneath the covers, and closed my

eyes. I was still sad and scared. I felt helpless. So, I did the only thing I knew to do. Pray.

"Mia is sleeping and I really don't want to disturb her. I'll tell her I talked to you. Okay, no problem." I heard Gary tell someone on the phone.

I sniffed and wiped away the tears that had been flowing for the past fifty minutes. I was curled into a fetal position with my body facing the middle of the bed.

Gary walked over to the bed and sat down. He pushed my hair away from my face. "You okay, baby? What's wrong?"

I shook my head. "No."

"What's wrong?" He looked concerned. The sadness showing in his eyes, he almost seemed as helpless as I did.

"I'm scared, Gary and I'm sad. I'm so sad. I'm so sorry I lost the baby and I know you really want a baby," I whimpered as I struggled to sit up straight.

"Mia. Honey," he sang and pulled me into his arms. "I was going to tell you later when I thought you were ready to hear it."

"I know. I heard you talk about it to somebody."

He looked disappointed in himself. "Oh my, God, honey. I am so sorry. I'm sad too but you don't have to apologize for that baby. It was not your fault." He continued to hug me. "I'm sorry, baby that we have to go through this, but we'll get through it together. Okay?"

He pushed back and rubbed my face with his thumbs.

I nodded and another tear fell.

He kissed me softly and hugged me again. "Listen. I want a baby but not at the risk of losing you, girl. Remember what I told you before we took the pregnancy test at your house?"

"But your aunt said…"

He was instantly irritated. "Look. It doesn't matter what that bi…it doesn't matter what she said. And when did you talk to her?"

"I overheard her when we were at your mom's house."

He sighed with so much irritation that I thought he was going to explode.

"Look I don't care what she said. Don't listen to her, Mia. She will forever have you upset if you do. She probably said that on purpose, because she knew you'd hear it. Look, as long as you want me, I'll never leave you, Mia. I love you too much." He pulled me into his arms again. He held on tight. "I love you."

"I love you, too." I pulled back and adjusted myself on the bed.

"We will try again, you know that right? We will try again regardless of the ridiculous odds that we'll face. Okay?"

"Okay." I nodded. "As much as you like to practice," I tried to joke through the tears.

He stopped ranting for a moment. We both chuckled.

He exhaled and looked at me with raised eyebrows as if he was waiting on me to make the next move. I scooted closer to him.

"Baby, I want you to hold me, hug me, and kiss my face."

"Of course, of course, sweetheart, I can definitely do that. I got you, baby. You don't have to be afraid either," he said as he started in reverse order of my request.

A few minutes later, we heard a soft knock on the door and the door opened. Gary's mother peeped her head in. "Hey, you two. I was hoping Mia was awake."

She walked over to the bed and Gary got up.

She smiled with her motherly warmth. "I wanted to give you a hug today. Can I get you anything? Warm milk usually relaxes you."

"Hi, Mrs. Matthews. No ma'am I'm fine." The tears started to flow again as she hugged me.

"Ohhh, what's wrong, honey?" She looked at Gary.

Gary chimed in. "Ma, we have something to tell you."

His tone caused her to look concerned at him and then back to me.

"First of all, if your sister-in-law comes up murdered, I did it. I almost hate her. She talks too much."

"What? Gary, don't talk like that. But, what did she do now?"

"She made sure Mia overheard her talking about I wanted a baby really badly and… you know what? I'm not wasting my time talking about that idiot."

"Gary!" His mother stopped him.

"Anyway, Ma, we found out that Mia was pregnant right before the accident." He paused to watch her expression.

Excitement.

"But, she miscarried after the accident."

Sadness.

She placed her hand over her heart, mouth agape, she reached for another tight hug and rocked me. She went through a myriad of emotions in a short span just as I had.

"Oh, honey, I am so sorry. Lord, I pray that we find out who did this."

"Mrs. Matthews, I have fibroid tumors and I've had surgery but they came back. My doctor said that I probably can't conceive but I did and she also said that if I conceived I probably wouldn't carry it to term, which could have been the reason for the miscarriage. We'll just have to see."

"Honey, that's quite all right. Whatever God has for you is for you, even if that means having a child, adopting a child or no child." She looked a Gary. "God's will, will be done, regardless. You two remember that. Okay? We have time for all of that. God will work this out in his time. Who knows, maybe after the wedding."

She grabbed Gary's hand and patted it. She stood up and Gary replaced her on the bed. "I got this, Ma."

"What do you want for dinner tonight? Emma and I are making dinner." She looked at Gary and then back at me.

"How much energy do you have? Just fix whatever you like. I'm sure I'll enjoy it and Mia will, too."

She leaned in to kiss me on the forehead and then kissed Gary. He squirmed.

"God's will. Remember that. I'm praying for both of you," she said as she sashayed out of the room.

I saw his mom lock the door before she walked out.

"Wow. She is pissed."

"Really? At us?"

"No, no, baby. Not at us. I know that lady like I know the back of my hand. She's mad because somebody tried to hurt you. And me. And she can't do anything about it because we don't know who did it. You see how she abruptly wrapped up the conversation. I know her. I'm telling you she's pissed. She's saved and prayerful but she's feisty, too. Then she dropped her little wedding bells and walked out." He chuckled. "Aih-yi-yi," he sighed.

"Do you think they will find who did it?" I said as I positioned myself to lie down and he continued my earlier request. It felt like he covered every part of my body with his body. I felt safe in his arms.

"Yes, baby. I do." He kissed my hair.

"Why do you think that?"

He sighed and rolled away from me, looked toward the ceiling then stood up and stretched. I didn't think it took all of that to answer the question but I guess it did.

"T.J. is relentless in his search, accompanied by Sean who has turned into a spy. V. is harassing his buddies at HPD, and Sam is intimidating everybody in Houston. Somebody will find whoever did it."

"They already know, don't they? You're just not telling me." I rose up on my elbows to look into his beautiful brown eyes. "I can tell by the look in your eyes. I know who did it. I told you it was Lynne. I wasn't hallucinating, it was her."

He climbed back into the bed behind me, inhaled, exhaled, kissed my hair, and held me. He still didn't respond. For whatever reason, I felt safe with no need to worry myself until the fruit of their labor unfolded. He was just what the doctor ordered. He brought me so much joy.

CHAPTER 31

GARY

Things happen so fast sometimes. I expected this whole ordeal to take months to resolve. Mia didn't feel safe unless I was right by her side. So, I couldn't offer much help. The first day Sam arrived he had slipped out of the room, got in touch with T.J., and went to my office to interrogate Lynne. He never made it to Nina. According to T.J., Lynne was scared shitless and Sam acted as if he knew nothing about it when I asked him. I guess that was for the best. The less I knew, the less I'd have to repeat. T.J. said that Sam threw a barrage of questions at Lynne, slammed his hand on the desk, pushed some things on the floor as T.J. had his office door closed pretending to be on an important conference call.

Sam, V. and my dad were in the media room watching a movie until they heard my mother and Ms. Emma yell, "Dinner is ready."

Mia and I made our way into the kitchen. All of us enjoyed the dinner that they prepared and just as we were getting ready for the best dessert ever, peach cobbler topped with vanilla ice cream,

T.J. and Sean showed up looking as if somebody chased them to my house. Sean immediately washed his hands and started to help himself to the food on the stove.

T.J. immediately started talking. "Man, I started to call but I decided to come over to tell you this. We need to go to the police station. You are not going to believe what you see and hear."

"What is it man? Tell me!"

V. was looking guilty as if he already knew what T.J. was talking about. I looked at my dad and Sam they had the same expression. T.J. had called while I was in the room with Mia and they decided not to tell me because T.J. was on his way to my house and they didn't want to muddle the story. I don't know if I appreciated that but it was not the time to fight over it.

"Man, Lynne was behind this whole thing," he said in an 'I'm so sorry' tone because he was the reason we hired her in the first place. I thought she was a bit mature for the job in the beginning but I came around quickly and actually appreciated what she brought to the table until recently.

"I knew it!" I said loudly then lowered my voice. "I knew it. She was on the tape wasn't she?"

"I told you it was her," Mia said.

"Yes, Mia you're right it was Lynne but she was not on the tape."

My eyes widened. Mia looked stunned by his reply. My mother remained calm and Ms. Emma tried to usher Mia toward the bedroom but to no avail. Mia wanted to hear everything.

"What? T.J. speak faster man, come on!" I was anxious.

"Lynne confessed actually. Nyla and Lynne's sons were on the tape from Dena's house."

"Nyla? What? Wait a minute, back up tell me the whole story.

What does Nyla have to do with this?"

"I'll tell you in the car." He opened the door. "Let's go."

There were six men preparing to leave for the police station. We thought that my mother would stay with Mia and Ms. Emma while the men went to handle whatever was about to happen. We were wrong. She wanted to go with us and headed for the door before anyone else did and no one stopped her.

"Wait a minute, where's Dena?" I all of a sudden thought she needed to be in the midst somewhere.

Sean spoke. "I can go get her and bring her over here," he said with a mouth full of food.

"Please do that." I frowned because he was speaking with food in his mouth.

Mia stopped me on the way out the door and whispered. "Honey, I really want to go but since I just took the pain pills. I won't fight it, but will you call me when you get in the car and put me on speaker phone so that I can hear the story when T.J. tells it?"

I must have given her a look that told her I didn't want to do that because she looked at me with the puppy dog eyes and said, "Please, Gary."

"Okay, baby, I will." I kissed her forehead and walked out the door.

We piled into T.J.'s Suburban and headed for the police station. I did as promised, I called Mia and put her on speaker.

T.J. began the story as we fastened our seat belts. "I had the tapes from Dena's house and was in the process of reviewing them. I saw three people, three different vehicles, on several different occasions putting notes on Dena's garage, ringing the doorbell, looking through her window or writing a note on her front door window around the same time for three straight days, not to mention the phone calls that she was getting. They were amateurs. I had a friend run the plates and found out, that the vehicles belonged to Nyla and Lynne's two sons. So then, I interrogated Lynne but didn't get much. But when Sam interrogated Lynne, or should I say threatened Lynne, she was scared and when I came back for the third interrogation, she didn't give any fuss, she just confessed. She said she was tired, it was too much to keep up with, and it was out of her character to act this way. She just couldn't keep her story straight. But she would not admit to going in Mia's room at the hospital. I think that confession will come out in the end, too."

"Hmmph. Did you run a background check on her? Does she have any criminal activity?"

"Yes, I ran it, but it was clean, now Nyla on the other hand has done minor jail time for petty thefts."

"What! Did Lynne know this, since she recommended her to Dena?"

"Yes, of course she did. That's why she highly recommended her." He paused, "Nyla is Lynne's granddaughter by marriage."

"What? I'm confused." I shook my head.

"Lynne has a step-son named Sylvester, her deceased husband's oldest son. He is Nyla's dad."

"Ohhhh," I sighed. "Oh my, God." My eyes were darting all over the place.

"Apparently, he hasn't been in Nyla's life that much. He was a teenage dad and the mother wouldn't allow him to see her. You know how some of that drama goes. Nyla loves her dad, craves his attention, and will do anything for him. That's why she did this."

This was all a coincidence. Sort of. The notes and phone

calls were not about Mia at all, it was about Dena and Sylvester wanting her back. Mia just happened to be Dena's best friend. Now Lynne on the other hand, would have tried her tactics on anyone that I was seriously dating because she wanted me to date her daughter. Any one of my ex-girlfriends would have endured this, Nina, Vonda, Angie, it didn't matter. I really didn't think Lynne was that serious.

The luncheon note was definitely from Lynne and one of her children and the note on Mia's car the night we met was done by Nyla from Sylvester but it was an attempt to get to Dena, and Dena would have hired Nyla regardless because of the way they... oh my, this is too much to try to think about. The bottom line was, Lynne, Nyla and Sylvester were all working this out together.

"Oh my, God," I heard Mia whisper. Then I heard Ms. Emma say, "What did he say?"

I almost chuckled at the thought of the two of them trying to remain quiet with all of the news coming from T.J. But this was no laughing matter. My mother was in the back seat squirming and showing her disgust at every sentence that came from T.J.'s mouth. My dad and Sam sat quietly but listening intently. Sam was proud of himself for scaring the shit out of Lynne, which consequently caused the confession.

T.J. continued. "Nyla started working for Dena at Sylvester's request. He had done some background work himself to find Dena. He used to work with her at a company in Dallas, I forgot the name of it. Nyla's role was to keep an eye on Dena. She listened every time Mia and Dena had a conversation, she knew their every move, and most of what was going on with them. She knew about every alarm, every note, everything. You following me?"

I nodded. "Yes."

He continued. "Lynne broke down because she couldn't handle the pressure anymore. But, I have a feeling that neither Nyla nor the sons would have ever confessed even with the evidence from the tapes. When Lynne started spilling, she ratted on everybody. Man, she really wanted you to date one of her crazy daughters."

I looked at T.J. with the most disgusted expression. It seemed as if T.J. had rambled on forever. Since he changed the pace, I asked, "Who hit Mia's car?"

He paused and sighed. "It was Lynne."

I put my head in my hands. Although from gut instinct and Mia's constantly saying it, I knew the truth but I still found it hard to believe.

I heard Mia gasp. I certainly did not want her to hear this without me being next to her, but this was her request that I hate I granted.

"You okay, baby?"

"Ummhmm," she tried to sound reassuring.

Then I heard Dena in the background. "Oooh, I'm gonna kick her a…, oooh just you wait!"

"Sean, got Dena that quickly?"

"No, she was already on her way when I left so I turned around," Sean chimed in. They were all huddled around the phone.

I turned my attention back to T.J. "So it was Lynne?" I was livid.

"Yes, so many coincidences. She saw Mia coming through the traffic light, obviously Mia's car is noticeable, right? So she went around the car at the intersection to try to scare Mia by acting as if she was going to hit her and actually did it. They were driving a pickup truck that she borrowed that morning to move some furniture to Nyla's new apartment. She said she didn't see you behind Mia. Nyla and one of Lynne's son's were in the truck and certainly encouraging her every step of the way. She said she was not trying to hurt Mia but was trying to scare her."

"Oh my, God. What did she think will happen if she plowed that big ass dump truck into Mia's car? What does she mean act as if she was going to hit her car?"

I was praying that I didn't try to kill Lynne when I saw her. I calmed myself enough since we were pulling up to the police station.

"Hey, Sean, please keep an eye on them until we're back?"

"Yeah man, of course."

I hung up before I heard Mia's voice, trying to convince me to stay on the phone the entire time. I know I couldn't handle what I needed to while holding a phone, but I regretted leaving her at home.

By the time I hung up the phone, my nerves were worked up again. I got out of the truck and started walking toward the door. I abruptly stopped. I wasn't ready. I needed to calm my nerves some more. The adrenaline within me would have taken over and I don't know what would have happened. I paced back and forth and started talking to no one in particular pounding my fist into my hand. "Man, I can't believe this! I finally find the woman of my dreams, no money drama, no baby drama, none of that sh--, I can't believe this! We don't have any of those issues, I am trying to give her my best and it's almost destroyed by this lunatic because she wants me to date one of her dumb ass daughters! Ugghhhh I can't believe this."

My dad suggested, "Maybe its best we don't all go in here together right now." He believed in allowing the law to handle what they were paid to handle without any help from citizens unless it was necessary.

"No, I think we should all go in right now. I know you're not suggesting that I stay out here." My mother said emphatically. She was beyond pissed.

"No Judy, Sweetheart, I was only saying that because Gary is visibly upset and he don't need to see that lady, try to hurt her, cause a scene," he tried to bargain.

"I want to kill her. I'm certainly gonna try. If I see her, I'm gonna to strangle her." I growled.

"No, no son. No need for that. We'll let the police handle it. We're in their territory." She rubbed my back.

"She's right, son, I know you're upset but please don't let a moment of anger have you regret something for the rest of your life. Mia wouldn't want that. You always say you want to give her your best and strangling Lynne is not it."

V. cosigned everything my dad said. "Listen to your parents son, they're imparting wisdom."

I leaned on T.J.'s truck trying to calm my nerves then thought, *the hell with it whatever happens will just go down in history.* Sam stood a few feet away with arms folded staring at me. I know he was ready for whatever I decided to do. Ready to make history.

We walked into the police station, all eyes on us. V. spotted one of his buddies that was helping with the case. T.J. walked over and asked for the detective that he had been working with.

A few minutes of waiting and coincidentally, they were moving all of the suspects in this situation to different interrogation rooms. And wouldn't you know, they walked Lynne past us as my parents were pacing the floor. I didn't know if my mother was pacing or actually searching for Lynne. She had met Lynne on one of her trips to Houston. She spotted Lynne and rushed down the corridor toward her, before I made a step in Lynne's direction. She grabbed her by the throat and slammed her into the wall. Lynne was in such shock that she didn't attempt to defend herself.

My mother was a lot smaller and shorter than Lynne was, with a similar style, but a classier demeanor and feisty as hell when pushed. She said Lynne smirked at her. That may have been true, but I think that she was so upset, Lynne could have smiled, and she would've gotten the same reaction.

All of us were stunned at my mother's reaction as we watched her straighten her clothes after we pulled her back. My dad tried to usher her outside. "Come on, Judy, let's go."

The cops acted as if they didn't see it. They thought this was such a bizarre story. One of them asked, "Am I on a Lifetime movie or am I standing here in Houston right now? Can somebody pinch me, please?" The other cop replied, "Both, a Lifetime movie in Houston." They both laughed. I wasn't sure I appreciated their attempt at humor.

"I thought you wanted to do something to Lynne but Aunt Judy was the secret weapon that even I didn't know we had," Sam joked.

Lynne's son tried to catch up to my mother before my father took her outside. "Did you try to hurt my mother?"

I lost it, before my dad or Sam had a chance to blink. I punched him and had him pinned down on a table beside the door trying to choke the life out of him. I was taking it out on him since I couldn't hit Lynne. The officer that was escorting them stood back for a moment, and then grabbed me. I didn't resist because I thought about what my dad said and I let him go, pushed him to the floor. Sam snarled at the other son, daring him to make a move. The officers eventually got them to their designated rooms.

They should've been in handcuffs anyway.

They needed statements from all of us so eventually Sean had to bring Mia, Dena, and Ms. Emma to the station. They made sure that they didn't bring the suspect crew back out because it would have been a melee for sure, especially with Dena there.

By the time they finished getting statements and questioning all of us, everybody was exhausted.

Lynne's daughters showed up with all of those bad ass kids and baby daddies but did not add to the drama. They wanted to, but the look on our faces told them not to.

Mia recognized Lynne's daughter, June, as the lady at the luncheon and December was the one that approached Dena at the gas station. We had to make sure Dena didn't try to get to them because she was furious. Mia was in no condition for any type of altercation so she just sat quietly.

June's goal, set up by her mother, was to "check Mia out" and report back to Lynne and her sister, December. Lynne told T.J. this during the confession. I guess her little dumb mission was accomplished or not, because apparently June became too nervous and didn't get all of the information that Lynne asked her to get. Lynne overheard me talk about one of Mia's speaking engagements and the mentoring that she does, so she sent June to see if she could get some personal information from Mia or a business card. The other daughter December tried to get information about Mia from Dena at the gas station, another plan not accomplished. The ultimate plan was to befriend Mia and try to somehow, break us up so I would want her daughter. This was the craziest mess I had ever heard. Lynne said that Mia got too close too soon. She thought Mia just wanted my money. I wondered what she thought her daughters wanted. The same damn thing.

As persistent, as Sylvester was in trying to get to Dena he had left town as quickly as he came, but he was behind the entire saga with the exception of Lynne wanting me to date one of her daughters. He broke into Dena's house, well actually, he just walked in. He had a key. I'm going to assume that he stole the key because I sure hope that Dena was not crazy enough to give him one. He probably had Nyla steal it. He had caused the alarms to go off at her house, twice. He left a note on the mirror and jumped the fence into the neighbor's yard. A grown ass man, walking into someone's house just to write on a mirror in lipstick, what the hell? I guess that's what stalkers do. This entire situation was wild and I couldn't believe I was in it. I thought I had left the craziness in New York.

Mia said, "Dena finally answered one of Sylvester calls when we were on our way here. He threatened to tell the cops that Dena shot him and left him to die. Dena threatened to tell the cops of all of the illegal activity, including his money printing fraud that he and his wife had gotten into over the years and never got caught."

I frowned because that was news to me.

Mia continued. "He had forgotten that he had told Dena all of his secrets in the heat of the moment. Sex, it can get you every time. Right?" She leaned her head on my shoulder. "Dena said her reputation was tight so she wasn't worried. She knows people and she'd even make up some things to make it worse for him if she had to."

I put my arm around her. "Wow. Dena told me some more things about Sylvester when we were at the hospital. You didn't tell me about the night at the club but I'll give you a pass on that for now. His wife Ari was abusive, and had been in and out of jail for some time for domestic disturbance. She's in some type of mental institution or rehabilitation facility to get help just recently as last week. This mess is crazy."

"Yep, it is Gary and how did I get all tied up in it? He told her he was lonely and needed someone to turn to, so he chose her. He said she owed him, since she shot him. He had heard that she was successful in Houston. Living large and had a new man that she was living with. He tried to contact her a few times over several months. She didn't recognize his number nor the name that he was using, Coleman or something, so when she refused the calls or didn't return the calls, he got pissed and started stalking or should I say harassing. But when she realized it was him calling, she still didn't answer. I guess that made him angrier. Just total chaos."

"Yep, baby it is."

"Wait a minute." She raised her head and looked as if she suddenly remembered something. "Hey, Dena, come here."

"What?" She walked over looking with a concerned stare.

"You said Sylvester was using the name Coleman?"

"Yeah, why?"

She stood up and grabbed both of Dena's arms. "Describe him to me, Dena."

"Tall, dark skinned, low haircut, grayish looking eyes, boyish look, why?"

"Oh my God, Dena. We need to find him! That is Brock!"

Dena looked alarmed and I stood up because I remembered the name from Mia's text message.

Both of them sat down, grabbed their heads, and kept whispering in unison, "Oh my, God, Oh my, God."

Mia placed her head in her lap. "Lord have mercy!"

"Ladies, do we need to let the cops know about this?"

"No!" They spoke in unison again. They stared at each other.

I was slightly confused but assumed that Sylvester and Brock was the same person. Trying to connect all of the pieces to the puzzle, S. Brock C. must have been Sylvester Brock Coleman. I was willing to bet they both had affairs with him in their past. I hope it wasn't at the same time. They didn't want to speak about it so I dropped it. For now.

Monty arrived at the police station in no time after Dena dropped the restraining order when she found out he wasn't the stalker. He looked at me and slightly tossed his head, "What's up?" but walked over to Dena.

After I was done talking to the detective, T.J. pulled me to the side, "Hey I have something more to tell you about Lynne, but I didn't want our business out in the open like that with emotions flying so high right now."

I frowned. "What is it now?" I wiped my hand down my face.

"Lynne didn't get far but she used the company credit card to purchase the dress for her daughter's ball that she wanted you to escort her to. It looks like she purchased three dresses. She agreed not to bring assault charges against your mother at her attorney's counsel, if we decided not to bring charges for using company funds. But both of us have to agree."

"How much did she spend?"

"A little over three-hundred dollars."

I paused for a moment. "I can agree to that, if that's all she spent. The charge was minor compared to what she was getting ready to deal with. And wouldn't be surprised if she has a concussion. Did you see how hard my mother slammed her into that wall?"

He chuckled. "Yes, I saw it and heard it, too."

"I can't imagine them cuffing my mother and finger printing her and all that crap. I'm glad my dad got her out of here."

"Yes, that was best."

If nothing else, I just wanted to slap Lynne but that would have brought another charge. She had confessed and while I certainly didn't want it to end the way it did, she had to go to jail for this mess she caused.

Mia walked over and eased her arm around my waist. "Gary, do you think Nina is capable of anything like this?"

I gave her a puzzled look. "Baby, uh, no. No. I don't think so. I sure hope not."

EPILOGUE

One month later, Gary and Mia were engaged. Although it wasn't when and how he originally planned it in St. Thomas. It was Thanksgiving weekend. One month after most of the drama settled. Gary had a big surprise proposal and engagement party in New York at the end of his parents thirty-fifth wedding anniversary celebration.

Gary took it upon himself to purchase Mia's dress for the evening. He googled "red cocktail dress" printed a picture and had Dena searching from Houston to New York to find it with shoes and a clutch to complement it. She was successful and Mia looked stunning in her red strapless dress with fitted bodice, and her four-inch stiletto healed shoes, still wearing the cast on her arm.

Gary's mother, Judy, assisted him in getting all of Mia's family to New York. Judy suggested they come to the anniversary celebration to get the families acquainted since both families were small. At least that was the story they conveyed to Mia and she easily believed it. Her family was her sister, her niece, her brother-in-law, aunt, and uncle.

He asked her for a dance to Luther Vandross' *"If This World Was Mine,"* he embraced her wholly and whispered in her ear. As part of the plan, all of the dancing couples left the floor one by one, leaving Gary and Mia on the floor alone. Halfway through the song, he got down on both knees to ask her to be his wife. She was pleasantly surprised when the banner was flipped, the music changed, and the lights were lowered. When she said "Yes," red and white rose petals and pearl white balloons dropped from the ceiling. It was truly a fairytale. Mia was amazed. Her eyes sparkled like a kid at Disney World. She covered her mouth in surprise and cried. She dropped to her knees in her short red dress and again shouted, "Yes, I will marry you, Gary!" while the crowd cheered and whistled with continuous applause as she hugged him tightly. "I love you so much, baby." She whispered in his ear.

Mia and Gary wanted to try to get pregnant again, but didn't know if there was much hope with Mia's fertility issues but they were willing to pray together and try it.

Everyone, especially Gary's dad, Clive was still teasing Gary's mom, for losing her temper at the police station and going all vigilante in the place. She replied, "Nobody messes with my babies."

Lynne's trial was coming up soon for something on the lines of conspiring to kill another human being. They released Nyla and Lynne's son on bond but she was still in jail for committing the act.

Dena and Monty were certainly meant for each other. They made up so maybe that meant she was ready for an open relationship or maybe he changed. They could possibly live happily ever after with no more drama, which was probably not possible with those two, though his demeanor seemed a lot more demure now. It was hard to understand why she wanted to be with him after he brought her so much humiliation. Sometimes love has no boundaries. Dwight was history since he decided to go back to his wife and kids.

Gary was still struggling with getting to know his biological mother, Karen. Mia was helping him. Karen had been trying to make contact but he was not ready to deal with her. She showed up at the anniversary celebration and had an opportunity to see the proposal but there was not much conversation going on after that. Karen tried to talk to Gary but he refused. He could not get over the fact that she was missing for so many years. He knew who raised him but felt like he didn't know who he really was.

"There are two whole families that I do not know simply because you decided to give me away. I don't know my family, Karen! Lucky for me, I haven't run off and married my cousin or something," he'd yelled at her.

He didn't know that that was exactly what he was getting ready to do.

Brenda A. White's

The Best I Have to Offer

Discussion Questions

1. Do you think Gary and Mia moved too fast into their relationship? Why or Why not?

2. Was Gary too controlling or just confidant? Was Mia too independent?

3. Have you ever had someone tell you he or she wanted you to complement the next steps in their life? How did it make you feel? Have you ever told someone the same thing?

4. Are you complementing someone's life now? If so, how? If not, do you plan to start? When? How?

5. Do you have a dream or vision that you want to pursue? If so, what is it? When do you plan to start? How will you go about it?

6. What did you think about Lynne? Do you know a mother that would go to these lengths for her daughter?

7. What do you think Dena's problem was? Or, do you think she had a problem?

8. Do you have a friend that you allow to pull you into their mess?

9. Why do you think Dena was so drawn to Monty despite the drama?

10. What experiences in your life have contributed to the person you are today?

11. Do you think Mia should have told Gary about Dena's trip to Chicago trip before Dena gave her permission?

12. Do you feel that Gary waited too long to tell Mia about his history? Did it matter? Why or Why not?

13. What's your view on living together prior to marriage? What is your mother's view?

14. How do you think Mia would have handled the situation, had it been reversed where Gary would have gotten hurt? How would you handle a situation like this?

15. What do you think about the proposal? Should they elope, have a large wedding, destination wedding? Why or Why not? Should they get married?